MW00610131

# JURY OF ONE

"In *Jury of One*, John Warley takes on the ultimate moral dilemma: a judge in a small Southern town, a decent and highly respected man of honor, is torn between doing what is right and doing what is just. His decision will not only affect the lives of others but also change the kind of person he sees each time he looks into a mirror. This fast-paced, skillfully rendered courtroom drama is filled with all-too-human characters who speak to the struggles all of us face in the age-old battle between right and wrong, justice and injustice."

—**Cassandra King**, author of *Tell Me a Story: My Life with Pat Conroy*

"John Warley's *Jury of One* is a penetrating tale that entertains while at the same time requiring us to reflect on our lives and the oft-stated maxim 'There but for the grace of God . . .' The story is built around a trial judge's idea for transforming the death penalty in an intriguing way that creates for him a potential path to South Carolina's highest court. But that path is clouded by one night's dalliance with an attractive woman that changes their lives forever. As the plot unfolds, you can see the inexorable finale coming in the judge's courtroom, but you have no idea how that fateful moment will arrive. John Warley is a master of his craft, as you will readily agree while turning the pages of this compelling story of people captured by their choices."

—**Wyatt Durrette**, Virginia trial attorney

"A promise made over a dead body conjoins two disparate lives in a compelling novel that's equal parts taut legal thriller and thought-provoking moral quandary. *Jury of One* keeps readers on their toes to the very end. A welcome addition to masterful storyteller John Warley's oeuvre."

—**Jonathan Haupt**, coeditor, *Our Prince of Scribes: Writers Remember Pat Conroy*

"From the first page to the last, *Jury of One* is a page turning thrill of a ride. Atmospheric and compelling, John Warley knows how to immerse the reader in a southern world where trust, betrayal, and secrets collide. Suspenseful and absorbing, *Jury of One* is your next can't-put-down legal thriller."

—**Patti Callahan Henry**, *New York Times* bestselling author of *Becoming Mrs. Lewis*

""Give me five minutes to clear out, then call 911; says Judge Daniel Borders. 'It's best we keep our distance.' And thus begins John Warley's powerhouse new novel. Part legal thriller, part excavation of life in the South Carolina Low Country, all moral quandary, Warley is as good at evoking a courtroom as he is the rural backroads of Beaufort. A page-turner in the spirit of John Grisham and Greg Iles, you won't put this one down until the very end.""

—**Mark Powell**, author of *Lioness*


"*Jury of One* tells the story of two people whose futures each depend upon the other keeping a promise made on the worst night of their lives. It will keep you guessing until the end, and thinking long after you close the book. John Warley demonstrates beyond dispute that he is a writer in full."

—**William P. Ritchie**, retired partner Jones Day

# JURY
# OF ONE

A NOVEL

JOHN WARLEY

VIRGINIA BEACH
CAPE CHARLES

*Jury of One*

by John Warley

© Copyright 2023 John Warley

ISBN 978-1-64663-928-1

Published by

**köehlerbooks**™

3705 Shore Drive
Virginia Beach, VA 23455
800-435-4811
www.koehlerbooks.com

*For Marilyn,*
*And for my siblings Shan, Rob, and Tom*

*". . . and suddenly the calm sea,*
*the sky without a cloud, appeared formidably*
*insecure in their immobility, as if poised on the*
*brow of yawning destruction."*

—Joseph Conrad, *Lord Jim*

# CHAPTER 1

# The Shooting

## *May 2010*

Two sets of headlights cut through the night on a rural, two-lane road in Beaufort County, South Carolina. The lead car, driven by Alana Morgan at a speed twenty miles per hour above the limit, gradually distanced itself from the trailing SUV, driven by Judge Daniel Borders. He hoped the deer, which usually grazed along this road, had bedded down for the night. The judge also hoped Alana hadn't lost him. If she did, she would have to face her drunk, armed, and violence-prone ex-husband Toby alone, as the judge did not know where she lived.

The distance from the dock, where Dan and Alana had been having dinner minutes earlier, to her home in a tiny smudge on the map designated as Seabrook, was twenty-five miles, giving him plenty of time to reflect on how foolish and utterly heedless of a risk he had taken in inviting her to dinner aboard his boat. His intentions had been honorable, like the way he lived his life, or at least that's what he told himself. But where Alana was concerned, he couldn't be too sure. A phone call from her daughter, Holly, had interrupted their dinner. What might have happened after dinner would be but one of several "what ifs" in the months to come, starting with, what had he been thinking? His prospects to become the next chief justice of the South Carolina Supreme Court had progressed well beyond a mere possibility. And tonight he, a dedicated family man, pillar of the community, and reliable reservoir of common sense, had stepped out of character into a dark pit, the depth of which he was learning now as he sped up to keep her taillights in sight.

Alana barreled through an intersection and red light onto Sea Island Parkway with only a flicker from her brakes. By the time Dan reached it, the light was green, so that was at least one traffic law he wouldn't break tonight. On Lady's Island, in her haste to reach the McTeer Bridge, she turned left into the path of an approaching car, narrowly avoiding a collision. On Parris Island Gateway, she would have to slow down, but she didn't. Dan said a silent prayer that the local cops and state troopers were taking the night off, as the county's circuit court judge roaring through the county seat at seventy-five miles per hour would be hard—no, impossible—to explain, especially with that glass of wine on his breath. But he'd never been to her house and had no hope of finding it unless he followed. Expecting flashing blue lights to appear in his rear-view mirror at any moment, he stopped checking it.

When she turned onto the main highway leading to Seabrook, her taillights were still visible but getting smaller as she sped up to eighty-five. He told himself to turn around. There was still time to avoid becoming mixed up in a messy spat between Alana and her ex, Toby, whose marriage had ended years before. What could he do but get in the way? On the other hand, his skill as a negotiator partly explained his elevation to the bench while still in his thirties. Maybe he could defuse a tense situation, put the pin back in the grenade, so to speak. He had done it often enough in his chambers at the courthouse to help bitter litigants reach a settlement. Perhaps, he thought, his mere presence tonight would be enough to calm things down.

She passed a tractor-trailer and disappeared from his view. The Marine Corps Air Station flanked the highway on his right, its runways welcoming back jets at speeds much faster than he was now traveling, though this was faster than he could ever remember driving. He whipped around the truck and caught sight of her again.

When Alana answered her daughter's ill-timed call, her eyes had narrowed in irritation before widening with alarm. Dan caught snatches of Holly's hysteria, "drunk" and "gun" and "whore." Her mother's attempt to calm her, drowned out by a wave of sobbing that bordered on incoherence. Shouting to be heard, Alana commanded her to lock herself in the bathroom. "I'll be there in a few minutes."

Dan knew that at least some of the affection for this schoolteacher he had known for five months had to do with her vulnerability at the hands of a bully. Dan had read her divorce file. At her most delicate stage of pregnancy, Toby's brutish punches and shoves showed what kind of man he was, the kind Dan despised. Toby's habit of tailgating her for miles, five feet off her bumper, proved his perverse need to keep her in constant terror. Their daughter, too.

On Dan's boat, she said, "Toby won't leave until I get home. I need to go."

"Should you call the sheriff?" the judge advised.

"I've called so often that by the time they get there, he's long gone. He normally would never hurt Holly, but a drunk with a gun—who knows? He's such a loser."

"He could hurt you," said Dan, stating the obvious.

She shook her head as her shoulders sagged. "I can handle Toby. I've been doing it for years. I'm so sorry about our evening." Her green eyes misted. "Rain check?"

She looked both lovely and vulnerable.

"I'm coming with you," he said.

"NO!" she protested. "This is all my fault. When my sitter canceled at the last minute, I should have called off our dinner. That's what a good mother does. But I had my heart set on seeing you. So no, you stay here. Toby is my problem, and I must deal with it. Besides, you can't afford to get any closer to my cesspool of a life. You have too much at stake."

"Maybe so," Dan had said, "but I'm coming anyway. I'll follow you."

She took the turn off Route 21, nearly swerving into the ditch bordering the oncoming lane. Her tires hugged the top of the embankment, the way drivers at a speedway took turns. For a moment, at his distance, Dan was afraid she would flip her car, but when he took the same curve, he saw her taillights. He had been born and raised in this county but wasn't sure he'd ever been on this road. At last, he saw her brake lights and a sudden veer to the left. *It must be the house*, he thought.

By the time Dan arrived, Toby stood in the glare of Alana's headlights ten yards in front of her car. He was tall, lean, with hair protruding sideways over his ears from a ball cap he wore backwards. Faded jeans sagged low on slender hips. A handgun hung by his side in his right hand. Dan pulled his car beside Alana's and stepped out onto the driveway.

"So," said Toby, weaving precariously and casting bloodshot eyes in Dan's direction, "is that the judge I see? You put me in jail, 'member? Nah, you probably don't. You put everybody in jail. What you doin' with my wife?"

Dan remained mum, trying to remember his court encounter with Toby.

"I'm not your wife, Toby," said Alana. "And Dan's just a friend."

Toby turned his fractured gaze back on her. "No fren' uh' mine," he slurred. "You been out whorin' again, spreadin' dem' pretty legs a' yours for the judge? Guess I ain't good enough for you like I was back in high school. 'Member those times? I was good enough then, won't I? You forgitten' where you came from, girl."

"Toby, drop the gun and let's talk," she said calmly.

He raised the gun and leveled it at Dan. "Git your ass outta here. This is 'tween me and my wife."

Outwardly, Dan mimicked the calm he heard in Alana's voice, but fear twisted his insides into a knot large enough to explode his chest. His goal went from mediating this marital dispute to surviving it.

"Leave him alone, Toby. I'm not sleeping with him or anyone else. Put down that gun and let's talk."

"Whatcha' wanna talk about?" Toby said. "Whoring in town? Wanna talk 'bout that? 'Bout how you been puttin' your sweet bidness up for sale?" In the glare of lights, Dan saw wildness in his eyes.

"I can't talk with a gun pointed at me, Toby. Drop it please."

He wobbled before steadying himself momentarily. "I come over to make sure you ain't takin' Holly to town wicha', teaching her the tricks of the trade."

With effort obvious to anyone who wasn't drunk, Alana struggled to modulate her voice. "That's disgusting. You know better."

"Do I? No, I don't think I do. You changed, girl."

"We can talk about who has changed when you've put the gun down."

"I've changed, Alana," Toby pleaded. "And I'm man enough to admit it. You know why I changed?"

"I don't want to know anything with a gun in my face."

"I changed 'cause I love you and want you back. I ain't the mean person I was. I swear I ain't. I been workin' on it real hard. I even seen some lady, a counselor. She said I been makin' good progress with anger management."

Dan heard Alana's voice drop into almost a whisper. "I'm glad to hear that, Toby. I suggested you see a counselor years ago and I congratulate you for doing it. But it's hard for me to believe you're making progress when you come here scaring Holly half to death and pointing a gun at her mother. That does not strike me as anger management. If you're making as much progress as you say you are, you'll hand over that gun."

Dan's eyes darted from Toby to Alana and back. As she coaxed Toby to negotiate, she moved to the front of her car and stood between the headlights shining on him, glinting off the gun, and casting his long shadow onto the front of the house. Dan measured the distance from where he stood to her, weighing his options if worse came to worst. Short of charging Toby, he could think of none.

For several moments, Toby fell silent, and the only sounds Dan heard were the chorus of cicadas coming from the woods behind the house. Then, as if recollecting what he wanted to say, Toby asked Alana in a plaintive voice, "You want to know my problem? You want to know?"

"Tell me," she said, her exasperation evident.

"My problem . . ." he started, "my problem is that I know you were the best thing I ever had. Okay, I didn't deserve you back then, but I'll make it up to you. We could be happy like we was in high school."

"Do you promise you won't hurt me?"

He raised the hand holding the gun to take his oath. "I swear. May God strike me down if I ever hurt a hair on your head."

"And Holly? You promise you won't hurt her?"

Arm still raised, he promised, "I won't hurt nobody."

"Then prove it by giving me the gun. Guns hurt people, and you're not going to do that again, right?"

Toby staggered but kept his balance. "So let me get this straight.

I'm gonna' give you my gun and we're going to talk like old times. Is that right?"

"That's right, Toby."

Toby swung the gun in Dan's direction. "What 'bout him? What 'bout the judge? He gonna throw me in jail again?"

"No one is going to jail if you do what she asks," Dan said softly.

Alana added, "He's a friend who wants to make sure I'm not hurt. Once you hand the gun over, I'll ask him to leave."

Toby's head dropped. For an instant, Dan couldn't tell if he was thinking or passed out on his feet. If there was to be a moment to rush him, this could be it. Dan felt his muscles tensing and his heart pounding, remeasuring the distance separating them and the time it would take to flatten Toby, if Dan wasn't flattened first. Just as suddenly, Toby raised his head. He dropped the gun to his side and walked to her. With his free hand, he grabbed the barrel, extending the butt-end to her.

"See there?" he said. "Man 'uh my word."

"Thank you," she said, accepting the gun. "You've done the right thing."

He turned and wobbled back toward his truck, swaying from side to side and stumbling. Over his shoulder, he said, "You gonna get rid of him and we gonna talk, so I need some more whiskey. Be right back, babe."

In the months to come, Dan would remember Alana's serene composure as she raised the gun and fired. Toby's right shoulder jerked forward, the force of the bullet or a drunken misstep or a combination of the two spinning his body back toward Alana. In the high beam of her headlights, Dan saw a dull incomprehension cross Toby's face in the second before she fired again. He fell, the back of his head slamming onto the driveway, his hat spun sideways, its bill parallel to his outstretched right arm.

Dan sprang to her side. Shaking, she handed him the gun. "I

can't take it anymore." She sobbed against his chest as he extended his arm around her.

"You'd better go inside and check on Holly," he said.

She ran toward the house, skirting Toby's still body. Minutes later, she emerged, running. Dan stood by his open car door.

"I heard a shot," she said, breathless.

"You handed me the gun, remember?" Dan said, looking confused. "My fingerprints were on it. I came to the car for a rag to wipe them. I could have touched the trigger when I went to clean it and the thing went off." He handed her the weapon. "I think I got all my prints off. I hope so."

Alana stared at Dan in the dimness of the SUV's interior light. "What now?" she asked.

Dan extended his hands to her shoulders. "I know you're in shock—so am I—but we need to think this through. Can you do that?"

She nodded.

"Then listen carefully. Did you tell anyone you were meeting me tonight?"

She shook her head, tears rolling down her cheeks.

"Trust me when I tell you this will all work out. With Toby's history, everyone will assume it was self-defense, and if they don't, I'll protect you. Remember, I'm a judge." He increased the pressure on her shoulders. "If you keep me out of this, we will both come out of it okay, even if they charge you with something. Probably, they won't. You'll have to give a statement, so just say he came at you, and you were terrified he would kill you. You got that?"

She wiped tears and nodded forcefully. "I was terrified he was going to kill me," she repeated.

"But I wasn't here. You understand? And Alana, in the unlikely event they try to hold you responsible for Toby's death, you can't tell a soul we were here together. Not your mother, not your priest, not your lawyer, not your best friend—no one. You're safe as long as you keep me out of this."

He looked toward the house. "Does Holly know I'm here?"

"No. I told her to stay locked in the bathroom."

"She didn't hear the shot you heard, are we clear? If she mentions it, investigators will know there was someone else here tonight, and they will need to find out who that was."

"Yes, I understand."

"Give me five minutes to clear out, then call 911. It's best we keep our distance."

He took his hands from her shoulders and put his arms around her, pulling her close. Her still-shaking body calmed in his embrace. When she looked up, he kissed her on the lips, a nervous but tender kiss that only hinted at what might have been.

"Try not to worry," he whispered. "It will work out."

# CHAPTER 2

# Monumental Meeting

## *Five months earlier*

The founder of the Beaufort County Historical Society said she organized it in 1935 because there was nothing else to do during the Depression. Society members would meet a lot or a little, depending on who served as president. And annual dues were twenty-five dollars, meetings or no meetings. In recent years, the club had become more active, having identified three locations in the county deserving of historical markers and supplying the state of South Carolina with enough background information to justify them.

Like the county itself, Society members consisted mainly of older, retired, life-long residents, but the past decade had seen a few new members described as "come heres." They were part of an influx who had sold their homes in New England and Ohio at prices affording waterfront property in Beaufort, with enough left over to buy a sporting yacht or fund their grandchildren's college tuition. Gradually, they homogenized with the locals, taking on the look, feel, and smell of lifers. They had traded their polo shirts emblazoned with the crests of their Connecticut or Rhode Island country clubs for the rural plaids that evoked life in the slow lane, their blood pressures fading with their jeans. Instead of ordering crab au gratin at a haute café in Newport or Greenwich, they threw crab pots off their docks. Three days and a bountiful harvest later, they might turn their heads at the sight and stench of chicken necks clawed by the crabs for their last supper, but that bisque that had cost eighteen dollars in yesterday's life now came in at a cool dollar-fifty. Judge Daniel Borders knew them all. He had grown up with the natives and instinctively reached out to newcomers.

By the time Darling Moore called to order the January meeting, Dan sat patiently among them in the public library's community room. He was conscious of a certain malaise he felt as he surveyed the room. These were the same people he saw at the Kiwanis Club or the potluck supper at the Methodist Church he attended. The reasons to gather changed, as did some participants, yet there was a sameness to them that had only recently begun to weigh on him.

That changed when Alana Morgan entered the room slightly out of breath. If she chose a seat in the back row so as not to call attention to her tardiness, it didn't work. Every person turned to look. *Exactly who*, Dan wondered, *is this*?

His answer came moments later when Darling Moore welcomed her as the Society's newest member. Alana blushed as she waved a hand, a jerky up-and-down acknowledgment that seemed designed to deflect the attention she had attracted. Dan tried not to stare.

Moore gave a light tap on her podium with a gavel. Named for the Darling family whose ancestors arrived in 1712, she stood tall with puffed silver hair, powdered cheeks similarly puffed, and matronly dress. She wore pearls.

"Before we begin tonight's meeting," Darling said, "we must take a moment to congratulate our own Judge Borders. I know you all saw or heard about the story in *The State* newspaper suggesting he's in line to become the next chief justice on our supreme court."

Directing her gaze to him, she continued, "Dan, this doesn't surprise anyone who knows you as we do, and it will be such a great honor when it happens."

He lowered his head in a modest deflection. "Thank you, Darling. You know what they say about counting those chickens. I continue to believe that others have a better chance, but I'm flattered to be mentioned, and we'll see where it goes."

"And now," said Darling, pressing a liver-spotted hand to her throat as if the greeting she was about to extend might leap from it before words could form on her lips, "we are delighted to welcome our newest member, Ms. Alana Morgan, who teaches government at Beaufort High." Polite applause. "Please come to the dais and tell us something about yourself, dear."

Alana stood and walked past the chair where Dan sat. With posture erect but not rigid, she approached Darling. When she turned to face the audience, Dan saw confidence and none of the apologetic hesitation of moments before. She wore little makeup, a touch of eyeliner which highlighted watchful green eyes. Her lips suggested a natural pout. Dark hair, framing what Dan perceived as a lovely face, fell to her shoulders.

She briefly sketched her background, focusing on her efforts to get a college degree after what she described only as "some early missteps." She stated her age at thirty-one, making her the youngest member of the Society by almost two decades. She attended Technical College of the Lowcountry until she earned enough credits to be admitted to the University of South Carolina at Beaufort, from which she graduated with a major in history.

"It took ten years," she said, "but I did it. As a single parent with a daughter to raise, getting that degree was a struggle." She expressed her love for the area, "where so much American history began."

"Well, we are delighted to have you," affirmed Darling. "And we are always open to new ways to honor our county's history, so speak up if you have any ideas."

"I have a question," Alana said. "Does the Society ever make recommendations to the city council?"

A perplexed look crossed Darling's face. "Not in my memory," she said uncertainly, scanning her listeners for affirmation. "I suppose we could if the need arose. Do you have something in mind?"

Alana glanced at the floor, hesitant. In a confessional tone, she said, "Being new, I'm reluctant to suggest it before we get to know each other. It seems presumptuous." When she looked up, she found all eyes looking back with a mix of curiosity and anticipation.

"Don't let that trouble you, dear. We are all adults here. Jump right in."

"It concerns the Confederate monument at the old courthouse. I think it's time to retire it to a museum."

The Beaufort monument was notable for two features: first, it did not occupy the courtyard's center as was the fashion in small Southern towns, and second, it lacked the gray-clad soldier, which was so common throughout Southern capitals. Instead, a marble obelisk, square in shape, rose from a solid base. Etched into it was a Confederate flag and the simple inscription, *To our Confederate Dead, 1861-1865.*

Darling froze. For several long, silent seconds, she stood mute. When she found her voice, it was only to say she was speechless.

"I know this is controversial," acknowledged Alana. "As I said, I hesitated to bring it up, this being my first meeting with you, but it's something I feel strongly about."

Frances Mellencamp, who wore a scarf to cover baldness resulting from recent chemotherapy and who often nodded off in meetings, expressed disbelief that any member, new or old, would make such a suggestion. Edgar Russ flashed her a thumbs-up.

Randal Stephens, bald, potbellied, and a member for a quarter of a century, spoke up. "I don't know a single person in this county who would support such an idea."

Alana replied evenly, "I have African Americans in my classes who support it."

Stephens pushed a raised hand dismissively, as if batting away the concept. "More nonsense from the radical left. I worry about what they are teaching in our schools."

"Well," offered Alana patiently, "I am a product of that same school system, and for many years, I thought as you do, but I've learned some things, and I think they have a point."

"No point I consider worth a tinker's damn, excuse my French. Lots of folks out there trying to erase our history, our heritage. Next thing you know, they'll be wanting to take Lee off Monument Avenue in Richmond, and then where would we be?" Heads nodded around the circle. "I move we reject this idea here and now." All hands went up except for those of Dan, Alana, and Darling, who seemed too stunned to move.

"Now just a moment," Dan said, feeling energized by Alana's presence, which struck him like a spice added to the bland recipe of these meetings. "That's not the way we do things here, and it's certainly not the way we treat a new member. This is a controversial topic, and none of us knows enough about it to decide anything tonight. Ms. Morgan has done us a favor by raising the issue. I have a suggestion. Why don't we form a committee to study the idea and report back? That way, we'll get to learn the pros and cons. I'll be happy to serve on it. Ms. Morgan, I assume you would serve?"

Alana nodded.

"Who else?" asked Dan.

Stephens raised his hand, though it was closer to a clinched fist. "I'll serve if I can take the cons." Frances Mellencamp clapped a hand over her mouth to keep from laughing.

"So there you have it," said Darling with a slight sniff, as if closing the door on an unpleasant odor. "We have a committee chaired by Judge Borders, which will study the matter and report back. Personally, I cannot claim to be unbiased in the matter, as I am a proud member of the United Daughters of the Confederacy, and we built that monument."

# CHAPTER 3

# Toby

The balance of the meeting was devoted to an archaeological dig recently begun outside Yemassee. A professor of archaeology at the University of Virginia suspected the remains of a colonial fort lay beneath it, but the discussion dragged, and as a practical matter, the meeting had ended with the formation of the monument study committee. Darling adjourned them early, making a hasty exit before she could be besieged by indignant reactions from members who had remained silent in the wake of Alana's suggestion. After everyone else left, Stephens, his arms folded across his chest, stood several feet apart from Dan and Alana, as if fearing contamination from infectious ideas.

"Let's get a plan," Dan suggested. "Alana, if I may call you Alana, why don't you recommend some reading that you think will help us discuss this more productively? I'll work with you on that. Randy, I know other communities are wrestling with this issue, so how about you look into how they are handling it? Maybe ask around in Summerville on your next trip." Stephens made weekly visits there to buy a hog, which he roasted over hickory wood to sell from a stand each Saturday at the Port Royal Farmers Market. His grill accommodated a pig weighing up to one-hundred-eighty-five pounds, and he sold out every Saturday.

"Judge, no offense, but I can tell you what those ol' boys in Summerville think of this idea, and I'd be embarrassed to ask them."

"Yeah, maybe you're right," Dan conceded. "Anyway, let's meet back here in two weeks."

Stephens had an afterthought. "Can that monument be moved? Legally, I mean. I read somewhere there was some law . . ." He looked at Dan.

"As a judge, I can't help you there," Dan said. "It's unlikely, but some legal issue could arise that I'd be called upon to decide. Check with the city attorney."

On their way to the parking lot, Dan told Alana that it was brave of her to propose what she did, knowing the hostility she would engender. "These are good folks," he said, "but they tend toward the rigid where certain subjects are concerned. I suspect you already know that from teaching their grandkids."

Alana gently chuckled. "I came tonight expecting what I got. What I didn't expect was finding an ally who would defend me, so thank you for that. Teaching high school has prepared me for hostility."

"I suppose I'm dating myself by saying this, but I walked those same halls and sat in those same classrooms as a student, and hostility isn't a word I would have associated with those days. Boring at times, but not hostile."

"It has changed even since I was a student there, which wasn't that long ago."

"Maybe it's your perspective. Mine, too. Perhaps our teachers felt hostility that we in our adolescent naivete were oblivious to."

"Maybe," Alana conceded. She stopped in mid-stride and turned to him. "I paid a big price for my 'adolescent naivete,' as you put it. His name is Toby."

As Dan headed to his SUV, she walked to her 2001 green Honda Civic, got in, and turned the key on an engine that would not start. She got out, slammed the driver's door, walked to the front, raised the hood, and stood peering down into the engine, her back to him, her feet planted slightly apart, her hands on her hips. Dan pulled up next to her, powered down the passenger window, and leaned toward her to ask if he could help. For an instant, he assumed she hadn't heard him as she stared down into the engine, her back still to him, her hands now at her side. Then she turned slowly, leaned back against the grill, and said with a slight grin, "Yes, shoot it or me. Right now, I don't care which."

"A bit dramatic, don't you think?"

Alana cocked her head lightly, ignoring the barb. "Do you have jumper cables?" she asked, looking over his passenger seat for eye contact. As she leaned, her dark, shoulder-length hair parted so that a small silver earring in the shape of the symbol for the Greek letter omega became visible.

Dan got out, retrieved cables from the trunk. She took them. "Pop your hood," she instructed. She seemed in no hurry but moved decisively and with confidence as she clipped the negative lead to the frame. Leaning into the engine compartment, she held one hand against her blouse to avoid stain.

"I've done this a few times," she said over her shoulder.

Finished, she handed the remaining leads to Dan. In the exchange, his hand brushed hers, and he wondered if she or the lead had imparted some fractional electric charge.

"Hook us up," she ordered.

Dan attached the leads and moments later heard her engine start. "Better let it idle a few minutes," he said. She nodded from the driver's seat, her left foot on the asphalt and her skirt hiked to mid-thigh. He came around to her side where, looking down, he caught a glimpse of her left calf, firmly tapered into the ankle with the athletic tone of a runner.

"Thanks," she said. "That's the third time this month. I need a new car." She hesitated, then added, "Obviously." Dan had noted rust on the fender.

"Do you have far to go? I could follow you for a while."

"Fifteen miles, to Seabrook," she said. "I don't want to put you out. Do you go west?"

"East," he said.

His gaze drew hers upward. With a note of recognition, she said, "As soon as I heard your name tonight, it hit me how I knew it. You signed my divorce back in '02. Most important document of my life," she added, "except for my daughter's birth certificate."

"Did we meet?"

"No. I never went to court. Only to some lawyer's office for a deposition. I better disconnect the cables before they burn up." She gathered in the cables as he lowered his hood.

"Why don't you take them with you?" he suggested. "If it conks out, you'll at least have something."

"Would you mind? I feel so stupid for not buying some. I'll bring them back, I promise."

"No hurry."

"I guess I know where you work," she said with a chuckle. "I'll drop them off unless this car won't start. Again." Her shoulders sagged. "How can I enjoy my job when getting back and forth to work is such a struggle?" Then, she brightened, and Dan detected something personal. "I suppose I should hold you responsible."

"Me?"

"You awarded this klunker to me in that divorce I mentioned."

"Did you ask for it?"

"Of course, but it was new then." An impishness crept into her voice. "So, you see? It's your fault."

He grinned. "A thousand apologies for giving you what you wanted."

She returned to the driver's side, opened the door, then paused before getting in. "I better get started. My daughter will think I've been kidnapped. Thanks again for the rescue."

"No trouble," he said, conscious of how sincerely he felt it.

"I'll return your jumpers. I really will."

# CHAPTER 4

# Bullshit Detector

D an studied a surface of aged oak, passing his fingertips along its splintered contours as a blind man might examine a face or tombstone. He found a fissure, set into it the leading corner of an iron wedge and tapped it firmly with a mall hammer. Stepping back, he brought the hammer down hard, broadcasting like a gunshot blast. In the salt marsh lining the creek, a startled blue heron lifted off in dignified protest, and an osprey took flight from its elevated nest in the top of a bald cypress. The wedge penetrated, the fissure widened, the crosscut yielded; the strength of a century sundered with a single blow. He righted one half, inserted the wedge, and repeated his motions, reducing the log to firewood.

He straightened, pressing the thumb of his free hand hard against a muscle in his lumbar back. Sweat beaded at his forehead. Sunlight of a new day spread across sawgrass, brown in winter's hibernation. Over the cove, a half-mile from where he stood, the osprey drifted effortlessly on air currents, the way his mind kept drifting to Alana Morgan and her principled opposition to the Confederate monument. *That took guts.* He had brought her divorce file home for a weekend read.

The judge wiped his brow with his sleeve. Around him lay massy crosscuts of an oak tree felled by a storm two winters back. Seasoned now, they rested like giant checkers flung aside an unseen board. In the distance, his house stood silent and dark. His wife, Claire, would be asleep for another hour.

Enoch's Cove, named for one of the county's original settlers, carved out a quarter-moon shore on Distant Island Creek where three homes stood. The Borders's house presided over a narrow channel leading from the Beaufort River into the upper reaches of the creek where, at low tide, a canoe risked stranding. Adjacent to the Borders property lived the Prescotts, centered on the Cove some two-hundred yards from where Dan chopped wood. The third house in the watery arc stood vacant, its owner having died two years earlier and his heirs, three grown children who lived out of state, still undecided about the fate of the place.

Dan embedded his axe in a stump, leaning backward to stretch muscles beginning to tense. Groaning in relief, he gazed toward the Prescott home, where chimney smoke swirled above a notch in the tree line. He whistled. Banjo, his black Lab, bounded from the brush, and together they started on a worn path. At the boundary line of his property, he picked a fistful of the daffodils he knew Wanda Prescott would want.

The Prescott home began as a two-story saltbox constructed in 1962. The basic design had been appended, over the ensuing decades, a haphazard sprawl of decks and porches, each representing Wanda Prescott's maturing opinion as to the best view of the cove, the optimum sunlight at her then-favored time of day, the most enthralling shadows in which to sip her chilled martinis after 5:00 p.m.

Dan approached French doors off the study as Banjo sniffed at Wanda's boxwoods in an uninspired meander. Dan knocked twice. "Daniel the Just," said Andy, throwing open one door. "Let's leave it open. A bit stuffy in here."

"Andrew the Celestial," acknowledged Dan in their custom of exaggerated greeting. Andy's nickname derived from the observatory he had constructed just after he sold his insurance agency. It was there that Andy spent clear evenings. Andy shook Dan's hand as they stepped inside.

"How about some coffee?"

"The blacker the better," said Dan, following Andy's lead across the study, oppressive in the heat generated in the fireplace, through a short corridor into the kitchen. At the breakfast table, Wanda sat eating toast.

"I heard you bright and early this morning," she said as they entered. A housecoat of Oriental design, cinched at the waist, accentuated her lean frame, which was beginning to show frailty. The kitchen smelled of coffee and warm cinnamon. As Andy poured, Dan joined her, handing her the daffodils as he sat.

"These are lovely. I keep threatening to plant them, but I'm spoiled by a thoughtful neighbor that knows me well. Thank you."

"I hope the sound of my mighty axe didn't wake you."

Wanda smiled, still looking at the flowers. "Not exactly, but what does it say about our little country compound when one neighbor gets up early to chop wood and the other to burn it?"

Andy, approaching Dan with a mug, said, "Not very resourceful of us, is it? I believe the cold weather may be behind us. You're welcome to what's left of my supply."

Dan shook his head. "I do it for exercise." He added sugar, then sipped. "I've noticed you burn what you don't use up. Why?"

"To keep my store of wood from falling into the hands of the Yankees."

Wanda scoffed. "To discourage termites. Andy has a theory they migrate from the woodpile to the house."

Dan eyed him skeptically. "Anything to that?"

"When have you known me to back up a theory with proof? That's why you're a judge and I'm an astronomer."

"But astronomy is all proof, the most exacting science there is."

"Not the way I practice it." Andy peered into his coffee mug. "When you get into all that higher math, I lose interest and it loses me. I don't care so much about how it works, only how it appears." A slight man, almost feminine in his facial features, Andy blinked as if to clear his soft gray eyes. Wrinkles gathered at his neck affirmed his age, but these melded seamlessly into smooth, glabrous cheeks and jaw, contrasting surfaces that suggested plastic surgery but were, in fact, natural.

"You haven't visited Star-Splitter lately. I've mapped out a new piece of sky that I plan to study until I'm the world's foremost expert. Long after I'm gone, astronomers everywhere will refer to it simply as 'the Prescott.'"

Wanda stood, walked to the sink, and pulled a vase from a cabinet. "He wants to be cremated and his ashes spread across his slice of sky," she said over the rush of water filling the vase. "But you haven't said how you expect us to get them there, have you, dear?" She returned to the table, centering the bouquet. Then, as if the mention of cremation put her in mind of lonely days ahead (the Prescotts were childless), she reached across and placed a hand on Andy's forearm.

He appeared not to notice. "That's the least my executor can do for me.'"

"How did we get on this morbid subject?" she asked, withdrawing her hand.

"Termites," answered Dan.

"You see?" Andy said, turning to his wife. "He's been sitting there the whole time tracking our chatter like a good judge would track evidence. He's listening for proof of my termite theory. It's a hunch, that's all. Don't you ever get them?"

"All the time," Dan acknowledged, "but I'm always thankful when there is some evidence to support my gut."

"Maybe it's just me, but I don't think I'd have the courage to lie to a judge," Wanda said. "Too intimidating."

"It's just you," said Andy. "Am I right, Daniel?"

"People lie more than ever," Dan acknowledged.

"People have lied since Moses," Andy said. "He lied too, by the way."

Dan shook his head. "I really believe it's worse."

"Or maybe you're just getting older and you notice it more."

Dan smiled. "I acknowledge getting older."

"It's your bullshit detector," said Andy. "I remember mine got pretty sensitive after forty years in the insurance business. That's why I love my telescope. No bullshit whatsoever out there." He raised one arm and pointed vaguely at the universe. "Now Columbia, on the other hand . . ."

Dan gave out a dismissive snort as he winked at Wanda. "If you're talking about that supreme court stuff, relax. You have as good a chance as I do of ending up there."

"Not according to what I read," Andy countered. "I've asked around. From what I hear, you have a real shot at it."

# CHAPTER 5

# Otis Hazzard

As Dan sipped coffee and Wanda again admired her flowers, he thought back to the death penalty case that represented a turning point in his judicial career. In *Hazzard v. State*, a Beaufort jury found Otis Odell Hazzard guilty of capital murder, and the same jury in a subsequent proceeding sentenced him to die by lethal injection. It fell to Judge Borders to impose the jury's verdict. Nothing in his life experience matched the weight on his shoulders when he instructed Hazzard to stand, asked if he knew of any reason why the jury's sentence should not be imposed (Hazzard remained mute), and set a date for his execution.

Capital murder cases in Beaufort County were exceedingly rare. The last one before Hazzard had come in 1963, before Dan had been born. Dan's predecessor on the circuit court had never encountered one in twenty-two years on the bench. South Carolina statutes left Dan no choice but to carry out the jury's pronouncement, but that didn't mean he had to like it. And he didn't. He had studied South Carolina's death penalty statue. Empirical evidence showed it was deeply flawed, biased against the poor and people of color, and arbitrarily applied by those bent more on vengeance than justice.

Which is not to say that he wasn't convinced that his family, his county, and the world wouldn't be better off without Hazzard in it. Twice convicted of armed robbery, Hazzard had been in and out of prison since he was seventeen. In the case that brought him before Judge Borders, overwhelming evidence showed he beat to death with a tire iron a nineteen-year-old shrimper after an argument in a pool hall. *If there is a Hell*, Judge Borders thought, *Hazzard deserved a seat nearest the furnace.*

But Dan did not feel it was within his power, or any jury's, or the sovereign state of South Carolina's, to send Hazzard there. Months after the trial and sentencing, while still very much under the influence of his doubts, he wrote an article for the University of South Carolina Law Review:

*The decline in executions, both in this state and nationally, represents a growing awareness of the difficulties presented by these cases. The present system's failure stems from the inability of any judge or jury to decide, with God's unerring certainty, whether a convicted defendant should live or die.*

*For those found guilty of society's most abhorred crimes and sentenced to life without hope of parole, I would provide a means to make that final decision which increasingly conflicts us as a civilized people. In our maximum-security facility, I would build a small chamber into which a prisoner could be admitted upon reasonable notice. In this room, I would make available the pharmacological means to end life with as much speed and little pain as possible. In such a chamber, a jury of one will decide what our juries of twelve should not.*

*A few felons, I predict, will rush to it, impatient to leave the world that, for whatever reasons, they rebelled against. Others will die of old age, living out bleak destinies within sight of the room that provides their only alternative. And some will enter the room in the belief that their minds are made up, only to linger with one hand on the door and the other on the instrument of their own demise, much as judges and capital punishment juries linger now.*

The article included some practical safeguards—psychological assessments, a waiting period before admission to the death chamber, legal and religious consultations—but it was the quoted paragraphs that drew attention. Some wondered if perhaps it signaled an intent by the judge to enter politics, as his suggestion so clearly would require extensive legislative initiative. Even the local newspaper, reliably supportive of its hometown judge, questioned whether the recommended solution more properly belonged in a letter to the editor than in an erudite legal analysis.

Nevertheless, the opinion received extensive publicity in legal circles and beyond. A Charleston *Post and Courier* editorial praised the idea as "worthy of debate." The Courts of Justice Committee in the legislature went so far as to name a task force to investigate the merits. Its public hearings attracted predictable choruses—pro-lifers, euthanasia advocates, moralists, and ethicists. Psychiatrists worried about the risk of a temporary, untreated depression producing fatal desperation. Penal experts pondered the effect of the room's mere presence on morale within the prison. Religions from Baptists to Buddhists weighed in. A support group for nursing homes voiced concern that the concept could spread beyond its original boundaries, for couldn't those homes be seen as a form of life without parole? At every debate, the name Dan

Borders surfaced as the carpenter who built the Pandora's box, as detractors of the idea branded it.

When Chief Justice Oliver Bidwell Cox announced his intention to retire from the South Carolina Supreme Court at year's end, the name of Judge Daniel Niles Borders as a replacement surfaced early. His selection, like his life and career, had an air of inevitability, a destiny Andy had sensed years earlier when he and the judge first became neighbors.

Dan said to Andy, "I'm flattered to be mentioned, but Sidney Callahan has been calling in IOUs he's been accumulating since I was in law school."

"Which only means he's old, like me," Andy said. "If they put you up there, you could serve long enough to make a difference."

"Maybe. But the legislature has the last say, and Sidney's influence there is a weapon I doubt I can match. I suspect he's got it locked up, or nearly so."

Andy lowered his coffee mug with a thud, as if pounding a nail in the question he was about to ask. "Let me put it to you directly, and none of that lying we were just talking about. Do you want it?"

Dan paused, then nodded decisively. "In all honesty, I'm troubled by how much I want it. I can't say I ever expected it, stuck out here in a county some legislators can't locate on a map, but a chance to serve on the state's highest court? I'd give my right arm, and that's the one I use to fly fish."

"I suspected as much," Andy said. "Let us know if we can help."

"Tell us about Claire," Wanda said. "I haven't seen her all week."

"The past few days have been rough."

Wanda shook her head slowly. "Poor doll. I don't see how she does it. Always so cheerful, so . . . positive."

"Not always," Dan muttered. "But were our situations reversed, I know my bad days would outnumber the good by a mile." His voice trailed off further. "I'm worried about her. Until recently, she was genuinely determined not to let her disease control her life."

"And now?" Wanda asked softly.

"She seems to have gone from disease management to anger management. Before MS, she loved her work for the altar guild at church. She prided herself on making the arrangements 'glow,' as she liked to say. Now she hates it because she can't go pick the flowers herself. All the joy is gone."

"Perhaps some counseling!"

"I've suggested that. She insists she got it when she was diagnosed. I don't think she appreciates how much things have changed."

Wanda moved her hand from her coffee mug to cover Dan's hand, patting it maternally. He felt radiant warmth. "Perhaps she realizes too well. I'd be furious," she said. "You can't begrudge Claire her anger."

"I worry she is now fighting a different enemy and doesn't realize it."

"But are they different enemies?" Andy piped. "Or just a distinction without a difference? I don't know; I'm asking."

"Anger's more pervasive," answered Dan. "It can take over your life more completely than a wheelchair. I don't say it has done that yet with Claire. She is fighting the good fight. I just see signs, small things that tell me she is dealing with a growing awareness of just how consuming her illness can be." He stood. "I need to get back. Thanks for the coffee and broad shoulders to cry on. I didn't come over to unburden myself."

"Of course, you didn't," said Andy, "but we hope you feel free to do so. I'll walk you back. I need to stretch my legs."

Wanda stood, tightened her housecoat at the waist, and walked them through the study. Outside, Dan let out a shrill whistle, which brought Banjo bounding from the woods toward which they walked. The dog fell in beside them. They entered the woods under a canopy of water oaks, Spanish moss hanging in profusion, with wrens and jays chirping unseen in higher branches. Dead leaves of winter lay just off the path. Banjo paused periodically, seemingly attuned to some mocking insult cast down by the birds.

From the corner of his eye, Dan saw a car driving slowly along the main road, past his driveway and approaching Andy's. In it, a girl appeared to be staring back at him, though, from this distance, he couldn't be sure of her age. She must have been young because her head came just within the passenger window. Again, because of the distance, he couldn't be certain, but the green car had some age on it and looked very much like the one Alana was trying to start on the night they had met. The car picked up speed, rounding a bend in the road.

# CHAPTER 6

# Friendship's Boundaries

As the green car vanished, Dan felt sure it must be the Honda he awarded Alana in her divorce. *What was she doing here?* he wondered. *Was that her daughter looking out the window?*

Dan turned his attention back to Andy. He valued his friend as much in silence as in conversation, but here Andy stopped and turned to him.

"Dan, something occurred to me back at the house. I didn't want to say anything in front of Wanda."

"Shoot."

"I hope I'm not overstepping some boundary between us."

"I wasn't aware of any, unless you count the property line."

Andy laughed patiently. "You're right. At any rate, as you described Claire, I couldn't help thinking that the same might be said of you."

"How so?"

"You've . . . changed. I see signs. Little things a friend might notice."

"For instance?"

"Your withdrawal at cocktail parties. I watched you over the Christmas holidays. Living in Beaufort, we tend to see each other socially, perhaps too much. You looked like you were tolerating the entire season. I intended to say something before now."

"But it does get tiresome, don't you think?"

"Of course, but it shouldn't start out tiresome. Again, I don't want to step on toes, but I got the impression you were disengaged from everyone around you, including your children, I might add. That's not like you."

Dan dropped his head. As he toed the ground with his boot, Banjo sniffed aggressively as if something pungent was about to be unearthed.

"It's very difficult," he acknowledged in a subdued tone. "Being a judge, you become isolated, and that isolation increases with time. But I'll be fine. It comes with the job."

"Yes, but you adapted to the job years ago. Perhaps the combination of the job and Claire . . . are you depressed?"

Dan shook his head. "My profession has given me a PhD in the causes and effects of depression, and I'm not depressed."

"Naturally, this situation with Claire would make anyone depressed. Let's be honest. It's an awful affliction. And Claire deserves our praise for how she's handled it. But what about you? How are you handling it?"

"It's been hard to see her go from a vibrant, active woman to a woman in a wheelchair."

"Yes, but that's you watching her, like you're in the crowd of a Roman amphitheater with sympathies for the gladiator. Like you're eighteen rows up and safely above the fray." Andy tapped his index finger decidedly on Dan's shirt pocket. Six inches shorter, Andy spoke directly into his chest. "I'm talking about you. You're in the ring along with Claire. Your battle is not just her battle, but your own. I mean, you lost your wife—not literally, of course, but you've lost what she's lost plus something."

"Plus what?"

"Control. Don't get so focused on her that you forget yourself. You must be selfish to survive. Unless you look out for yourself, you won't be able to look out for her."

"I have my work. I have the children."

"They're not children anymore, and they're not here."

"You know what I mean."

"Does your work give you pleasure?"

Dan paused and raised his gaze over Andy's head, searching the far shore of the creek for his reply. "Had you asked me that a year ago, I would have said I like being a judge."

"And now you don't?"

"It's the supreme court business. In my wildest dreams, I never expected the buzz my Jury of One idea is getting. People are calling from all over the state. And the country. What I told you and Wanda about Sidney Callahan is true, but what I failed to mention were the calls I've had from the lieutenant governor on down telling me I've got a realistic shot at it. Me! A little 'ole circuit court judge from Beaufort nobody ever heard of until the *Hazzard* case. I know better than to count my chickens, but I meant it when I said it troubles me how much I want it."

"Nothing wrong with ambition unless, of course, it destroys you."

Dan's face registered a patient indulgence. "Right."

A squirrel crossed the path ahead. Banjo sprinted for it. The men laughed as the Lab stood at the base of the tree oscillating his head between them and the refuged squirrel.

"Thanks for the visit, Daniel the Just," Andy said as they resumed walking. "If you ever feel the need to unload, I promise

I'll be mute. Come down and look at the sky with me some night. It will do you good."

At the head of the path, they shook hands. Andy turned toward home. Dan eyed his axe embedded in the stout oak stump. He started toward it, changed his mind, and walked instead to the side door of his house. With Claire still asleep, now would be a good time to learn about that divorce he entered years ago that Alana had described as the second most important document in her life.

# Making Her Mark

The house was as quiet as he had hoped. Claire still slept. He entered his study and sat at his desk. The *Morgan v. Morgan* divorce file rested before him. He opened it, extracting a deposition transcript thicker than what he had expected. Alana, duly sworn, testified that she had been born Alana Suzanne Saunders on January 16, 1979, in Edgefield, South Carolina. In 1991, her family moved to Beaufort County, where she attended high school, graduating in 1998. She married Toby Morgan that summer and gave birth in the fall to a daughter, who they called Holly.

"And did there come a time in your marriage," her lawyer had asked, "when you came to fear Toby Morgan, your husband?"

Answer: "Yes. Within the first month. He was fine as long as he wasn't drinking, but he drank often. Heavily, I'd say."

Question: "He had not done this when you were dating?"

**Answer:** "He drank a few beers now and then, but nothing like his habit after we were married."

**Question:** "Describe his behavior after you married him."

**Answer:** "He worked construction. He got off about four and drank with his buddies until eight or nine. Then he'd come home, usually with beer, sometimes with vodka. He would drink some more, until he passed out. I was trying to make a family budget work, and every week it seemed we were short of money because he drank it up."

**Question:** "And when he came home drunk, did he make demands upon you?"

**Answer:** "Yes. He wanted dinner and sex. I usually gave him dinner."

**Question:** "Did there come a time when he became violent?"

**Answer:** "About three months after we were married, he threw a beer bottle at me."

**Question:** "At this point, you were . . . what . . . five months pregnant?"

**Answer:** "Seven. The bottle missed me, but it hit the TV. Then he broke a chair by kicking it. He wore those steel-toed work boots, and the chair just shattered. It was old but sturdy. This was my first real taste of his temper."

Question: "But not the last?"

Answer: "A few weeks later, after he broke the chair, he came home drunk and angry. He had been in a fight on the job. Almost got fired. I tried to calm him down. He punched a toaster. I was afraid he would break the few things we had. I tried to stop him. He pushed me down. I fell pretty hard. I put on my coat and told him I was leaving."

Question: "What did he do then?"

Answer: "He"—witness paused.

Question: "Do you need a few minutes?"

Answer: "No. Let's get this over with. What was the question?"

Question: "He pushed you down hard. You put on your coat to leave. What did he do then?"

Answer: "He grabbed me. I was at the door, just at the top of the stairs. We lived in this garage apartment, and the stairs were steep. I fought him. He put his hands around my throat. I couldn't breathe, so I kneed him in the nuts. Pardon me, in the groin. I pushed him away but lost my balance."

Question: "He pushed you down the stairs?"

Answer: "He did. I ended up at the bottom. I went into

labor immediately. I called up to him, to tell him I was hurt, that my water had broken, and that I needed to get to the hospital fast."

Question: "And what was his reaction?"

Answer: "He looked down at me, then reached in his pocket. He threw down the keys to the truck and slammed the door. My daughter Holly was born the next morning."

Question: "Was it a normal birth?"

Answer: "If you mean, 'is she normal?' the answer is yes. I hemorrhaged and almost died."

Question: "Did he come to see you in the hospital?"

Answer: "No."

Question: "What happened next?"

Answer: "I spent two weeks in the hospital. They let my daughter stay with me. When we were discharged, I asked my parents for help, just for a while, but they had been dead set against him from the beginning. They offered to take in Holly . . . only. I decided to go back. I had no choice. But it didn't work. I knew it wouldn't. His drinking got worse, even with a new baby in the house."

Question: "And when was the last time you cohabitated as man and wife?"

Answer: "Do you mean slept together?"

**Question:** "Yes."

**Answer:** "Not after that night on the stairs. I told him I'd live with him, but I'd kill him if he touched me or my daughter."

**Question:** "Did there come a time when he left?"

**Answer:** "Fifteen months ago. I haven't seen him since."

The judge read to the end, adjusting his glasses as he scanned the testimony related to property. She had asked for the car, the household effects, sole custody of Holly, and that her husband be ordered to pay monthly child support and the judgment against her taken by the hospital stemming from the birth of their daughter. She had no life insurance and feared leaving Holly penniless if the worst happened, so he ordered Toby to keep in force a policy of $50,000 naming her as beneficiary, and to send her proof he paid the premiums.

Reading her deposition revived in him a memory he carried from it, of a young woman at the bottom of steep stairs soaked in amniotic fluid. He never expected to meet her, but now he had. He tried to conjure up a picture of the brutish man at the top of the stairs, tossing down the keys, but it blurred into an indistinct mass of wanton cruelty. Had he ever personally known someone capable of such behavior? He couldn't think of one, though any number of them had come before him as a judge. Early in his law practice, he had been court appointed to represent a child abuser to whom he took an instant dislike. No legal ethic required a lawyer to like his client, only to zealously represent him. Dan struggled to find the requisite zeal, and silently rejoiced when his client was found guilty. Perhaps that convicted felon was the closest he had come to someone capable of Toby Morgan's evil.

Alana's testimony must have moved him in 2002, when he entered the final decree. Of other divorces he had entered since, he had no memory. Violence, like so many things, faded over time, so that only the most bizarre rapes, murders, or arsons retained distinctive outline. Yet eight years later, he was still able to summon the memory of the woman at the bottom of the stairs. Not her face but her plight.

◉  ◉  ◉

As it was Saturday morning, his odds were good of finding Lucille Taylor at home. He punched in her number from an old rolodex on the desk. Taylor had been the Beaufort High guidance counselor for forty years.

"Why, Daniel Borders, what a pleasant surprise."

"Good morning, Mrs. Taylor."

"Mrs. Taylor? You know better than to call me that. If any of my students has earned the right to call me Lucille, it's you, Dan Borders. And haven't I been thrilled to read about this supreme court appointment? Not to brag, but I predicted it when you were a sophomore! Well, maybe not the supreme court exactly, but great things. You remember I predicted great things."

Lucille Taylor was hardly alone in predicting a bright future for Dan. It was said among many who noticed such things. Certainly, his third-grade teacher saw it in the way Dan organized his pencils on his desk and printed his name in neat block letters in the upper right corner, as she had repeatedly asked the class to do. Sarah Trout, known to her sixth graders as Miss Fish when her back was turned, noted the way boys and girls alike gravitated toward Dan, especially impressive at an age when, as Miss Fish well knew, social circles were beginning to be drawn by the kids determined to ensure they landed within those circles. Coach Bennett told Coach Higgins after the first day of JV football practice that there was something about the Borders boy. "Seems too nice, but give him a few pounds and a couple of years and he'll be a good 'un." A "good 'un" was about the highest praise you could earn from Coach Bennett. And Pastor Kanney at the First Methodist Church said to the bishop on more than one occasion that his youth group might have dissolved had it not been for Dan's regular presence and inspired participation. "It all begins at home," the pastor said, referring to Dan's parents, William and Molly Borders, widely respected throughout the county.

"I'm grateful . . . Lucille. You boosted my confidence."

"Not that you ever lacked it. How can I help you this fine morning?"

"I'm calling about Alana Morgan."

"You know, I still want to call her Alana Saunders because that was her name when I advised her back in, let's see, class of '98, I think. I hope she's not in trouble."

"No, nothing like that. She recently joined the Historical Society, and we're working together on a project involving our Civil War monument."

"Ouch. I wouldn't want to touch that one."

Dan laughed. "No kidding. I suspect it will be a thankless task, but as they say, someone has to do it. Since I will be working with her, I was hoping you could give me some background."

"On or off the record?"

"Let's start with on."

"She's an excellent teacher, very bright and well-liked by her students and other teachers. Personally and professionally, I consider her one of my biggest accomplishments. But she is also one of my biggest failures, and here we need to go off the record . . . and you never heard this from me."

"Understood," Dan said.

"Alana was one of those students, and she was by no means

the only one we dealt with, who came from such a troubled home life that struggling should have been her middle name. I call it troubled. Today they would say dysfunctional. Father couldn't hold a job, drank himself silly, arrested for forging a check and other things I can't recall. As a judge, you've seen your share of them."

"I certainly have."

"I only met her mother a couple of times, and the way she spoke, I doubt the poor thing made it past eighth grade, with bad teeth and clothes that . . . well, you get the picture. And don't get me started on her brother. So, with all that chaos at home, I didn't give Alana much of a chance, but she proved me wrong because she studied hard and applied herself and kept her skirts clean. Back in her day, we called in the better students, you know, the ones we felt were college material, in the fall of junior year to ask about their plans after graduation. I could tell right away that Alana was embarrassed, and of course, I knew why. If they had any money, daddy would drink it up before she could matriculate even at the community college. But she had the grades and the extracurriculars for a very good school if we could find the money, so together we explored every scholarship imaginable and just about the time it all came together—"

"Toby Morgan showed up?"

"Bingo. From the moment he arrived senior year, I knew he was trouble. But Alana, she was moonstruck and all over him. It broke my heart because I had seen it happen more than once. You remember that Mary Sue Peterson from your class?"

"I remember Mary Sue very well, but not in the way some of my male classmates remember her."

"Well, there you go. So, Alana was pregnant at graduation, married with a child and stuck with a husband who lacked enough sense or maturity to earn a merit badge in the Boy Scouts. I tried to warn her. Called her in and told her the future was so bright for her with a college degree and so limited without one. But I could tell by the look in her eyes that her mind was a mile away, probably thinking about Toby."

"Sad," agreed Dan, "and not uncommon, as you know better than most."

A pause on Lucille Taylor's end. "So, I count Alana a failure on my part. But you know that when she returned to Beaufort as a teacher, she stopped by my office on her first day, closed the door, and told me I had been right and that she had been a fool not to listen. I thought she was going to cry, and I did cry after she left. Sweet thing. She's going to make her mark in this world yet. That's my prediction, and it's on the record."

As he closed Alana's divorce file, he heard Claire's chairlift descending to the living room.

# Feeling Worse

Dan spent the afternoon cleaning out an upstairs closet located between bedrooms. It had become a magnet for the clutter accumulated by a family of four. He set aside for discard an old, rarely used set of golf clubs, a ceramic lamp he had been intending to mend for at least three years, and an ancient Waring blender whose motor had burned out not long after Christina had been born. Twenty years had now passed. Dan gripped a tennis racquet with strings frayed and slackened, its wooden press loosely affixed. He had been a strong player in his twenties, with a murderous serve and competent ground strokes.

Reaching behind a shoe rack, his elbow struck a hard object in a zipped compartment of a garment bag suspended among Claire's old clothes. He opened it to find a bottle of gin, half empty.

He turned the bottle over in his hands, mulling the portent of this minor treason. Treason, because her repugnance to alcohol as a source of strength or solace had been so vocal. To all appearance, she needed no anesthetic, and in Claire's world, appearance was nothing short of displayed reality, although a few in Beaufort, prior to her illness, might have termed it flaunted reality. She had embraced her illness as openly as she had welcomed Christina's recognition as a National Merit Scholarship finalist, Ethan's athletic awards, Dan's judgeship, or her own nomination and selection as Converse College's Alumnae of the Year. MS was a disease, nothing more or less; she had it, and she was dealing with it. Drugs were essential allies in the fight, of course, but the real war was one of the spirit, fought during long evenings reading or watching television, and in early morning hours when she repeatedly shifted her head on the pillow, as she had always done when sleepless. Throughout it all, she had refused whatever comfort others found in hard drinking, an occasional glass of wine or a token cocktail marking the outer limit of her indulgence. Dan stared down at the bottle, balanced between his thumb and forefinger, letting the gin run one way, then the other, as if it was a tide. Had he been subconsciously looking for something in this closet?

Later, after he had showered and dressed, he went downstairs to find Claire reading in the family room. She looked up as he entered.

"Going somewhere?" she asked.

"Only the video store if you still want that Meryl Streep movie."

"I do. You want to see it, don't you?" She closed her book, resting it on her lap.

"I'm happy to get it, if I can remember the name."

"*Doubt.*"

"Oh, yes. *Doubt.* Do you need anything else while I'm out?"

"Dan, you're pouting. We don't have to watch it. I know it doesn't interest you."

"I didn't say that."

"You don't have to. Let's forget it. It's a long ride into town, and besides, I've seen it. Really."

Dan walked by her chair, momentarily resting his hand on her shoulder. "Then perhaps I'll fix a drink."

"Yes, do that, darling. You've worked hard today. I saw you carrying all those things to the garage. Is there anything left upstairs?"

"More than you can imagine. Can I fix you a drink, too?"

"You know I've sworn off booze." A voice inflexion seemed to creep into Claire's speech, something that happened when she adopted what he had come to think of as her good-soldier attitude. Such remarks, pitched half a key higher than her conversational tone and spoken with a barely audible underscoring by slowing her diction and accenting hard syllables, were not affectations, Dan had concluded. Rather, they represented something akin to official pronouncements, Claire's considered view of whatever had been asked, said, or intimated. She was unconscious of this pattern, but Dan knew it surfaced whenever she felt her moral authority, her personal credibility, called forth. He heard it now, in her answer.

"If I take comfort in a bottle," she said at her measured pace, "where would it end? I'm in this chair for a long sit." She paused, and when she resumed, her voice returned to normalcy. "I'm surprised that you would encourage me that way."

Dan crossed his legs and shook his head slowly. "Not encourage, exactly. We all need a little relief from stress. You used to enjoy a cocktail on nights like tonight—the kids out, the house to ourselves."

"I enjoyed tennis, too." Her expression changed into something unpleasant. "Oh, Dan, forget I said that. It's just the kind of indulgent self-pity I've taken a vow against. You promised you'd shoot me if I begin wallowing, didn't you?"

"Feeling sorry for yourself is like drinking . . . a little won't hurt you."

"It's exactly like drinking. They're both addictive. The last thing we need on our hands is a wallowing lush."

Dan stood. "Well, at the risk of lushness, I'm going to fix a bourbon. You're sure you won't have one?"

"Don't mock me. I'm being prudent for both of us."

"Don't take this wrong, dear, but I spend my week being prudent. On Saturday night, I'm not above encouraging a little depravity, or engaging in it either."

He started to the bar, feeling her eyes follow him. As he dropped ice into a cocktail glass, he knew she was waiting for him to turn, to face her. He covered the ice with two fingers of bourbon.

"Dan," she said upon eye contact, her voice hard and flat. "Why make me feel worse? I can't help it. On those nights you mentioned, when the house was quiet and we had a few drinks, I could walk upstairs with you, and when we got into bed, I could enjoy it. Why are you doing this?"

"What am I doing?"

"You're hinting, and it's making me feel bad."

# CHAPTER 9

# Alluding to Sex

Dan sat quietly, sipping his drink and swirling the ice in his glass. He studied the tiny rivulets of water bleeding from the cubes. Waves like elevation lines on a map of mountainous terrain melted into the whiskey, a lighter amber on top but darker, purer at the bottom of his glass. He felt the first effervescence from bourbon entering his bloodstream. He watched Claire adjust the cotton afghan covering her legs. Her body seemed to be aging in segments. Her neck and face appeared younger than forty-eight, particularly this evening in the indirect lighting offered by nearby lamps. Here, the lines forming at her eyes and the corners of her mouth were muted. Her hair was no longer the lustrous brown of a decade ago, but he liked her refusal to color it, and the gray now emerging provided a subtly variegated frame for a face still strong and earnest. Below the neck, her body held its essential shape despite her disease. A modest weight gain brought on by mandatory sedentariness might have been appealing had it been produced by exercise. As it was, however, this weight clung, and for the first time, her movements and gestures evoked in him the impression of a woman nearing sixty.

"Something Andy said hit me," he said. "He reminded me not to forget about myself in this process."

"Process?" Her voice rose. "Is that what our lives have become, a process? A process you'd discuss with the Prescotts?"

"Claire, don't seize on semantics. The point was only that I too am affected by your condition. Andy was being a friend, that's all. He loves you, you know that. He and Wanda both."

"And have you forgotten about yourself in this process, Dan?"

"Possibly. I'm not sure what's wrong. I'm . . ." His voice trailed off.

"Well, whatever it is, join the club. At least you have your work. Everyone looks up to you. Just look at all the discussion you've generated with that death chamber idea. And even though you poo-poo it, I still think you'll be appointed to the supreme court vacancy. You make important decisions that have real impact on people's lives. Your life goes on."

"You were very much a part of my life."

"Were?"

"Were in the sense that things have changed."

"Have I ever pretended things haven't changed?"

"No. You've acknowledged that."

"So what's your point?"

"That we haven't adapted. As a couple, anyway."

"Are you alluding to sex? Is that what this is about, because if it is, it's cruelty. We had a decent sex life before I got sick, and this chair is the only thing preventing us from having one now. I know it's not easy for you, but I've got all I can handle to make it day-to-day without that bottle you're urging on me."

"It's more than sex, Claire. It's somehow feeling, or being made to feel, that I can't demand . . . no, I can't even suggest my needs to you. Telling you my troubles seems like describing a cavity to someone undergoing a root canal."

"Oh, poor baby. Do you need a little sympathy?"

The word *sympathy* hovered between them, the first note in a dirge that was not new. He sighed, anticipating the exchange about to ensue, searching for words that could alter the refrain, however slightly. "Belittling me is not helping," he said. "We need to be able to talk about our lives, and that includes mine."

"Of course it includes yours," she said mechanically, her mind already on the next question. "Dan, do you think God is testing me?"

"No. I don't think it works that way."

"Well, something is testing me. I feel I'm being tested."

"You've shown great courage, Claire. If you're being tested, you've passed."

"So far, darling. Still so far to go."

"Day at a time, remember?"

"But what if—"

"Day at a time."

Dan watched as tears welled. Taking her hand, he said, "You're heroic. Few people could handle this the way you've managed. I couldn't."

"You're sweet," she said, in that voice half-a-pitch higher.

"I mean it, Claire."

"I know. That means so much. It's just . . ."

"What?"

"I'm such a poor candidate for a heroine. I really am. I'm learning that. When this thing first hit me, I almost welcomed it. Did you know that?"

"Tell me why."

"Because it all seemed a little too perfect, you know. Our lives, our children, our futures."

"You built that. You worked for it."

"Did I? I wonder. I remember, when I was small, asking my

mother what things would be like for me. She said I'd grow up, marry a wonderful man, have two wonderful children, be admired by friends . . . as immodest as it sounds, it's all true."

"Mothers say such things."

"This was different, Dan. My mother had my number. She knew me better than I knew me. Of course, she never predicted this."

"No one would."

"I think that's why I welcomed it at first. I said to myself, 'Okay, here's a chance to show what you are made of. Anybody can thrive with everything I have, so it's time to prove I'm not just a fair-weather sailor.' That's why I asked if you think God's testing me."

"You are no fair-weather sailor. You've proved that."

"No. I *am* a fair-weather sailor. I loved my old life. I was born to live the life I've led. I was so good at it." Her voice broke. "I'm no good for this. No good at all."

Dan knelt in front of the cold chair, leaning toward her and holding her as she sobbed. After a time, she grew still. He disengaged but remained kneeling.

"Sorry," she said, dabbing her eyes.

"Nonsense."

"A good cry won't hurt me."

"Neither will a drink. You're sure?"

"Just one. Gin, if we have any."

Dan rose, walked to the bar. He refilled his bourbon and mixed her a stiff gin and tonic. When he handed it to her, she took a long, grateful pull. Dan returned to his chair.

"Claire, you paint your life as one long, grand parade, but don't overlook the other changes. MS hit you at a particularly vulnerable moment. The kids leaving the nest, menopause, looking hard at fifty, the Millers moving to Florida . . . all these changes would have been difficult enough without a disease thrown into the mix. In that sense, you've borne a double burden."

"I suppose," she said with an insouciant flip of her free hand, as if swatting a mosquito. "I do miss Betsy Miller. She's the one friend I have who didn't seem fazed, put off somehow, by my condition." She raised her glass. "This is good. Thank you for persisting."

"You're welcome. Hey, I have an idea. Why don't we ride up to the lake one of these days? We haven't been there in so long."

Claire wheeled over to her lounge chair. "Do you remember how we used to plan the house we were going to build up there?"

He smiled. "Yes, I remember you telling Wanda that if you ever saw a sunrise there, it would be because you'd been up all night."

"And that I would own the sunsets. Sunrise on the Atlantic is lovely, don't get me wrong, but sunsets! Remember the trip we took there with the architect, and she showed me about where the master bedroom would be, and I stood on the hood of the car just as the sun was setting? That's the view I wanted."

"And could still have."

"Only now when I think about that house it's only to plan access ramps and elevators and space for a night nurse when I get sicker. I feel like I'm designing the wing of a hospital rather than a retirement home." She paused. "So you don't think God is testing me?"

"Maybe you're testing Him."

She eyed him skeptically. "Why would I do that?"

Dan stood. "Who knows. Guilt."

"I beg your pardon. What do I have to feel guilty about?"

"A perfect life. You said so yourself."

"Yes, but I don't feel guilty. Besides, how would I test God?"

"Don't you pray for a cure?"

"You know I do. Every night and every morning and often in between."

"So, see?" He paced in front of her, his drink suspended from his hand. "You're testing His power to cure you."

"Oh, Dan, you can't be serious. Don't be sacrilegious. Don't you pray for me?"

"Frankly, dear, I haven't prayed in quite some time. Months. Maybe a couple of years."

"You go to church."

"Physically."

"I had no idea. Why didn't you say something?"

"I'm sorting it out."

"Is this Andy's influence? He's such a raging atheist."

"I think agnostic comes closer to describing him, but this has nothing to do with Andy, at least as far as I'm aware. Give me enough credit to be the chief patron of my own faith crisis."

"Agnostic my eye. He told me once that religions were responsible for most of the world's problems, that they were all superstitious nonsense, and the sooner we get rid of them, the happier we'd be. That sounds like a man who has made up his mind."

"About religions, yes. But God? I think he's still undecided."

"I would be terrified without my faith," she said with a dread as palpable as his own doubts.

Dan halted his pacing at a window. Staring out into the night beyond, he felt again the disconnection that had become predictable in conversations with Claire, as if she suffered from a compulsion to hang up the phone at a critical juncture of any dialogue personal to him. She had just done it again. His reference to his faith crisis had handed her the leading inch of a metaphoric twine that squeezed him to a spiritual numbness. He needed her to follow that twine. Peering through the window into the darkness, his drink hanging by his side and his back to her, he acknowledged that need, but she wasn't going to meet it—not now or tomorrow or next month. Her own needs were too great.

"Damn," he muttered, not certain why.

"What, darling? What did you say?"

"Nothing," he replied without turning around. He supposed he was damning himself. He felt greedy and ashamed. *It isn't fair*, he reminded himself. *It isn't fair to ask her to fight on two fronts. It's unfair to ask her to handle my feeble little disorientation when she is coping with her own survival. Focus on her*, he ordered himself. Yes, he had needs, perhaps more than he acknowledged, but all need was relative. His were manageable. *Focus on her*, he repeated.

He thought back to the call from the lieutenant governor, urging him to make the rounds of legislators and offering a prediction. "If you quote me, I'll deny it," the lieutenant governor said, "but my guess is you'll be our next chief justice." After the conversation ended, Dan sat in contemplation of being selected. "You have your work," Claire had reminded him, and that work had sustained him for years, but the prospect of appointment to the state's highest court gave him fresh insights. Andy had noticed Dan's retreat into himself, the erosion of enthusiasm for his work and even his family. Why hadn't Claire noticed? For that matter, why hadn't Dan himself noticed? It took a neighbor and a call from the lieutenant governor to revive him. *Bad timing*, he thought, with Claire feeling weak and vulnerable while he was beginning to feel newly energized.

"And now," Claire said, "on top of all the rest of it, Ethan is talking about going to Haiti. Do you think he's serious?" Ethan Borders, their twenty-two-year-old son, had been on a post-graduation tour of Europe when the earthquake devastated Port-au-Prince.

"His email sounded serious. We should be proud of him for wanting to help. God knows those poor people have the world's biggest mess on their hands."

"And I feel I have all I can handle, and I'll worry myself sick if he ends up there."

"I can see the appeal. He's at an age when he can take some risks, do some good. I wish I'd done more of it."

"But where will he sleep? What will he eat? The images on the news make it seem like there is hardly any civilization left."

"He can get by with a toothbrush and a change of clothes. It could turn out to be one of those defining life experiences."

"Have you encouraged him to go there?"

"I encouraged him only to let us know what he decides."

Claire sighed as if Ethan, naked to the waist, was already in an overflowing tent city with cholera raging amidst gang gunfire. "Another thing for my prayer list," she said in a whisper.

Conversation lagged. Dan renewed his suggestion for a trip to the lake, getting her to agree that a trip would do her good. They found an old movie on one of the satellite channels, an early Paul Newman with one of those actresses so familiar he could never remember her name. He fell asleep on the couch. Later, the whir of Claire's chairlift roused him vaguely, but he slept until an early morning drop in the room's temperature shivered him awake. He mounted the stairs to his room, where he undressed and fell into bed. At nine, he reminded Claire that they should get to church early in anticipation of the crowd. She mumbled something unintelligible. He brought coffee, and she roused grudgingly. He helped her dress. Walking by the closet he had cleaned the previous afternoon, he spied the garment bag. The compartment that held the gin was partly unzipped, and the bottle gone.

# CHAPTER 10

# Witness for the Prosecution

Brock Jamerson left Columbia on I-26 headed east, carrying with him a veteran reporter's skepticism that Judge Borders could measure up to the hype being generated by his "Jury of One" idea. Jamerson's boss, the editor of *The State* newspaper, thought it worth a trip to Beaufort to find out. Jamerson, who covered the local courts, looked forward to seeing Judge Daniel Borders mete out justice in his element.

A phone call to the clerk of court had given Jamerson a bonus for making the trip today. On the court's docket would be a motion to suppress the introduction into evidence at trial of the knife allegedly used to kill store clerk Hazel Hudgins, who happened to be among the county's most beloved residents. Jamerson had read about it several months back, but it wasn't his beat and hardly justified a trip to Beaufort absent the chance to take the measure of Judge Borders.

The courthouse in Beaufort, the county seat, was a red brick affair, its lines traceable to no known style of architecture, boxy with severely pitched roofs. Lintels over vaguely Romanesque arches, painted white, resembled sharply bent eyebrows. He walked past the Confederate monument without a glance.

He had accustomed himself to metal detectors. They still struck him as unseemly, but as he found them in every courthouse he visited, it hardly surprised him to confront one here. Between him and the yawning detector waited men, a mix of corduroys, denim, work boots, keys suspended from chains, and postponed barber appointments, all of whom could have as easily been gawkers at the state fair.

To one side of the detector sat Deputy Boyette, a massive man who filled his chair to the point of obscurity, its back, side arms, and legs eclipsed by his abundance. Outsized thighs stretched his cotton pants. He stared with half-closed, is-it-five-o'clock-yet? eyes.

"Keep moving," instructed Deputy Boyette. No one emptied pockets or purses. A briefcase went unexamined. The machine dutifully belched its warning with each trespasser. After Jamerson passed through, predictably triggering the alarm, he stopped at the chair occupied by the deputy.

"Good morning," he said.

"Morning," Boyette said in the same bored "move along" voice.

"I'm from Columbia. Couldn't help noticing your screening procedure."

The deputy tilted his melon-shaped head in the direction of the metal detector. "You mean that thing? I know all these folks."

Jamerson grinned. "But you don't know me."

"You're right," Boyette said, still seated, his drowsy eyes focused on where Jamerson had stood in line before passing through the detector. "You got anything we need to worry about?"

"Just a notebook and a couple of pens."

"There. I feel safe. What brings you to our neck of the woods?"

"The Hudgins murder. I want to hear the argument on the motion filed by Rodrigo Lopez."

"That guilty bastard?"

"So I'm told," said Jamerson. "Which way to the circuit court?"

"Up the stairs behind me. Only courtroom on the second floor."

At the top of the stairs, he perused the docket. Three arraignments, all scheduled for 9:00 a.m., preceded the 10:00 a.m. hearing on the Lopez motion. As he pushed through double doors separating the courtroom from a bench-lined foyer, the reporter received his second surprise of the morning. Standing at one counsel table was a woman who appeared to be not yet thirty. Long black hair fell to the shoulders of her neatly tailored dark suit. A pile of folders rested in front of her, a slim briefcase to one side, and when she turned her back to the still-vacant bench, as if seeking someone in the crowd, he noticed serious, dark eyes set against lovely, flawless copper skin. She scanned the ten or twelve people seated, glanced briefly at him as he walked toward the railing separating them, then turned her back, studying the folder she opened as she pivoted. In an arena where sharp elbows and heated disputes prevailed, her movements were fluid, feline, and graceful, like a ballerina in a boxing gym.

He chose a seat near the front. On the wall to his left hung an enormous plaque dedicated to the mothers of Southern soldiers by the United Daughters of the Confederacy. Beneath it hung a rendering of *Lee and his Generals.* Bearded jurists of yesteryear stared out at him and at their counterparts adorning the opposite wall. Except for these, the courtroom was spare enough to have been designed and furnished by Amish. A simple elevated bench dominated the far wall. A door behind it led to the judge's chambers. A jury box with a dozen straight-back chairs stood empty. Hot water radiators, painted white, lined the walls beneath windows that lacked ornamentation of any kind. The public seating area consisted of church-stark pews, ten to a side, with dark wood accented by glistening white paint.

Shortly before 9:00, a hulking bailiff entered, followed by the clerk, who took her seat to the right of the judge's bench. The bailiff kept a religious eye on the wall clock, and when the second hand swept past the hour, announced, "Oyez, oyez, silence is commanded on pain of imprisonment while the Honorable Daniel Borders presides. All those with business before the court come forward and you shall be heard. Turn off all cell phones. God save the state of South Carolina and this honorable court. Ladies and gentlemen, you may be seated."

From the door behind his bench, Judge Borders entered. He approached his chair and seemed to make eye contact with everyone at once. He had the square set of shoulders Jamerson associated with tennis players. Erect, almost rigid posture. When he reached his chair, he stood for a moment, a beat, nodding faintly to the Indian woman. Then, he sat. Jamerson waited for a gavel. Instead, the judge spoke.

"Ladies and gentlemen, my name is Dan Borders. It is my honor to be the judge of this court. Courtrooms can be intimidating, and I want each of you to relax. While we need to observe certain formalities during the session, we who work here remind ourselves that you, the citizens, pay the taxes that support us. We work for you. The man who called the court to order this morning is Deputy McKinsey. He's the bailiff and in charge of courtroom security, and during a recess he'll be happy to answer any questions you have. Beside me today is the court's clerk, Mrs. Vivian Patterson. She keeps track of everything that goes on here. Ms. Jillian Pillai, standing at the counsel table, is the county solicitor. She is your elected representative and prosecutes criminal cases on behalf of the state. Ms. Pillai, call your first case."

"State against Reid Wallace, Your Honor."

Deputy McKinsey walked to a side door, gave two sharp raps, opened it, and returned with a man wearing an orange jumpsuit. The accused, a stocky man who managed to strut despite his apparent lack of leverage, looked hard at Jillian Pillai. A trailing deputy from lockup flanked him as he turned to face Judge Borders. Yes, Wallace understood the charge of grand larceny could result in his confinement in the penitentiary, and yes, he wished to be represented by a lawyer, and no, he didn't have a lawyer and couldn't afford one, and yes, he wished to have one appointed.

After concluding arraignments, the court took its first recess, during which Jamerson learned that Jillian Pillai was the only Indian solicitor in South Carolina but also, at the moment, the youngest, her long-serving predecessor having died several months before. He made a note to spend some time with her.

# CHAPTER 11

# A Knife and Hazel Hudgins

In the courtroom, a steady influx of older folks and friends and admirers of the late Hazel Hudgins filled the available seats. Like Deputy Boyette, they had already convicted Rodrigo Lopez among themselves, so today's brigade of Hazel's admirers came to honor her rather than from curiosity over the motion. They knew of her blood donations over the years amounting to over ten gallons, her tireless efforts for Mobile Meals, and her regular visits to shut-ins. Loving hours spent at hospice work earned her gratitude from three generations. Hazel, it seemed, found a way to touch everyone in the county.

As reporter Brock Jamerson sat, a man entered the courtroom brusquely, banged his briefcase on the table opposite Jillian Pillai and opened it with a flourish. Reaching in, he withdrew a folder and slapped it onto the table with the force of finality.

"Good morning, Mr. Roan," Pillai said in a lilting tongue. "Roan" came out closer to "Run."

Joe Roan turned and bowed slightly at the waist. "Miss Pillai, always a pleasure."

"Even today?"

"Especially today, when you learn your so-called evidence is inadmissible."

Pillai giggled faintly. "Admitted or not, it is evidence regardless."

"What's the point of evidence if you can't use it?" Roan asked.

"It tells us we have our man," she replied. "Even we heartless prosecutors like to know we have indicted the guilty."

"You're wrong on this one, Jillie. You'll see." Roan moved like a man accustomed to breaking things, heavy-handed and brawling like his jaw, slightly too large for his face and jutting out beneath determined brown eyes. Dressed in a single-breasted suit, he sported a florid silk tie and matching breast pocket square. In keeping with his habit, his suit was cut a half-size too small, accentuating his gym-intensive physique. He had just turned forty, and if weight-burdened lifts and squats three times a week could keep a man looking like someone a decade younger, Roan was all-in.

The bailiff, Mrs. Patterson, and Judge Borders returned. Seated near Roan in the first row, a woman in her mid-fifties drummed her fingers silently on the bench.

"Good morning, Mr. Roan," said Judge Borders. "Are we ready on Rodrigo Lopez?"

Roan stood. "We are, Your Honor."

"Is the state ready?" the judge asked.

"Yes, Your Honor."

"Deputy McKinsey, bring in Mr. Lopez."

Lopez entered from the lock-up door, shuffling as though already convicted. Dwarfed by Deputy McKinsey, he looked like a ninth grader trying out for varsity football, peering out of a helmet two sizes too big and bracing for impact. He wore a clean plaid shirt and jeans. His jet-black hair swept back from his temples.

"Mrs. Patterson, please swear the translator."

A Hispanic woman came forward and was sworn, then took a chair between Roan and Lopez at the defense table.

"Ms. Pillai," said Judge Borders, "does the state concede that the knife at issue was seized pursuant to a warrantless search?"

Jillian stood. "We do, Your Honor. The state will offer evidence that on the night of February 19, the defendant stabbed to death Hazel Hudgins as she worked at The Happy Clam convenience store, and that the weapon used was properly and legally seized by Deputy Carl Flock shortly after this horrible crime."

"Very well. Call your first witness."

As Martha Hudgins, daughter of the victim, approached the witness stand, the door at the back of the courtroom opened, and Alana Morgan came through it, holding a plastic bag emblazoned with the logo of Turner & Feinberg, a Columbia department store that closed a decade earlier. She walked toward the front and took a seat in a row opposite the one in which Brock Jamerson sat taking notes.

Jamerson's eyes strayed to his co-spectator seated a few feet away. Completely absorbed, she leaned forward with her legs crossed, her back straight. She had great legs, tanned and toned, with a lushness about her that appealed to him. Rounded nicely in the right places. As he watched, she reached down with her hand to finger the shopping bag she had set on the floor. No ring, he noted.

The clerk swore in Martha Hudgins, who had heard her mother's scream and held her as she died. "I saw a man run out of the store. I couldn't see his face 'cause his back was to me, but you could tell he was a Mexican by his hair and skin and all."

Joe Roan jumped to his feet, his arms raised beseechingly over his head, objecting to the label of Mexican applied to a man she saw fleetingly. Judge Borders sustained the objection while reminding Roan that no jury was present, an unmistakable signal that the judge was in no mood for courtroom dramatics, which were staples of defense counsels.

Jillian asked, "What happened next?"

"I couldn't follow him," Martha said, beginning to sob. "Momma needed me, and I was holding her." A microphone nearby amplified her agony.

"I know how difficult this is," Jillian said in a voice full of empathy.

"He, that man, Lopez, ran to the migrants camp."

"Objection!" said Roan.

Without waiting for a ruling, Jillian asked, "Do you mean you saw a man you believed to be Mexican run in the direction of the migrants camp?"

"Yes, in that direction. That's what I meant to say."

"Then what happened?" Jillian asked.

"A few minutes later, I don't know how long because I was so upset and Momma had stopped breathing, Deputy Flock showed up. He pretty much took over things from there."

Deputy Carl Flock entered from a side door. A bird-like man whose uniform hung awkwardly from skeletal limbs, he resembled a disheveled heron settling on a nest as he seated himself in the witness chair. He adjusted the microphone precisely in front of him, and Jillian led him through the events of February 19, beginning with his response to a 911 dispatch: robbery and possible homicide at The Happy Clam. He arrived minutes before 9:00 p.m. to find Hazel Hudgins, the owner, behind the counter, bleeding from a large wound to the chest. Her daughter Martha, crying and distraught, cradled her mother's head and whispered words of comfort that Flock was pretty sure could not be heard. He felt no pulse. Minutes later, EMTs arrived.

"Did you ask Martha Hudgins what happened?" Jillian asked.

"I did."

"As a result of that conversation, what did you do?"

Carl Flock testified that he drove to the trailer park on Penman Road where Lopez lived with other migrants working for a large landscaping company. Just as he got out of his vehicle, he saw a man emerge from one of the backlot trailers and run toward the woods behind it.

"There's a shed back there, and Lopez must have thought I didn't see him go in it, but I did. I pulled my weapon and told him to come out. He didn't give me no trouble after that."

"You spoke to him in English, I assume?" Prosecutor Pillai asked.

"Yep. My Spanish ain't so good."

"What was he wearing?"

"A T-shirt and jeans."

"A white T-shirt?"

Flock nodded, then replied, "Yes," after being reminded by the judge that the court reporter needed a vocal response.

As Flock testified, Lopez gazed downward into his lap, the translator at his ear repeating things that, by his shrug, seemed to confuse him.

"What happened next?"

"Backup come by then," Flock replied. "I turned him over. Then I searched his trailer."

"The one you saw him come out of?"

"The same."

"I see," said Pillai, squinting slightly. "What did you find inside?"

Flock detailed a space almost devoid of furniture, with mattresses on the floors of the two bedrooms. "Under his mattress, I found a knife. A big knife."

"How did you know the mattress was his?"

"The company they work for, All Green, gives them shirts with their names on 'em. Found two 'Rodrigo' shirts on top of his mattress."

The prosecutor opened her briefcase, extracting a large, clear, sealed freezer bag containing what appeared to be a hunting knife, with a black lacquered handle, an upturned blade, and a serrated top edge. A dark stain covered the blade near its point. She unsealed the bag, extracted the weapon, and walked deliberately to the witness stand. "This knife?"

He turned the weapon over in his hands to examine a green tag on the handle. "That's it."

"And did you consider getting a search warrant?"

"No time for that. I had a pretty good idea I'd find a knife, and I wasn't gonna give them Mexicans a chance to get rid of it."

Jillian Pillai shifted her attention from the witness to Judge Borders. "Your Honor, I proffer that forensic tests will establish this as the weapon used to murder Hazel Hudgins."

Judge Borders said, "Very well. Mr. Roan, you may cross-examine."

# CHAPTER 12

# No Warrant

Roan's gaze as he stood had the steely concentration of a jackal pursuing prey. His monogrammed French cuffs put him at odds with the standard couture of the Beaufort bar.

"Now, Deputy Flock, you've testified a man came out of a trailer. Was this the man?" Roan asked, pointing to his client.

"It was."

"Had you ever seen him before?"

"I'd seen him in the store a time or two, him and his buddies."

"And was the shed where you arrested him behind the trailer he came out of?"

"That shed is in back of the row of trailers, more or less behind the trailer next door to the one he came out of."

"How far is the shed from what you are calling the Lopez trailer?"

"I'd say maybe ninety, a hundred feet."

"Did you go in that shed?"

"After I turned Lopez over to backup, I went inside, yeah. Lawnmower and yard equipment mostly. Didn't find nothin' I was looking for."

"You testified that you saw several mattresses on the floor of the trailer. How many?"

"I didn't count them . . . but at least eight."

"Was the trailer empty when you found the knife?"

"No people, if that's what you mean."

"Was there anything other than the All Green shirts that suggested to you that it was Lopez's mattress?" Without waiting for an answer, Roan pressed on. "Isn't it true, Deputy Flock, that migrants come and go in all those trailers, living like one big family?"

Jillian Pillai rose. "Objection. Calls for speculation."

"Sustained," Judge Borders ruled.

Roan proceeded. "Deputy, I think you testified to this, but I want to be clear on your answer. At the time you found this knife, where was Mr. Lopez?"

"Like I said, I turned him over to backup. They had the cuffs on him in the back seat of the squad car."

"Thank you. No further questions." Roan started toward his chair, then stopped abruptly. "One more thing. You liked Hazel Hudgins, didn't you?"

"Everybody in the county loved Miss Hazel."

Jamerson continued scribblings notes on a pad resting on his knee, but he struggled to concentrate. The nearby presence of Alana Morgan distracted the newsman. The more she focused on the back-and-forth between the lawyers and the judge, the more he found himself glancing over, admiring her profile.

"Counsel, I'll hear your arguments now," the judge announced. "Mr. Roan."

Roan stood, looked briefly at Pillai, and outlined the defense's theory of why the search must be held invalid. "To search that trailer, judge, they needed a search warrant, and they didn't get one. Deputy Flock's testimony shows at least eight people sleeping there, proving everyone and his brother had access to those trailers and to the mattresses."

Alana leaned forward, intently focused on Judge Borders as he questioned Roan about two evidence cases on which the defense clearly relied. A slight bob of Alana's head seemed to signal agreement.

When it was Jillian Pillai's turn, she attacked. "Your honor, Mr. Roan is using the tired tactic of putting law enforcement on trial. Deputy Flock's conduct was entirely appropriate, as was this search." She dismissed the court cases Roan had cited as factually distinguishable, underscoring a recent Fourth Circuit Court of Appeals search and seizure ruling.

"He was directed to the migrant quarters by the victim's daughter. When he arrived, Mr. Lopez, a migrant, ran away, as a guilty man would. Deputy Flock apprehended him. The case law is clear that a search conducted incident to a lawful arrest is constitutionally permissible. The State requests that Mr. Roan's motion be denied." She sat, glancing at Roan as if to say, "I warned you." Pillai exuded the confidence of a good poker player with a strong hand.

When Judge Borders said, "Ms. Pillai," his tone was such that her confidence slipped visibly. "I'm having trouble with your argument. From the testimony, the shed where the defendant was arrested was not located in his yard, what the law refers to as curtilage. Deputy Flock stated that it was located behind the trailer next door and contained the type of lawn maintenance equipment that could be used to service the trailer park. Doesn't that fact dictate the need for a search warrant?"

Pillai jumped to her feet and replied immediately. "In the *Ragland* case I cited, the chase took over two hours, Your Honor. Thirty minutes is entirely within reason here."

"But in *Ragland*, there was just what you mentioned, a chase, whereas here we simply have a lapse of time. Rather than a suspect being pursued, we have a police officer headed off in search of a possible culprit, as you might have in any crime. Doesn't that make a difference?"

Pillai, still standing, tried to sound accommodating, but her voice, rising, betrayed her. "Not at all, Your Honor. He was directed to a specific place to a man who just happened to have the murder weapon under his mattress. And all this occurred in half an hour."

Judge Borders looked at her evenly. "Let's keep the record straight, Ms. Pillai. It will be easier on all of us. As I understood his testimony, he was not directed to a specific place, but only in a general direction. Isn't that what your witness said? That Martha Hudgins pointed in the direction of the migrant camp? And he went there, not looking for Mr. Lopez specifically, but for a Mexican. Deputy Flock admitted on cross-examination that there may well have been other Mexicans present along with Mr. Lopez."

"But only one ran into the woods, Your Honor. That should tell us something. And once the defendant ran, Deputy Flock was in hot pursuit when they entered the woods, even if he wasn't when he first arrived at the migrant quarters."

A resigned smile flickered on the face of Judge Borders. "That's a good argument, Ms. Pillai, and had Deputy Flock found the knife in the shed, or searched the area within the immediate control of Mr. Lopez, I might accept it. But the arrest took place at least fifty yards from the living quarters. He's using that arrest as justification for searching what amounts to Mr. Lopez's home, humble as it is. Suppose someone is pulled over and arrested for hit and run three blocks from their house. The officer can search the suspect, and his or her car, but I fail to see how such an arrest could serve as a basis for a warrantless search of the home."

"He told you why he didn't get a warrant, Judge." Desperation seeped into her voice, and its volume increased yet again. "He was afraid the other Mexicans would destroy evidence. It's no secret they cover for each other. Potential destruction of evidence is a legitimate exception to the requirement for a warrant."

He replied, his voice softer than before, "The evidence is that a backup unit was on the scene. That would have made it difficult for anyone to enter or leave the trailer. You're asking me to believe that the other migrants knew of the knife, knew of its hiding place, and would have moved it to protect Lopez?"

"Exactly so," she responded.

"If that's true, isn't it just as logical that someone other than Lopez put it there in the first place? Everyone who lives in those quarters fits the description of a Mexican. There are no locks on the doors, so Lopez is hardly the only person with access to where the knife was found. If I've just committed murder, I might be more inclined to put the weapon under anyone's mattress but my own. Wouldn't you?"

Pillai slumped, her voice turning plaintive. "I must tell you, Judge, that the case against Mr. Lopez is circumstantial, even if the court admits this knife into evidence. Without it, however, the state will have a most difficult time establishing his guilt. I want to be perfectly frank on this point."

Judge Borders sighed. "I take that comment to mean that in the view of the state, a ruling adverse to it would be tantamount to acquitting Mr. Lopez and possibly letting a guilty man go free. The court is aware of the implications. And, just so the record is clear, Hazel Hudgins was as dear to me as anyone in this county. She sold me bottle rockets for the Fourth of July from the time I was old enough to reach her counter, back in the days when fireworks were illegal. I don't know three people who haven't got special memories of her, and her murder has been an unspeakable tragedy for us all. But I'm bound by the law, and I've got problems with this search. Specifically, I'm having trouble seeing why Deputy Flock couldn't take a few minutes to get a search warrant. I'm going to rule it inadmissible. Mr. Roan, please draw an order."

Pillai was on her feet again. "But Your Honor! This can't be . . ." she stammered. "It's outrageous to suppress such evidence."

"Careful, Ms. Pillai. You are courting contempt with those comments." With his rigid stare and fixed facial features, the judge made it clear he was not a man to be disrespected.

"But sir, this man is guilty. A murderer. This is the kind of technicality—"

"Enough," commanded the judge. "Ms. Pillai, approach the bench."

She stepped from behind her table and walked reluctantly forward. Arriving in front of the judge, she folded her arms. He towered over her, leaning forward and whispering, but entirely composed and in tones more suggestive of a chat between father and daughter than a verbal blistering. She nodded several times before returning to her place at the table.

"Anything further from the state?" he asked.

"No, Your Honor," she replied in a voice barely audible. Then, as she sank into her chair, she said, "Note our objection."

"So noted," Judge Borders replied. "The court stands in recess."

Alana, shopping bag in hand, joined a throng of people walking to the exit. Not far behind was Jamerson. His height made it easy for him to track her. He followed at a distance, determined to find a way to introduce himself. When she entered the clerk's office, a line at the clerk's window caused her to pause.

Jamerson saw his chance. Approaching from behind, he said casually, "Never thought I'd see one of those again."

Alana turned to face him. "Beg your pardon?"

He pointed to the bag. "Turner & Feinberg. Sad day when they went out of business."

"Oh, this," she said with a momentary glance at the bag and a casual titter. "My mother used to hoard them. I should put them on eBay."

He was about to introduce himself when she turned back toward the clerk. "I'd like to see Judge Borders," she said. "A personal matter." The clerk motioned for her to follow. Jamerson could only watch her walk away.

# CHAPTER 13

# Jumper Cables Come Home

After his Lopez ruling, Judge Borders, back in his chambers, took off his robe and hung it on an old hat rack in his unpretentious office. On the walls, a fading aerial photo of his home taken by a grateful client with a pilot license, a framed certificate of appreciation for pro bono services rendered to the NAACP Legal Defense Fund before he went on the bench, a pastel drawing made by Christina in the second grade, a gift for Father's Day, a photo of his college fraternity at their twenty-year reunion, and his appointment to the circuit court by the governor. Without intending to do so, he had arrayed a pictorial biography of sorts—home, family, service, fellowship, profession.

He lowered himself into his chair, mentally picturing Alana Morgan, whom he had noticed as soon as she entered the courtroom. In his peripheral vision, he had noted her studied attention and her leg faintly bouncing as if keeping time with the hearing's ebb and flow. A knock at his door brought him back to the moment. "Come in."

Alana opened the door cautiously, her head appearing before the rest of her. "Am I intruding?"

"Not at all." He stood and motioned her to one of the two chairs in front of his desk, eyeing the Turner & Feinberg bag in her hand. "Did you bring me lunch?"

She smiled as she sat, back straight, legs crossed. "I promised I'd return them."

"So you did. I hope you now own a pair."

"And a new battery. And, one day, a new car." She paused before saying, "I find this case very interesting. I've been in The Happy Clam many times."

"Most people in the county have as well. Hazel Hudgins was a popular woman in these parts."

"Will Lopez go free?"

"I'm sorry, but I can't discuss a pending case."

Alana blushed. "I didn't mean to—"

"No harm done," he said. "How goes the teaching war?"

She turned her head slightly and looked at him with a faint smirk. "I'm sorry, but I can't discuss my pending classroom."

Dan laughed. "Well played, and touché."

"The kids are restless, as they get every year at this time. Summer vacation can't come soon enough for them or for me. I'll bet you didn't know that Charleston is the capital of the state, which was an answer I got on a paper I graded last night." She raised her hands in a gesture of futility. "Maybe you should come talk to my class. They would love to hear from a future supreme court justice."

"That's enough of that, but I'd be happy to speak to your students. I haven't been to the school in a couple of years now. Law Day is coming. Maybe then?"

"Perfect," she said. "I'll let the administration know you're coming. Maybe we'll combine some classes to take full advantage of having such a distinguished visitor."

"You flatter me, but I'll take it." Maintaining the eye contact, Dan said he had a confession to make.

"Let me guess," she said. "You bought a new set of jumper cables because you were sure I wouldn't bring these back."

He leaned forward in his chair. "I read your divorce file to see if I actually awarded you that car. You went through a difficult time."

She dropped her head and spoke into her lap. "Horrible. Worse than the physical pain was the realization I had married my father. Several of my high school teachers tried to warn me, but like some kids I teach today, I knew it all."

"We do at that age," he said.

She looked up and past him, and for a moment, he sensed she would tear up, but she remained composed, and the eye contact returned. "It's funny," she said with a wry grin, "a couple of those same teachers are now my colleagues. After Toby and I split, they encouraged me to return to school, even taking care of Holly a few times so I wouldn't miss an exam because my childcare fell through."

"Is that how you ended up back at Beaufort High?"

"Exactly. It has done me good to return to the scene of the crime, so to speak."

There was an awkward pause, during which Dan inclined toward asking about the crime, but thought better of it.

"Is that your family?" she asked, pointing to the photo on his desk.

He leaned back philosophically, hands joined behind his head. "Just before my son went off to college. Seems like yesterday, but the picture says it wasn't."

"Your wife is lovely," she said, cocking her head to one side as if to get a better view of Claire.

"Indeed she is. We're empty nesters now."

"Holly, my daughter, is eleven. I can't imagine life without her."

"We said the same about ours, but you hope you've trained them to fly so you can be only so disappointed when they do. It sneaks up on you. Be prepared. Changing subjects, let me say again how glad I am you decided to join the Historical Society."

She cringed with a simultaneous roll of her eyes and exhale through pursed lips. "Judging by reception the other night, you may be the only one. I thought that Stephens guy might have a stroke, and Darling Moore certainly isn't a fan."

"I suggest you lower your expectations. You're in a conservative county in an even more conservative state. One of my more progressive friends suggested we include the words *sic non est* in the county seal. Loosely translated, it means 'I don't approve.' They are solid citizens, but getting them to move that monument may be a bridge too far."

She nodded but did not reply. Into the lull that followed, she placed the bag on his desk. "I know you're busy, so I'll let you go. Thank you again for coming to my rescue."

"My pleasure," he said, standing. He reached for her hand, which she extended across the desk. "Now that you're a member of the Society, don't miss a meeting . . . we'll elect you president."

She grinned, looking at him squarely, her handshake firm yet supple.

As she turned to go, he asked if by chance she had driven her car in his neighborhood a couple of weeks earlier. "No," she said matter-of-factly. "Why?"

"Nothing really. I thought I recognized your car one Saturday morning."

She shrugged. "Wasn't me. I don't know where you live."

As she turned back toward the door, he admired her curves and toned calves he had noticed in the library parking lot. He thought back to her deposition, trying to picture the smartly dressed, seemingly assured woman just leaving his office lying at the bottom of a stairway, pregnant and desperate. *She must be a survivor.* He wondered if there was a man in her life and, if so, a better choice than the brute at the top of those stairs. Experience had taught him how often the abused boomeranged back to the abuser. He hoped she had better sense. He wanted her to be happy, though he couldn't say why. Didn't he want everyone to be happy? Yes, but why her in particular?

He stood, put on his coat, picked up the bag holding the jumper cables, and headed to his parking place behind his office.

# CHAPTER 14

# A Tough Spot

Brock Jamerson approached Joe Roan, introduced himself, and asked if he could spare some time to talk about Judge Dan Borders. Jamerson had met very few defense attorneys who avoided the press. Roan suggested lunch at Rosanne's Grill for the seafood. Jamerson accepted his invitation to ride, trying to remember the last time he had been a passenger in a pickup truck driven by someone wearing cufflinks.

"Did you get Lopez off?" Jamerson asked. They were traveling along a three-lane highway headed east toward the barrier islands and the ocean beyond.

Roan shrugged. "The whole enchilada was the knife. Keeping that out as evidence was a big win. I'd be surprised if Jillian doesn't drop this case." Roan's confidential tone struck Jamerson as cocky and unprompted. Roan was clearly relishing his victory and the battle ahead. "Jillie freaked a little when Borders ruled in my favor, which, by the way, I thought likely. I don't often have the law on my side, but this time I did," he said over a Willie Nelson lament on the radio. "Jillie's in a tough spot. Hazel Hudgins was a saint in this county, and if Jillie doesn't get a conviction, she'll be toast in the special election to fill Frank Walthall's term. He was elected solicitor when I was in grammar school. She's a better lawyer than Frank was, to tell you the truth, but she's still green."

"Can an Indian woman be elected here?" Jamerson wanted to know.

Roan smiled, staring straight ahead. "If you had asked me that a year ago, I'd have said no. Most people in this county have never even seen an Indian, much less voted for one. But she's sharp, people like her, and she just might pull it off."

"Unless she blows the Hazel Hudgins case."

"You got it."

"You may not be the most popular guy around if you get this Lopez off."

"But I'm not on any ballot, now or ever. I've got better sense."

"I'm surprised Lopez can afford you. Are you court appointed?"

Roan took his eyes off the road long enough to flash Jamerson a quick smirk. "Listen, pal, those Mexicans have money. They send a lot of it home, but there's a lot more of it here in places you and I wouldn't look. I quoted Lopez a big retainer, thinking there would be no way he could come up with it, but a week later, there it was. His buddies ponied up, I'm sure. Bond is set too high to get him out, but he's living better in jail than he lived on the outside."

The countryside gave no hints of the magnificent water that lay on either side of the highway. A mix of trailers, fabricated ranchers, and old farmhouses predominated but set off the road at a distance, surrounded by acreage, so whatever they lacked in pretension seemed offset by space, light, and air.

At Rosanne's Grill, they struck an unvoiced agreement to leave discussion of Judge Borders until after the entrée of broiled shrimp in a white wine garlic sauce. Roan was several inches shorter than his companion, with powerful arms that bulged beneath his shirt and an ego just as obvious to Jamerson. Except to eat and fidget briefly with the saltshaker, he kept his hands below the table, folded in his lap. At this hour, he was still clean-shaven, but already a closely cropped beard had begun to emerge, its symmetry perfect. Jamerson guessed the growth worked in Roan's favor before juries—clean-cut early and tougher as the day wore on. He had an odd laugh, a stifled, guttural release of air in short bursts from the back of his throat. He struck Jamerson as a man who missed little. His eye contact held but from willing it so rather than natural predisposition.

"You married?" Roan asked.

Jamerson swallowed a shrimp, dabbed his mouth with a napkin, and with a smile, asked Roan who was interviewing whom. "Tried it twice," Jamerson said. "I must not be any good at it. You?"

"Tried it once," Roan said. "Finalized my divorce last year. We had a few good years, but in the end, we couldn't make it work. We both saw it coming. Thank God no kids. I've been thinking of spending time in Charleston to meet some women. The pickings are pretty slim in a county this small. How hot is Columbia?"

"Lots of women, that's for sure. In the old days, it was legal secretaries, like my first wife. Now your chances are better with lady lawyers. Then there's USC and lady doctors. No shortage."

"Doctor, maybe," Roan said. "I know too much about lawyers to want to date one."

"That Indian chick is easy on the eyes. Maybe you should make an exception for a prosecutor."

Roan's mouth puckered in a toothless grin. Shaking his head, he said, "I've thought about it, to tell the truth. She's attractive, no doubt. And she's available, from what I hear. But then it comes down to mixing business with pleasure. As one of my fraternity brothers used to say, crudely but accurately, it isn't a good idea to get your meat where you get your bread."

Roan casually inquired about Jamerson's work, his hobbies, and in the exchange that followed, Roan guarded himself well, knowing there was nothing casual about this lunch. Jamerson had come to size up Dan Borders, and Roan didn't intend to cross a future supreme court chief justice with a slip to the press.

When they had eaten, Roan looked up expectantly. "You're in tight with the legislature," he said, "so what are his chances?"

"Hard to say exactly. I hear good things about him. Naturally, these seats don't open up every day, so it isn't like no one else has an eye on it. An ex-legislator named Sidney Callahan, part of Columbia's good-ol'-boy's club, is pulling out all the stops for it. What can you tell me about Borders?"

"I'm in his courtroom several times a month. He usually gets it right. That's key for a judge."

"Does he prepare?"

"Does he ever. I've never, and I stress *never*, cited a South Carolina case he wasn't conversant with, and when I say conversant, I mean facts, holding, majority opinion, dissents, the entire enchilada. He . . . absorbs them."

"Photographic memory?"

"Possibly," Roan said. "He just has the best legal foundation I've run across. Once he fits a case into that mental structure of his, he doesn't forget."

Jamerson ordered a refill of coffee. "What else does he offer?"

"He can read a witness like an open book. See, our clients lie a lot. I know that, but unless they tell me they're lying, I can't do anything about it. He sniffs them out. That may or may not cut any ice at the appellate level, but it sure makes for one hell of a trial judge. Have you met him?"

"No," Jamerson replied. "I hope to, maybe today. What about his personal life? Wife, kids?"

"I'm not the best one to talk to there. His wife has MS, that much I know. Nice lady. I see him socially here and there, but he insulates himself from lawyers. You might want to look up Andrew Prescott. They've been buddies for years. Andy might talk to you if he thought it would help the judge's prospects."

Jamerson made a note. "Thanks. I thought I'd drop in on Jillian Pillai as well."

They split the bill and returned to Roan's truck. On the trip back, Roan talked of his obsession with NASCAR, pointing to a number 88 Dale Earnhardt Jr. decal Jamerson had already noticed. Back in the parking lot, Jamerson got out, shook Roan's hand, and went in search of Jillian Pillai.

"She left for the day," her secretary said. "Can I tell her what it's about?"

"No," said Jamerson. "I'll call her tomorrow."

⊙ ⊙ ⊙

Jillian had impressed the newsman with her indignation at the suppression of the knife as evidence, as if the ghost of Hazel Hudgins had been perched on her shoulder cheering her on. And, as he had told Roan, Jillian was no slouch in the looks department.

What interested Jamerson more than her strengths were any unseen weaknesses. His innate radar locked onto the foibles and vulnerabilities in others for the simple reason that his own missteps had calibrated it with near-atomic precision. He was twice divorced, supporting both ex-wives and a child born to each, once bankrupt, frequently on the losing end of Atlantic City larks, hard drinking, and currently living with a registered nurse to whom he found it impossible to be faithful. He held an advanced degree of sorts in wrong turns, bad decisions, dead-end streets. His most admirable trait, aside from the professionalism he brought to his work, was his ability to take responsibility for the mess his personal life had become. His least desirable trait, at least in his private view of himself, was the satisfaction he derived in skewering others, a form of Schadenfreude that brought them down to a level closer to his own. This "one-downsmanship," as he termed it, hardly mitigated his own shortcomings, but he was powerless against the urge to point them out anyway, and the newsroom of the capital city's newspaper was the perfect place from which to do it. His only truly close friend was his editor, the friendship accounting for his employment. Driving to Beaufort, he had predicted it might take as much as half a day to debunk the Judge Borders myth.

In the clerk's office, he debated whether to approach the judge's chambers, deciding against it. He lacked the information necessary to conduct an interview, for which preparation was essential. Through a window, he saw the judge emerge from the rear of the building and walk into the parking lot, to the spaces reserved for court personnel. Suspended from his right hand was a plastic bag emblazoned with the logo of Turner & Feinberg. Brock Jamerson found that interesting.

# CHAPTER 15

# Jillian Seethes

In the days following the Lopez hearing, Jillian Pillai appeared routinely in Judge Borders's court. He appreciated the effort she made to hide her hostility, but he sensed it. "Yes, Your Honor" and "No, Your Honor" were delivered with pointed, undue crispness. Her smiles, rare though they came, concealed gritted teeth. To her habitually polite treatment of witnesses, defendants, and opposing counsel, she added a flourish that Dan perceived directed at him, a passive-aggressive expression of her refusal to let the Lopez ruling go. In hopes of clearing the air, he asked to see her in his chambers.

"Please be seated," he said, nodding toward the closest chair. "I want to talk to you about Lopez. Because we're discussing an active case, I invited Mr. Roan to be present. He waived that right. I know you're upset. Lopez was a tough argument to lose." He walked around his desk and took the chair beside her, five feet away. "For what it's worth, I think you did an excellent job. Even great arguments don't always win."

"Thank you, but with all due respect, Your Honor . . ." The

judge could tell that even with the lapse of time, she was fighting for control. "It was the piece of evidence we need to convict, and without it, a guilty man may walk."

"I suspect you are right, and you hold me responsible. I took no pleasure from excluding the knife."

"Because the knife won't be in evidence, we can't show a jury the report from the state crime lab matching blood on the knife to Hazel Hudgins. And Lopez's fingerprints are on the handle." Her dark eyes blazed with indignation.

Judge Borders paused before asking if other fingerprints were also present.

She inhaled, let her breath out slowly, then admitted, "Two other sets. By the way, Lopez is here illegally. No green card. He probably swam the Rio Grande."

Dan nodded. "Which may also explain why he ran into that shed when Deputy Flock showed up. Without papers, they avoid anyone with a badge."

Her mouth puckered as if tasting something sour. "And now I will likely lose the special election because of this. Jerry Higginson is praying Lopez gets off so he can remind anyone who will listen that I'm the one who let Hazel's murderer go free."

"Don't be too discouraged by this setback. I've heard many people say nice things about you and the job you're doing."

"But . . . but Lopez is guilty!"

Judge Borders held up a flat palm. "When you have been doing this as long as I have, it is inevitable you will make rulings leading to results that seem unfair." His eyes shifted to the window. "But until they change the law . . ." Then, looking at her again, he said, "I asked you to join me in chambers to reassure you that you have a great legal career ahead of you, regardless of what happens in this case or the election, so don't let this one ruling get you down. Or if it gets you down, don't stay down."

She stood. "Thank you. I will try to take your advice." She offered her hand, which he shook.

Back in her office, Jillian seethed. Whatever peace she thought she had made with herself after the ruling had been fractured by the conference just concluded. She remained convinced that Judge Borders got it wrong. She threw the file on her desk with enough force to scatter the papers within. She was on the verge of losing a case she had to win. It was that simple. She ran her fingers through her jet-black hair, a habit when under stress. Joe Roan's smug smile at the ruling would stay with her until she beat him next time, and in this business, there was always a next time.

# CHAPTER 16

# Karma

Jillian had been born in Virginia as the third child of Indian parents who immigrated from Mumbai in 1975, back when it had been Bombay. Her father engineered software for a Northern Virginia think tank while her mother worked in retail when she wasn't raising Jillian and her two older brothers, which was most of the time. Her parents retired to Bluffton the same year Jillian began law school at the University of South Carolina. Between her second and third years, she interned (unpaid) for the local solicitor and discovered she loved prosecuting. After graduating magna cum laude and law review, she moved back home to insulate herself from the financial need to accept one of the many offers she received from law firms in Atlanta, Washington, DC, and beyond. Before worshipping at the altar of the almighty dollar, she decided to explore prosecutorial opportunities in this watery part of the state. Perhaps, she reasoned, a lower profile job at lesser pay would mean greater opportunity, and in this assessment, she proved entirely correct.

It could only have been karma that landed her the interview with Beaufort Solicitor Frank Walthall. A friendly man with a welcoming smile, Walthall greeted her and suggested she remain outside the office while he reviewed her resume. Minutes later, when the door opened, he summoned her with the wave of his hand, pointing to a seat in front of his cluttered desk.

"We don't pay much," were his first words.

"I don't need much," she replied.

"No big student loans to pay?"

"I'm blessed by very frugal parents who would have spent their last dime for my education but didn't have to because they had been saving for it since I was born."

"That makes you fortunate," Walthall agreed. From his desk drawer, he extracted a red rubber ball and began to squeeze it. "Tell me why you want to be a prosecutor."

"Because I like to win."

Walthall shifted the ball to the other hand as he nodded. "Fair enough. We win most of 'em. If we don't, we're doing something wrong, because most of the people we charge with crimes are guilty as sin." Another ball shift. "Just remember that it isn't our job to convict. The judge or the jury gets paid to do that. It's our job to bring the best case we can, and deciding which cases to bring requires brains and judgment. You impress me as having both. I'll start you out in the general district courts."

"Is that an offer?"

"It is, indeed, young lady. When would you like to start?"

"When do you need me?"

"Today. Now."

Walthall was tired, he told her. Recently reelected to his fifth six-year term, he said it had been a mistake to run again. "There are some fish out there with my name on 'em, and I need to catch 'em. You'll have more work than you can handle, but I won't throw you to the wolves until you're ready." Early on a Friday afternoon, while fishing, he dropped dead of a heart attack. A hunter found him facedown in the creek. Jillian cried at his funeral.

She wished her mentor could be here now to advise her on what to do about Lopez. She paced as she sorted through the wreckage of her case. All her hopes now rested with a man named Miguel Fernandez who lived in the same trailer complex as Lopez and claimed to have seen him run from The Happy Clam as Hazel Hudgins's screams grew increasingly faint. Fernandez even claimed to have seen what looked like blood on the white T-shirt Lopez wore. But her investigation of Fernandez and his purported eyewitness account had revealed problems, chiefly Fernandez himself. He and Lopez shared bad blood. Each had competed for the affections of a local woman named Camilla Ordonez, and according to Jillian's sources, Fernandez had finished second. A fight between the two men a few days before the Hudgins murder had served as amusement for the migrant community until Fernandez pulled a knife.

Jillian couldn't be positive Fernandez hadn't killed Hudgins. He had put himself at the scene at the time of her murder, and she wouldn't have been shocked to find his fingerprints on the knife along with those of Lopez. When the lab report came back, neither of the two sets of prints belonging to someone other than Lopez belonged to Fernandez, but that didn't make him a better witness. Given his hostility to Lopez, Joe Roan could be expected to tear him limb from limb on the witness stand. And Camilla, the ingénue, had not been seen in weeks, so it was anyone's guess as to what she could add.

Jillian ceased pacing, as if nearing resolution. Prosecutors resorted to *nolle prosequi* when they dropped charges against a criminal defendant. It represented a form of surrender they resisted but sometimes felt compelled to exercise, and it was not without its benefits. Not only did it spare the prosecution the humiliation of defeat, but it preserved the option of bringing the charge again should new evidence develop. Maybe, reasoned Jillian, another more credible eyewitness would come forward. Perhaps Lopez had made an admission to a cellmate during his time in jail that further investigation would uncover. If anything turned up before Lopez was deported back to Mexico, she might yet achieve justice for Hazel Hudgins. Or so she reasoned in pondering her decision whether to "nolle pross," as it was commonly known. It would be, she realized, the single toughest decision she would be called upon to make since becoming the youngest solicitor in South Carolina.

# CHAPTER 17

# Sidney Callahan

Dan merged into Saturday morning traffic on I-26 headed to Columbia. With light traffic and the sun behind him, he could spend a reflective hour contemplating the meeting to which he had been summoned. Members of this influential group would go out of their way to make him comfortable, as if they had finished a round of golf at the country club and now relaxed at the 19th hole over something smooth and amber. The sole reason for his presence, the only reason some other judge wasn't at that moment driving toward Columbia, was his Jury of One concept and the publicity that it occasioned.

How much should he share with them about his inspiration for the idea? It had not begun the moment he signed Otis Hazzard's death warrant, though that solemn act made it more immediate. He traced its origins to a college literature class and the study of Camus's *The Stranger*. He began it as just another mandatory read, one of two dozen books in the syllabus, but on some early page, it drew him in as others had not. Because it was short, he could polish it off on a Sunday afternoon and still make it to dinner before the cafeteria closed, and had it not been for certain sentences and the thoughts they engendered, he would have. But those sentences and thoughts had been the equivalent of walking into a dark basement and being suddenly assaulted by a blinding light. He had never considered "the gentle indifference of the world," for example. His universe, from his first breath, had been ordered. With love and support at home, role models as parents, a strong work ethic instilled early, and a sound education, he was destined to reap rewards, and it had never occurred to him that the world he inhabited couldn't care less about any of that, or that those rewards he assumed were inevitable could prove as impossible as lightning in a bottle, made unforeseeable by forces beyond his control. He credited *The Stranger* with an awakening empathy that matured as he did.

And it was empathy that compelled him to take a hard look at the death penalty. As the penalty phase of Otis Hazzard's trial made clear, the indifference of the universe had been for him not so gentle. His mother, age nineteen, died of a heroin overdose in her public housing apartment. She had been dead for a day and a half when the stench alerted her next-door neighbor, who called 911. EMS found Otis, naked and dehydrated, on the floor of the kitchen. He had just turned three. A loveless aunt reluctantly took him in, exposing him to a string of her boyfriends, one of whom beat him for crying during a particularly inopportune moment with the aunt. Hazzard escaped his hunger and needs by sniffing glue from a brown bag. Over time, it reduced what might have been average intelligence to borderline. Social Services removed him from his aunt's, beginning a series of foster homes hopelessly unequipped to deal with the challenges he presented. By fifteen, he lived on the streets of Savannah, functionally illiterate and angry. *Where would I be,* Dan wondered, *had this been my childhood and youth?*

Leaving aside the fact that death penalty juries had been shown to convict those later proved innocent, the ultimate sanction demonstrably targeted the poor, minorities, and those with lesser lawyers, as if their lots in life somehow made their crimes more reprehensible. When a few commentators criticized Dan's Jury of One as a judge's way to avoid responsibilities that came with the job, he could only wonder in what obscure closet their empathy had been locked away.

Around a highly polished mahogany conference table in a downtown Columbia law firm, Dan faced an informal gathering of men who would largely determine the next supreme court chief justice. They sat in tufted leather chairs, the aroma of tobacco still faintly detectible despite the ban on smoking instituted a decade earlier, and then only because the firm no longer represented the major cigarette manufacturer that had turned a staid, silk-stocking partnership of good ol' boys into a legal piranha, gobbling up talent from rival firms. On the walls were prints of scarlet-clad riders on horses chasing hounds in pursuit of invisible foxes. Oak paneling gave the room a dark warmth, swaddling clients in the arms of competence at six-hundred-dollars an hour.

This meeting had been arranged by Kennedy Mosby, the state senator who represented Beaufort County. As a practicing attorney, Dan Borders had supported Mosby in his first bid for public office fifteen years earlier. While Dan and Mosby enjoyed a cordial relationship, it was Mosby's close connection to William Reynolds, general counsel to the senate Judiciary Committee, that held the key to this Saturday morning showdown. Dan couldn't lock up a seat on the court here, but he could lose it.

Over intermittent clinks of china coffee cups, idle chatter about Clemson's football prospects in the fall gave way to the business that brought them there. "What concerns folks," Reynolds said, "is your view of the death penalty." In choppy, clipped sentences, either a cause or effect of his habit of moving a flattened hand up and down, he spoke as if dividing the world before him, his listeners, into hemispheres. It reminded Dan of a Braves fan's tomahawk chop.

"We all know the death penalty is flawed. Most of us see a day when it will be abolished. But that day isn't today. Or next week." Right hand waving up and down, he continued, "It may take a generation. Personally, I like your Jury of One idea. And the death-with-dignity folks are running with it. Biggest blowback is the law-and-order crowd. The worst of the worst getting to live off the public teat for forty or fifty years. They like the idea of citizens giving the emperor's thumb down." Ironically, his thumb went up as he said this. "Want a shorter appeal process. Earlier date with Old Sparky. The electric chair." Having advocated the devil's position, he lowered his hands to his lap, then turned a piercing gaze on Dan. "But many I've spoken with think it solves the thorniest problems, so I give you full credit for an inventive solution."

"Thank you," Dan replied. "There are still some questions about the pharmacology. A prisoner opting for the cure must be able to end it as quickly and painlessly as possible. Some new drugs could help us there. Cyanide derivatives."

Mosby spoke next. His deep tan nicely complemented his maroon polo shirt and silvering hair. "I've spoken to some representatives in the House. They wonder if a vote to confirm you for the high court will be seen by their voters as an endorsement of your capital punishment views. Obviously, you would bring a lot more to the seat than just your Jury of One idea, but given the media coverage it's getting, it may be hard to separate the man from the plan, so to speak."

Reynolds laughed. "The man from the plan. You should go into politics."

Now it was Mosby's turn to laugh. "I should get out of politics is what I should do."

"Not before the vote on this seat," Dan said with a grin. "What about Sidney Callahan? How do you fellows assess his chances?"

"Sidney's so old school," Reynolds said. "Always fighting the last war. As a person, he's fine, but the general impression I get from those I've spoken with is that they don't think he would add much to the court. Very traditional thinker, and not a deep one. Still, I can't deny he has support. Kennedy?"

Mosby agreed. "Don't sell him short when it comes to his former colleagues in the legislature. He's working them hard. His buddies leave me alone because they know where I stand, but they are busy reaching out to others who don't know Dan. That smoke-filled back room everyone talks about is still open for business. I've been in it a few times myself." When the laughter quelled, Mosby summed up the situation as he saw it. "This is likely to come down to a two-man race. Sidney's old South Carolina against Dan's new South Carolina. I think we've got a shot."

*A two-man race?* Dan felt more optimistic. This group, as politically savvy as any he could have assembled, had just confirmed that the lone obstacle standing between him and a seat on the state's highest court was Sidney Callahan.

Callahan lived on a two-hundred-acre estate outside Aiken. Miles of neatly maintained, freshly painted fences enclosed thoroughbreds worth almost as much as Callahan's wife, Isabell, heiress to a pharmaceutical fortune. Through years of riding and untold amounts of money, she acquired an international reputation in dressage. Decades earlier, she had urged Sidney to run for the state senate and funded his successful campaign. When he retired after serving four terms, he assumed he would have ample time at home and at the 19th hole of his country club, but Isabell reportedly had other ideas. Gossip said she pushed him toward the supreme court vacancy to keep him away from home, where she entertained a handsome thirty-year-old trainer.

# CHAPTER 18

# Growing Intimacy

O n his drive home, Dan's thoughts should have been on the encouraging meeting he had just left. Instead, he dwelled on his sessions with Alana Morgan at the library to discuss the Confederate monument. She had arrived with the zeal of a reformer, carrying books on her reading list. But Dan had read most of them, and it was soon apparent, from exchanges of "so true" and "I couldn't agree more," that their minds ran in parallel where the monument was concerned. He admired her passion for the subjects.

"I didn't expect you to be so open-minded," she said, a comment that nicked his pride, but not enough to show it.

"You assumed I was some mossback rebel?" he asked with a wink.

"A rebel, anyway."

They met in a small study room off the main floor of the library with a small table and chair. Opening the glass-paneled door inward usually required a chair to be moved. A fluorescent light overhead gave off an irritating hum. The room stayed cool even in summer, the lone air-conditioning vent positioned directly above the table where they sat.

"It's not that I don't believe in honoring history," she said. "I'm a history junkie, and I get that we Southerners think that by ditching our monuments we are somehow being disloyal to the ghosts of our ancestors. But they fought against their own country, for God's sake. This has to be the only place that builds monuments to losers."

"Perhaps," said Dan, tilting his head as if looking at her words from another angle. "But to survive, they couldn't think of themselves as losers. They had to find comfort and meaning from the effort, not to mention banishing the thought that their sons and husbands had died in vain."

"A truly lost cause," Alana added.

In their time together, they found mutual admiration for Frederick Douglass, and for each other. Exchanges about Reconstruction gradually led them into personal stories, histories, and opinions. Dan found himself revealing matters close to him, the ones he deflected at cocktail parties. His family, for example. He spoke of Claire and the challenges of MS, mostly for her but also for him. His daughter, Christina, clung to a romance both he and Claire feared had no future, while his son Ethan had cut short his backpacking in Europe, looking for whatever it is that draws young men there, to join an NGO in Haiti, where the suffering from the earthquake continued unabated. Absorption with his job, Dan confessed, may have kept him from being the father he should have been, and now it was too late to be otherwise. He had never admitted that, even to himself. He admitted, too, that his desire for the chief justiceship had reached a near obsession. He told her he believed he had earned it, and that within a few years he would put his mark on the court, making it a model across the South and the nation. He wasn't bragging, he insisted. The fact that he had never uttered those words, even to Claire, punctuated the intimacy he felt with Alana.

For her part, Alana spoke in aspirational tones of an advanced degree she hoped to pursue. She wanted to teach at the college level someday. A better house, closer to the high school, ranked at the top of her list of priorities. She spoke longingly of a village in Italy she had never visited. "How can you miss a place you've never actually seen?" she asked Dan rhetorically. She confessed her absorption with travel videos and her determination to hone closer to a Mediterranean diet. She wanted to learn tennis. When Holly got a little older, they could team up for doubles to become a formidable mother-daughter duo. Such conversational musings were so compulsively futuristic that Dan began to suspect they were her defense against the past, a suspicion confirmed when, in a voice of modulated pain, Alana described Toby's sporadic, alcohol-fueled harassment, at times following her car from school five feet off her rear bumper.

"He needs to get a life, and he seems to think he can't do that unless I'm part of it, which isn't going to happen, as I've told him repeatedly. He's pathetic. He wants to save his life by bringing me back into it, and I want to save mine by keeping him as far away as possible. I still find it hard to believe that a single act of intercourse can have such long-term consequences, although I've known that intellectually since I learned about sex. Have you ever wished someone would just vanish?"

Dan found her simple clinical reference to sex and intercourse titillating. As he passed exit signs leading him home, he thought about how he had wanted to ask what she knew about sex, whether she enjoyed intercourse, when she last had it, did she miss it. He had asked none of those questions, conscious of how inappropriate they would have been. But how inappropriate was it for him to ponder them? For all he knew, she had a boyfriend who satisfied her romantic desires. That Dan could find stimulation in a couple of random allusions spoke more to his needs than hers.

And then there was the relationship between Toby and Holly. "For a time," Alana had said in a tone that would have been appropriate from the couch of a psychiatrist, "I encouraged Holly to meet him on Saturday mornings at least once a month because it was important for a girl to know her father, even *that* father. I drove her to Hardees and waited in the car, grateful for the large plate glass windows that allowed me to monitor hand gestures and, at close range, facial expressions as they faced each other across the table." Dan had watched her tear up at the recollection of these scenes, surprised to find himself so affected as to put himself in her place. "It was awful," Alana said. "I should have known it would make things worse. He preached. Holly listened. You'd think the least he could do was ask a couple of questions about her school, her life. He really didn't know her at all. But no. Big bad Toby had to blather on about how great he was and how much he wanted me back and how he tried to make things up to me and how cruel I was in ignoring him. Then he'd lay down the law about how the poor girl should dress and act. What a joke coming from someone who thinks and acts like laws are for others. Through that big window, I could watch the spirit drain out of her. She hardly touched those breakfast biscuits Toby made such a big deal out of buying for her. When he'd finally had his say, he tried to hug her, and she just stood there stiff as concrete. It took all the control I had to stay in the car, as I promised her I'd do. She held herself together as she walked back across the parking lot, but I could see the effort it took. We drove home in silence until she said, 'I hate him' and began to cry. Nightmares became more common. When I awoke to find her in bed with me, shaking from another Toby nightmare, I stopped those Saturday visits. That enraged him into incessant phone calls. We didn't answer."

His time on the bench had exposed Judge Borders to infinite variations of familial dysfunction and human frailty, so Alana's account should not have moved him, yet it did. Being pulled into the pathos surrounding the Morgans heightened Dan's growing sense of intimacy with her. Eye contact became more intense. Hands clasped at departing, brief as they were, became something to look forward to. It was this building attraction that both absorbed and troubled him on the drive back to Beaufort. *What is happening?* he asked himself. *Where is this going?*

*Nowhere,* came his answer, with determination not to be some middle-aged fool with a crush. *Buy a Harley. Take flying lessons. Anything but this.* Yet every time he considered resigning from the Historical Society, pleading workload, he balked. When she asked him about their next session, he scheduled it. An unspoken but mutually felt gravity was at work, drawing them closer. And it was after the fourth session that he considered a social meeting, a dinner perhaps. But where? Meeting at a restaurant in the county where everyone knew him seemed likely to generate gossip, with some awkward greetings and questions about Claire. On the other hand, being spotted in Columbia or Camden, huddled over a candlelit meal, could defy explanation and invite publicity he didn't need.

Then Dan got an idea. An uncharacteristically bad idea.

# CHAPTER 19

# Glory Days

E very May 1, as part of Law Day, the Beaufort County Bar Association sponsored an annual essay contest. Dan Borders judged it, reading through piles of entries to announce the winner of a three-hundred-dollar first prize. In past years, he had also hosted receptions for legal secretaries, delivered a public service announcement for a television station in Greenville, judged a moot court contest at USC's law school, given a guest reading of the Constitution at a bar association luncheon, and spoken to numerous high school classes on the centrality of law to America's gestation and future.

As a young man, he had been drawn to the system in which he now played so integral a part by what he regarded as an essential nobility. Lawyers mattered, and by becoming one, he mattered. His idealism in those days embarrassed him now. During his years as a practicing attorney, he had been at ground zero when the system failed to function perfectly, or well, or at all in extreme cases. Money purchased professional competence, including his own. Armed with a consummate knowledge of legal procedure, he out-maneuvered those less astute. He learned the value of delay when defending, and how to cut through that same delay when his plaintiff clients paid for a quick result.

In the year prior to his appointment to the bench, he defended a fuel oil company in a contract dispute with its wholesaler. The wholesaler's lawyer amended the suit three times to satisfy Dan's objections, and when it appeared the court would grant his newest objections, requiring yet another amendment, the frustrated and embarrassed attorney turned to Dan, meekly asking his advice on how to do it right. Dan helped him. After the case settled, the wholesaler retained Dan, which added one more corporate client to his burgeoning practice.

But by this time, his view of the law, or at least his role in it, had shifted. The shift had been gradual, nearly imperceptible, and he owed it to his habit of compulsively assessing the legitimacy and fairness of his own clients' positions. As with most lawyers, he did his best to represent a client who was wrong as vigorously as those who were right, yet he never lost sight of the equities, the essential justice of the client's cause. By the standard of essential justice, he had prevailed in cases he and his client didn't deserve to win, and neither the grateful litigant nor generous fees soothed the guilt he felt at using his considerable talents to bring about an unjust result. As he gradually became aware of this habit, he took more pains to conceal it from clients, other lawyers, and judges. But one who noticed was Kennedy Mosby, a lawyer Dan had supported for election to the state senate from Beaufort County. When a circuit court judgeship opened, Mosby called to ask Dan's permission to submit his name. A day later, after talking it over with Claire, Dan called back to confirm his interest. He was destined to be a judge, as Mosby had perceived and Dan had decided, because his talents were best employed to equalize odds. In his first month as a jurist, he knew he had come home. His idealism returned, more precious for its tempering, and he prized his membership in a black-robed fraternity bound together by respect for precedent, fundamental fairness, and, above all, impartiality.

As a trial judge, he rendered few written opinions, although he willingly seized what opportunities he found. A dominant strength was his ability to identify the nub of the issue on which any given case turned, and the decisions he had authored explored these hinge issues in analytic fullness, to the satisfaction of the lawyers participating, if not always their clients. Lawyers liked to know why they won or lost a case, and his opinions, often characterized as "closely reasoned," satisfied such curiosity. Several years prior, he had issued an opinion in a case applying a statute of limitations to particularly gnarled facts. On appeal, the South Carolina Supreme Court upheld his decision and adopted portions of his opinion verbatim. That case, *Owens v. Sontag Motors, Inc.*, was still considered the leading case on the point decided, and for the reasons he articulated.

Dan read the *Owens* opinion with a mixture of pleasure and frustration. Pleasure that the court had seen fit to quote him, and frustration that Oliver Bidwell Cox, who wrote the majority opinion, failed to adequately articulate a key argument to guide future decisions. *Cox is getting old,* Dan thought at the time, and Cox, as if overhearing Dan's thoughts, announced his retirement a year later. It was his seat that Dan, at age fifty, hoped to fill.

On this Law Day, Dan answered the invitation extended by Alana to speak to her class. Beaufort High stood a mile southeast of the courthouse. Structurally, it looked and felt very much as it did when he, at age seventeen, graduated in its class of 1979. Wide corridors, expansive windows, and vaulted ceilings spoke of Depression-era design and construction. As the largest public works project undertaken up to that time, it made a rural county's declaration of progress, to be measured in minds. He had loved the school—still loved it—for it was there, in the halls, classrooms, and athletic fields, that his adolescence played out in small highs and lows which, combined, added up to an experience he treasured.

The football field had been rearranged somewhat, the bleachers now standing in what had been the outfield of the baseball diamond in his day, but the grass smelled the same, and he could walk it on an autumn night with fall's echo in the air and enough humidity in the freshly mowed grass to yield the aroma implanted forever in his senses, a sickly-sweet bouquet that somehow combined the cheers of the crowd with the sweat in his uniform and the youthful scent of a cheerleader named Nanci, so that in an October just after Claire's diagnosis, he had come here late at night, in an hour of acute loneliness, and in no more than a few strides across the field had been transported back to the fall of 1978 as surely as he had lived it. He paused in the north end zone, imagining the crowd's celebration, blue and gold pom-poms waving, heat rising from his body, and the press of Nanci's breasts against him in the crush of fans after a victory over rival Estill High.

Simple nostalgia, he convinced himself. "I can almost hear the band," he said to no one. How silly for a man of his age and responsibilities. He looked around. Utter darkness. Overhead, stars littered a moonless heaven. He listened. No sound. Yet he felt it, 1978, as real to him as his hands and feet. The nearness of the memories jolted him, like a small but acute detonation within, and he compared it to the night he was knocked out in the last quarter of a football game his junior year and Doc Vandencamp had waved smelling salts under his nose—that kind of jolt, that brings consciousness from unconsciousness, and he wondered if what he was experiencing could be a panic attack, which he'd heard described by witnesses in his courtroom. He wasn't sure, didn't know quite what to make of the episode, and told no one about it. But he sensed, from that night forward, a certain introspection ebb into his daily routine. He began a rhetorical dialogue of sorts, posing to himself questions about his happiness, his ambition, his worth. *Am I living or merely marking time? What do I need to do before I die? My God!* he thought. *Am I writing my own eulogy?*

Concern for Claire had allowed him to postpone such thoughts for a time, but like water in a basement which has not been sealed, they ebbed and seeped back, creating a kind of mildew in his spirit. Then, out of the blue came the *Hazzard* case, his widely circulated Jury of One essay, and thereafter Oliver Cox's announced intention to retire. Overnight, or so it seemed to Dan, his rudderless malaise transformed into a focused ambition to succeed Cox as chief justice. In his mind, such progression became inevitable, though his innate modesty kept such ruminations hidden, even from Claire. But not, to his surprise, from Alana.

# CHAPTER 20

# Third Base

She met him at the door of her senior government class with a broad smile. In a hunter-green skirt, white blouse, and multicolored neck scarf, she resembled no teacher Dan could remember, and he wondered how he would have been able to concentrate on anything but her in class. She introduced him as "one of our own."

In addressing the last class of the day, he knew he would be competing against both fatigue and restlessness for the students' attention. He spoke without notes about the extraordinary qualifications possessed by framers of the Constitution. Of the fifty-six signers, thirty-two had been lawyers. "The Constitutional Convention brought together the brightest, the best educated, the most seasoned men the colonies possessed, even with Jefferson in Paris. Never in the history of mankind had so formidable a group assembled to cut a new government from whole cloth." He listed from memory the leading men and women who had put their lives and fortunes at risk for the great experiment, citing Washington as an example and inspiration.

From his imagination, he painted a scene of Washington at Mt. Vernon, retired from public life and immersed in farming that was his livelihood. He asked the students to picture Washington standing at a rail fence. Suddenly, an overseer shouted and pointed to the long lane, to a horseman approaching at full gallop with dust in his wake. As Washington's eyes followed the rider's advance, he sensed in his urgency a sea change of his own fortunes.

Dan paused to survey the students, who listened attentively and who, he wanted to believe, were themselves at that moment with Washington waiting to learn the identity of the rider, the nature of the crisis. "Washington's instinct proved only too accurate," he said. "The rider came with news of Shay's Rebellion in Massachusetts, which Ms. Morgan tells me you've studied. Washington recognized that a grassroots insurrection by farmers, long expected and much feared by framers of the Constitution, signaled the end of his retirement. His nation, a nation on paper only, needed him. He had no choice but to respond. One day, you, too, like Washington, may be called upon to put aside something valuable for something more urgent."

He had repeated the Shay's Rebellion episode many times in church groups, book clubs, and civic organizations, which often invited him to speak, but never had he related Washington's sense of the moment to his own. *Am I being called upon to put aside something valuable, my role as a trial judge, for something more urgent, chief justice of the South Carolina Supreme Court?* It felt so.

At his close, students asked questions, mostly tinged with the cynicism of their times. "Could a Black person get a fair trial in your courtroom?" a Black girl asked, without condescension. "What happens if you can't afford a lawyer?" another wanted to know. When a thin, pock-plagued boy in the back asked the punishment for possession of marijuana, first offense, Dan smiled, and the students snickered.

When the hour's end neared, Alana thanked him, the class applauded, and he left. In the hallway, he encountered the principal, Bart Easton, who thanked him for coming. Easton, a short, pudgy man with a penchant for bow ties, worked often with the courts. They chatted briefly, and by the time they shook hands, the school stood in a stillness of virtual abandonment. Easton's heavy steps returned him toward his office, while Dan paused at a display case to examine an exhibit of photographs from the 1950s. The school's annual staff had assembled old prom snapshots, a progression of sideburns and hemlines. He lingered, smiling in recognition of many still living in and around the county.

He greeted a janitor just beginning his chores, then exited the school from the door nearest the parking lot. He got in his car, started the engine, and adjusted the radio. Looking up, he saw Alana crossing the parking lot carrying a satchel. He powered down his window and called. Moments later, she stood at the door.

"I enjoyed today," he said. "Appreciate the invitation."

"You were quite the topic after you left. My girls were buzzing about how handsome you are."

"Oh, yeah? That does this old heart good."

She winked at him. "Don't bother telling me you don't hear that a lot because I know better."

He smiled, resting his arm on the door. "You're headed home?"

"Yep. I need to pick up Holly, and there is a mountain of papers waiting to be graded. But I'm glad you're here because you can witness me starting my car without using your jumpers or mine because I bought a new battery. Thanks again for coming today."

He watched her walk away. Images came back to him of his fumbling teenage discoveries with Nanci, who wore his high school ring on a chain around her neck. Late one afternoon, after he finished with football and her cheerleading practice ended, they drove in her car to a secluded spot at the end of a remote lane. She shifted into park, then looked at him in a way he did not recognize. "More room in the back," she urged breathlessly. In his haste to climb over the seat, his leg hit the pine tree air freshener suspended from the mirror. He heard giggling. "What?" he demanded, nervous and unsure of himself. She opened the driver's door, got out, closed the door, opened the back seat door, and climbed in laughing. Locked in a frantic embrace, pressed pelvis-to-pelvis as the strains of "Three Times a Lady" melted around them, she blew warm air into his ear and moved his hand to her breast, brushing aside the suspended ring. The breast felt firm and full. As windows in her old Ford fogged, she urged his willing hand. She seemed to have too much breath, and he not enough. No one had instructed him on the mechanics of sex, so it was all new and wildly erotic. When they surfaced for air, she told him no one had instructed her either. At age twelve, menstruating began without warning, and her shy mother stumbled over vague allusions to birds and bees, ending the discussion abruptly. "Talk to your father about boys," she instructed. So, Nanci did. Manifestly fond of sports metaphors and clearly as uncomfortable as her mother, her father warned her that boys were determined to get to something he called "third base," though he never said exactly where third base resided, leaving Nanci to guess. The important thing—"don't ever forget this"—was to never allow them to get to home plate, "because then you could get pregnant."

"So you see," she whispered to Dan, with the windows of her Ford now opaque, "I can't let you get to home plate because we could become parents, and you'll just have to figure out where third base is. I'll help you."

His thoughts returned to the present. *What would it be like if Alana circled around to his passenger seat, and he drove to the dead-end road where he used to park with Nanci?* On impulse, he called to her just as she reached her car. "Hold on a sec."

# CHAPTER 21

# A Private Dock

"I have an idea," he said as Alana sat in the precise place he had fantasized about moments before.

"Let's hear it."

"Suppose I was to return your invitation to the school by an invitation to dinner on my boat?"

"I didn't know you had a boat."

"At a private dock on Lands End."

Her answer did not come as quickly as he expected, nor as enthusiastically, leading him to wonder if perhaps there was a man, a relationship, in her life to be considered, though she had never mentioned one. After a pause, she said, "I suppose that would be okay."

"No pressure," he said, a bit defensively. "We enjoy each other's company, and I won't pretend it's a strictly business dinner, but I can also assure you I'll behave like the married gentleman I am. You need not worry where that is concerned."

"Actually, I'm worried I'll behave like the unmarried woman I am, and that might not be fair to you. I've loved our time together, as you know."

"I'm flattered, and yes, it has been great to connect like we have. Is that a yes to dinner? How about next Wednesday, say seven?"

"A private dock, you said?"

"There's a large house on Timber Gate Lane. You can't see it from the road, and the mailbox is on its last leg, but if you look closely, you'll see the number 240. The actual address is 2401, but the one fell off years ago. It's owned by an old client of mine who lives in Maine and lets me keep the boat there."

"Sounds lovely. Can I bring anything?"

"Just an appetite for steak."

"Then I'll see you Wednesday."

In the ten minutes it took him to drive home, he knew his impulsive overture was a mistake. He would call her in the morning to say so. A Harley or flying lessons were better choices, not that he had an interest in either. She would understand. But the next day, he vacillated. Yes, a judge entertaining an attractive divorced woman in such a private setting was unusual. No argument there. But as long as he kept his head clear and his moral compass pointed north, what was the harm? Claire was unlikely to learn of it, since no one used that stretch of Timber Gate Lane except its few residents. Even if she did, he could rationalize it as a fitting reward for someone taking her time, unpaid, to help the county wrestle with the difficult and controversial topic that monuments presented. Perhaps, he decided, he would tell Claire about it after the fact, further evidence of how transparent his life was when he was away from home. He wasn't giving himself the credit he deserved for will power that had sustained him in his adult life, and he felt certain he could restrain himself from anything that would complicate his relationship with Alana or with Claire. *Lighten up,* he told himself. *Didn't Andy remind me of the need to look after myself as well as Claire? Live a little?*

# CHAPTER 22

# Last, Best Chance

Dan's last, best chance to avoid the disaster looming just offshore on his personal and professional horizon occurred when Claire threw him a surprise birthday party. On the Friday after his Law Day talk, he came home from a brutal week in court. The sight of Christina's car in the driveway gave the first inkling that something was up. As soon as he walked inside, she called from the kitchen. "Daddykins!" For an instant, the young woman who strode forward evoked in him the eight-year-old girl who kept watch fifteen years before. The same generous smile, the same impish hug. For all her twenty-three years, people had remarked on how much she resembled Dan, with the lanky frame, serious eyes, and open, engaging personality.

"What a lovely surprise," Dan said.

"More to come," Christina said. "One more big one."

"Another?" Dan asked, taking Christina's hand and walking into the kitchen, where Claire stood leaning on the counter. "What did I do to deserve this? My birthday isn't for another month."

Claire smiled pleasantly. "Turning fifty is a biggie," she said, "and I figured the only way to really surprise you was to jump the gun, so to speak." In front of her rested the bowls, mixer, flour, butter, and chocolate she would need to assemble a cake. Her wheelchair stood in a door to the pantry.

"Well," Dan said, still holding Christina's hand. "It worked. I'm blindsided in the best possible way. If you tell me the big surprise left is Ethan coming home, I'll have to sit down."

"He arrives in Charleston at seven-thirty tonight. Andy volunteered to pick him up. Very sweet of him. Now you and Christina clear out of my kitchen so I can work. I'll call you if I need you."

Dan and Christina walked into his study, where he mixed a drink and she sipped the white wine she brought from the kitchen. When they were seated, she asked if she should begin addressing him as "Chief Justice Dad."

"That is quite enough of that, young lady. It's not at all clear I'll be appointed. A man named Sidney Callahan has a much better chance than I do. I'm trying not to get my hopes up."

Christina suppressed a smirk. "I should have known you'd be your modest self. Mom says your chances are very good. She thinks you'll get it."

"As good as your mother's instincts for such things can be, she may not fully appreciate the efforts being made by some to make sure I don't get it. I'm a long shot, but it's nice to be in the running. Enough about me. Tell me about life in Boston."

"I have to begin with a confession."

"Uh-oh. This doesn't concern your artist friend, does it?"

"Wait here. I'll be right back."

She went upstairs and returned with one hand behind her back. "Prepare yourself for a shock," she instructed. "Close your eyes."

When he opened them, he saw she was wearing a baseball cap with the Boston Red Sox logo.

Dan dropped his head into his hands. "I was afraid of this. How could you?"

"I told you it would be a shock. Joel, my artist friend, started taking me to games this spring. Believe me, Dad, tickets are hard to come by, and they aren't cheap."

"But the Braves?"

"I know. I grew up a fan just like you, but now I have to support the home team. We've been to twelve games, so I'm getting to know all the players. It is so much fun. And Joel knows batting averages and all kinds of stuff about the game. Did I tell you he played in college?"

"You did not."

"Four years at Brown. MVP his senior year. How's that?"

"I must admit I'm impressed. I can't fault his taste in girls, but I sure wish he had better taste in teams."

"Women, Dad. I'm a woman now."

"And a bright and beautiful one at that."

"Awww. Dads say such things."

Dan sipped his drink. "With all this baseball in your life, has there been any time to work?"

"Plenty. I think I told you my boss is a woman. I'd bet the ranch she'll end up as CEO of the hospital. She's urging me to go to grad school in hospital administration. And there are so many great schools in Boston. What do you think?"

"I think you'll do well at whatever you set your sights on."

"I've learned I love the business side of hospitals. The staffing, the finance, the latest high-tech equipment, those kinds of things."

"What about the patients?"

She flattened her hand toward the floor, as if warding off some unwanted pest about to jump into her lap. "I could never be a doctor or a nurse. Not my thing."

Before Dan got home, Christina had ordered Chinese takeout. Just as a delivery driver brought it into the kitchen, Ethan arrived. After an exchange of greetings and hugs, they all sat at the dining room table, which had taken Claire an hour to set after Dan left for court that morning. Takeout on her best china seemed to fit the mood of the occasion.

"I can't wait to hear of your adventures in Haiti," Claire said to Ethan, who was so deeply tanned that Dan found the whiteness of his teeth a bit startling.

"I know I've been out of touch," he said. "Communications there pretty well suck, like everything else. Those poor people had it bad enough before the big one hit."

"It was very . . . noble of you to interrupt your time in Europe to help," his mother said. "Yes, I can't think of a better word than noble."

"Not everyone there thought so," he replied. "Some of the locals resented me, accusing me of adding to the chaos. I guess I did for the first couple of weeks. Arriving without a job or a place to eat and sleep wasn't too smart."

Dan said, "You must have had some memorable adventures."

Ethan put down his fork and flashed his father a quick thumbs-up. "The first week, I walked around looking for a way to be helpful. This woman called out to me, 'Hey, man, hey man,' she said. That was the only English she knew. I'd picked up enough French to understand she had a sister somewhere outside Port-au-Prince, and she didn't know if she was dead or alive, and she would be gone a couple of hours and could I watch her three kids. This was about eleven in the morning. The kids were small, maybe four and three and one just crawling. So I said to myself, 'Ethan, you came to Haiti to help, and here's a woman who needs it,' so I said, 'Sure, I'll watch them. Two hours, right?'"

"Let me guess," Christina said, sounding a note of alarm. "She never came back."

"The kids got hungry. Hell, they were hungry when I got there. I had nothing to feed them, no idea of what they ate or where to find it. I couldn't leave to find help, and the few people who walked near the place kept walking. Kids crying, the little one naked, no water or food and no mother. So, Mom, when you say I did a noble thing, I wasn't feeling too noble that day."

"What did you do?" Claire asked.

"By late afternoon, I knew the mother wasn't coming back. For all I knew, she was hanging out in some bar or searching for her sister in a pile of rubble, or maybe there was no sister and never had been. Who knows? Picked up the baby and walked back the way I had come with the two little ones following. We made about half a mile per hour, and the little girl kept turning around to wander. When I saw the Red Cross First Aid station, I knew how seasick immigrants felt when they caught sight of the Statue of Liberty. The Red Cross folks were great. They offered me a job. We never located the mother, or we haven't yet. Maybe she'll turn up."

Dan stared down the table at his son with a mixture of pride, respect, and a touch of envy that he had what it took to stray from the path Dan had followed at that age. He guessed Claire would be having the same thought about Christina. These two young people had a sense of direction if not yet a destination. Their parents were entitled to some credit, and Dan mentally took some, giving the rest to the woman sitting at the other end of the table.

"You'll return to Haiti?" Dan asked.

Ethan nodded. "I fly back on Monday."

Dan turned to Christina. "What would you like to do while you're home?"

"I'm meeting Jenny Cooper tomorrow morning to catch up.

Other than that, Ethan and I were hoping we could talk you and Mom into a sail." She looked first at Ethan, then at Claire.

"A wonderful idea," Claire said. "I can't be the first mate I used to be, but some time on the water would be glorious."

"Great. Dad? You're up for a sail, aren't you?"

"I am, indeed. I'll check the weather first thing tomorrow."

# CHAPTER 23

# Car Pay Diem

In Beaufort County, nearly all roads eventually lead to water. As a boy, Dan learned to sail on a thirteen-foot sunfish with a lateen sail and daggerboard keel. With its three-foot draft, it could go virtually anywhere deeper than a bathtub and was light enough to drag or carry if stranded. During countless hours, he honed his feel for the ever-shifting relationship between wind, tide, and sail so that by age ten he could tack in gentle waters propelled by a breeze barely strong enough to flicker a candle. Years before he settled on a career, he set his heart on a boat. When Christina and Ethan were still young children, he bought one. A particularly large plaintiff's settlement in a multi-vehicle auto accident accounted for both the cash to buy it and the boat's name—*Car Pay Diem*.

Miles of shore-seeking roads separated Dan's house from the dock where he kept *Car Pay Diem*, a Vancouver 32 cutter. Shortly after he purchased it, a wealthy client named Gilroy, who spent most of the year in Maine, offered Dan docking privileges. Dan would have liked to have kept it closer, but while the front porch of his home on Enoch's Cove afforded a pristine view of Distant Island

Creek, the depth at water's edge was too shallow to accommodate any vessel larger than a canoe or dinghy.

By noon on the day planned for sailing, *Car Pay Diem* had been stocked with enough water, soft drinks, and snacks to provision a cruise to Bermuda, though it would never leave the confines of the Beaufort River and Port Royal Sound. With Christina supporting Claire's left arm and Ethan holding fast to the right one, Claire made shuffling but steady progress across Gilroy's dock. The step from the dock onto the boat posed the greatest risk. Dan stood on deck, extending both hands to her as Christina and Ethan guided her gently from behind, alert to a possible veer or falling back. Safely aboard, she sat in a deck chair.

They were about to cast off when Claire said to Christina, "Honey, go see if Edna wants to come. She loves to be included, and it's the least we can do to repay her for keeping an eye on the boat." Edna Poindexter lived next door to Gilroy and had for years been the unofficial watchdog for *Car Pay Diem*. Minutes later, Christina returned to say that Edna was not at home. "I should have thought to ask her yesterday," Claire said.

Ideal sailing conditions promised a pleasant voyage to Daufuskie Island, where an old dock sold crabs that had been crawling in their sideways fashion below the surface that morning. Under full sail, Dan skillfully piloted the boat to that dock, where on each piling sat a seagull with expectant eyes. Christina secured the lines and Ethan negotiated the purchase of half a bushel.

"Doesn't get any better than this," Ethan said as he cracked a particularly meaty claw. The four of them sat around a portable table arrayed with paper towels, cocktail sauce containers, and a generous quantity of drawn butter.

Claire said, "I am trying to remember the last time we all sailed together. Not since my little heath hiccup, so that's been at least three years."

"I was in college," Christina recalled.

"So, Dad," Ethan said, "you haven't mentioned the court."

"What court?" Dan asked with a wink at Christina.

"You know what court. The supreme court. Do you know the other justices?"

"I've met them all at bar functions, judicial conferences, things like that. Can't say I know any of them personally."

"That's going to change," Christina predicted.

"Maybe, maybe not," her father said. "If it's meant to happen, it will."

"That's pretty old school, Pop," Ethan said. "Much too philosophic for 2010."

"Well, I'm pretty old school," Dan said.

Christina sighed. "I love picking crabs, but it takes such a toll on my nails. Mom, how about you and I get a manicure next week."

"I'd love that," Claire said. "I'll get us an appointment."

The return to Gilroy's dock, aided by a breeze out of the east, took less time than the crossing. As they disembarked, Edna Poindexter arrived. A frail woman in her early eighties, she hugged Christina and Ethan, saying she had missed them and lamenting the loss of bygone days when summer sails were routine. She waved to Claire as Dan helped her from the boat.

For the rest of the weekend, old patterns of family cohesion reasserted themselves, like pieces of a jigsaw puzzle sliding into place. That night, Dan grilled salmon, Claire and Christina sang a duet from Girl Scout days, and Ethan regaled them with stories from Haiti that managed both tragic comedy and comic tragedy. They finished the evening with an old Chevy Chase movie they had seen years before, paused halfway through for Claire's birthday cake and fifty candles. When it ended, all said goodnight to Dan as he lingered, telling Claire he would "be along shortly."

Dan relished nights like this, when he knew the kids were safely off the roads and sleeping peacefully upstairs. A wave of contentment washed over him—contentment and gratitude that he had lived long enough to enjoy the satisfaction of a job well done by Claire and him in raising them. In that hour of solitude, he figured he had pretty much everything a man could want within the confines of three thousand square feet. Every comfort of home and hearth were, in those minutes, real enough for him to touch. *So why am I pressing my luck with Alana? I have everything a man could want. Is that not enough?*

He had no answer, only a resolve to call off dinner with her. The day his family had just spent together was a clear reminder of what he had at stake. Reflecting, he found it hard to believe he had ever entertained the notion of an intimate dinner with a woman other than his wife. He had needed this weekend as a wake-up summons to his old life, a life centered on his family. He sensed relief, his vision at last cleared of the temptations that had been clouding it, leaving him positive that on Monday morning he would call Alana to let her know that the invitation must regretfully be withdrawn.

But he didn't.

# CHAPTER 24

# Small Talk

Ethan returned to Haiti on Monday, and Christina left on Tuesday. On the Wednesday of his dinner with Alana, Dan told Claire he had a meeting in town and might be late getting home. He didn't say what meeting, and she didn't ask. "Drive carefully," she said as he left. He stopped at the local market for provisions. In the back seat, his jumper cables still inside the Turner & Feinberg bag reminded him of how long it had been since he had cleaned his SUV. He opened the trunk, put the cables on the floor, and carried the bag inside for his purchases. He bought steaks, asparagus, a lemon, and an arugula salad with oil and vinegar dressing packaged inside.

He wound down Gilroy's lane until the house loomed ahead, half in shadow from the setting sun on what would be a cool, moonless night. He circled the house, carrying in one hand a flashlight he would need later and in the other the Turner & Feinberg bag. Gilroy's lawn sloped down to the water at an angle steep enough to make croquet impractical. At the end of the dock, *Car Pay Diem* rocked on a gentle tide.

As he stepped aboard, he heard Edna Poindexter call his name. Turning, he saw her standing on the deck of her home next door. He returned her wave. She cupped her hands to amplify her voice, calling to him. "It was wonderful to see you and the family last weekend. I'm so sorry I missed the cruise." Her voice carried in the stillness.

"We're sorry, too," Dan yelled, suddenly aware that Alana could arrive at any moment. If she did, he'd have to introduce her, and how would that look? "Please, Edna," he muttered to himself, "go inside. Now." He glanced nervously in the direction from which Alana would come.

"I'll bet that time on the boat was just what Claire needed," Edna said.

Dan felt his blood pressure rising. A discussion with Edna of Claire's health was likely to go on and on, increasing the chances of the awkward introduction he dreaded. He needed to change the subject. He called back, "It did wonders for her. I just stopped by to do some maintenance. You know boats. Something always needs attention." He stepped toward the hatch, hoping to signal an end to the exchange.

"And Ethan has grown a foot since I saw him last," Edna persisted.

For a moment, Dan considered unlocking the hatch, pretending he hadn't heard her. He stole another look at the corner of Gilroy's house, where Alana might appear at any moment. He gritted his teeth as if to will Edna inside.

"And Christina is as lovely as ever," Edna called.

"Very proud of them both," Dan managed.

"Well, I'll let you get to work. It's a treat to see you again. Twice in one week!" She turned and retreated through the sliding glass door which accessed the deck from the family room. Moments later, a light went on in the room Dan knew to be the Poindexter library. By now, he thought with relief, Edna is probably curled up with a book. He wouldn't have to make that awkward introduction after all. It was nearly dark. He unlocked the cabin hatch and ducked inside.

# CHAPTER 25

# Prying Eyes

By 7:30, Dan decided Alana wasn't coming, and the relief he felt should have been another revelation about the wisdom of inviting her. Just as he was about to begin packing things up, thinking he could cook one steak when he got home, he saw a flash from the lane and, moments later, a car door slammed. He met her on the dock.

She arrived out of breath wearing clothes appropriate for boating if not for dining. White pants fit snuggly on her hips, and a blouse tied above her midriff accentuated firm breasts. Deck shoes, no socks. A sweater tied at her waist anticipated a drop in the temperature. She brought on her a hint of gardenia that lingered in their greeting, an awkward near-embrace closer to ballroom dancing than to budding friendship.

"So sorry to be late," she said as she stepped aboard. "My sitter canceled at the last second, and I wasn't sure I should come. I leave Holly alone sometimes if I'm just running to the store, but otherwise I want someone else there."

"No harm done," Dan said. "I waited for you. Can I get you a glass of wine?"

"You bet. Red if you have it."

With his attention now on Alana, Dan failed to notice that the Poindexter library had gone dark. Edna stood at the window, as she often did to make sure *Car Pay Diem* was securely moored. With the lights off, she got a better view through the binoculars she kept handy. *Who is that with Dan?* she wondered.

Dan went below deck, returning with two glasses of wine. "To monuments," he said, raising his glass and meeting Alana's at the rim. They looked out over the river, the setting sun casting a golden glow on smoothly undulating water. The boat rocked casually against its bumpers.

"That house looks haunted," Alana said, turning back toward shore and staring at Gilroy's. "A little creepy with no lights. You were right about that mailbox. I couldn't find it so that's another reason I'm late."

Dan may have had guilt on his mind because his reply was to confess that he hadn't fixed Gilroy's mailbox. "It's the least I can do for a man that lets me use his dock. I'll do it this weekend."

He raised the cover to a gas grill mounted on the stern. After removing a platter holding two filets and a dish where asparagus marinated in olive oil and lemon zest, he lit the grill, closed the cover, and waited several minutes before again raising the cover. When the steaks hit the grill with a hiss, the aroma wafted around them. As the steaks cooked, Venus made its first appearance in the darkening sky. After turning the steaks, he tonged the asparagus onto the grill, and pronounced all ready.

"You're a pro," she said.

"A practiced amateur," he assured her.

He invited her to go below deck and followed her down the short steps. From behind her, he wondered if her gaze took in the furnishings or the closed door that separated the galley from the berth in the bow.

She sat across from him at a table already set. They toasted again, this time holding their gaze a beat longer. After complimenting him on steaks "done perfectly," she mentioned the Historical Society. "Even though I've managed to make myself its least popular member, I've needed an engagement like that. It gives me a sense of purpose. And with your help, we'll bring those rebels around to our way of thinking about the monument."

He flashed an ironic grin. "Even Randy Stephens?" He laughed when she said that might be one miracle too many.

Turning more serious, she said, "My life revolves in a loop. I carpool Holly, teach, fix meals, grade papers, sleep. Pretty boring except for all the drama Toby creates by his phone calls and insane tailgating. I must find a way to put a stop to that."

"I've mentioned a restraining order."

Alana sighed, her shoulders slumping in synch with her pout. "I got one years ago, and he ignored it. He's like that. He has no respect for authority. I called the cops, and by the time they came out, he was gone and denied ever being there. It was an infantile game to him. The cops said to call earlier next time, and the whole thing was a useless pain in the butt."

"And now," Dan added, "you have the added drama of a monument, or as the bad punster might put it, a monumental drama."

Her pout lifted into a radiant smile. "Can I tell you how much I enjoy talking to you?"

Dan's hand, which had been curled loosely on the table, raised up as his palm flattened toward her. "Oh, please," he said lightly, "no flattering. You'll embarrass me."

"Well, it's true. I can speak truth to power, can't I? Isn't that what they are always urging us to do? You have no idea what it's like to marry someone like Toby because you're young and stupid and your hormones are on fire, and then you wake up one day to the utter mess you've made of things. And you tell yourself you deserve to be in the hole you've dug and that the future holds more of the same, and sometimes you get so discouraged and depressed, you want to die."

"But you climbed out of that hole you say you dug."

"I got an education, and with it came some desperately needed self-esteem. But Toby's still there to remind me. What's that great line from the Eagles' song? 'You're still the same old girl you used to be.' Then someone like you comes along, the kind of person I never imagined having as a good friend, and I start thinking maybe I'm not the same old girl I used to be. Maybe I'm better than that."

"You're much better than that, and don't let anyone tell you otherwise."

She reached across, where beside his plate his cupped hand had returned to its position. She could have easily grasped it, but instead placed hers on top of it in a gesture that might have been inspired by the intimacy of the conversation, or perhaps it was merely a tactile exclamation point to his assertion that she was better than that, a physical "damn right!" Whatever prompted it, after several seconds, she removed her hand.

With her hand on his, and not before, he recognized what a biblically bad decision it had been to invite her aboard. Her mere touch had lit a fuse, pulled the pin on a grenade, unleashed urges he had at first denied having and then insisted he could control. Another glass of wine would pour gasoline on an already hot fire, one that had been smoldering for weeks.

But the second glass of wine never came. In mid-sentence, he had been interrupted by a buzz from Alana's purse. She blew out a short burst of frustration, rolling her eyes. "Hold that thought," she said. "It's my daughter. I told her to call me only if it was an emergency, so I have to take it."

Dan nodded toward the phone, now in her hand. "Of course."

"Yes, Holly," Alana said, her voice business-like.

Given their proximity, Dan heard Holly's voice, anything but business-like. In fact, she was hysterical. Between her sobs, he

heard snatches of "dad" and "drunk" and "gun." Alana's face turned
to cold slate as she urged her daughter to calm down. She mouthed
at Dan, "I'm sorry," stood, and walked to the stairs, then back on
deck, from which he heard only Alana's aggressive voice, her words
indistinguishable. She returned to the table. As she put the phone
back in her purse, she said, "Toby's at the house. He's very drunk,
and he has a gun. Holly is terrified. The doors are locked, but he's
banging and yelling that he won't leave until I get home. I need to
go."

"Should you call the sheriff?"

"I've done that before. Useless. He won't hurt Holly, but a
drunk with a gun—who knows? He's such a loser."

"He could hurt you," said Dan, stating the obvious.

She shook her head, squaring her shoulders like a good soldier.
"I can handle Toby. I've been doing it for years. I'm so sorry about
our evening." Her green eyes misted. "Rain check?" Dan thought
she looked both lovely and vulnerable.

"I'm coming with you," he said.

"No," she protested with a voice harsh and insistent. "This is
all my fault. When my sitter canceled at the last minute, I should
have called off our dinner. That's what a good mother does. But I
had my heart set on seeing you. So no, you stay here. Toby is my
problem, and I must deal with it. Besides, you can't afford to get
any closer to my cesspool of a life. You have the supreme court at
stake."

"Maybe so," he said, "but I'm coming anyway. I'll follow you."

# CHAPTER 26

# Quicksand

After the shooting, Dan drove from Alana's house, going the speed limit, his mind a tumble of haunted disbelief in what he had just been through and the frozen image of Alana's composure as she leveled the gun at a retreating Toby. As he neared Grays Hill, on the opposite side of the same road he had raced up thirty minutes earlier, he saw a squad car, lights flashing and siren blaring, headed toward Seabrook. *Her 911 call*, he assumed. It had all happened so quickly, and he now began the mental agony over a man dead, a woman in jeopardy, and the possibility—perhaps a likelihood—that his involvement in the mess he just left would be discovered. Arriving at his house, he entered in time to catch sight of Claire as she ascended the stairs in her chairlift.

"Oh, Dan, you're home. I'm headed to bed. There's some dinner on the stove. Christina called but nothing that can't wait until I see you in the morning." He heard the chair's distinctive click as it reached the top of the stairs. The fact that he didn't have to engage in conversation answered a prayer he had not uttered.

Restless, jittery, and pulse still elevated, he roused Banjo, and together they walked to the creek, as calm and unruffled as it had been when he floated on the river a short time ago. He thought back to an expression—a cliché, really—that his mother often repeated. *"Trouble comes from the direction you least expect."* He had taken a mighty risk in being on the boat with Alana, but what were the odds the call would come from Holly at that moment? Alana's hand on his was about to complicate things. If, instead of removing hers, she had seized his and led him to the berth she surely knew waited behind the shut cabin door, could he have resisted? For the sake of his long marriage to Claire, would some alarm bell in his head have sounded, clanging with the urgency of conscience, to call him back to himself?

But perhaps her hand had been an innocent gesture suggesting affection, but not sex. They had never kissed except in his dreams, when far more than kissing roiled his sleep and woke him panting. Or even hugged, those lengthening handshakes being the outer limits of physical contact. Not that he hadn't been tempted in the hug department. In their last meeting at the library, not long before he had suggested dinner, he caught a glimpse of a sight that stirred him then and for nights thereafter. She wore a plain white cotton shirt, and the room was unduly cold, as usual. For no reason apparent to him, her nipples hardened within her bra. They stared out at him, wide-eyed and all-seeing, as if reading his mind. He did his best to maintain eye contact as she spoke about Seneca Falls, seemingly unconscious of this mammillary tumescence. What could she be thinking that caused it? After what might have been a minute, the nipples retreated, but his urge to hug her had never been stronger.

But now, all thought of lust and longing disgusted him. He felt cheap, an emotion as foreign to him as Farsi.

He and Banjo returned to the house. After refrigerating the food Claire left on the stove, he tried to read a chapter in a novel as a way of marking time until the late news. News he dreaded, postponing sleeplessness, which he dreaded more.

A local broadcaster, in a funereal voice pitched to airplane crashes and school shootings, threw the telecast to her on-the-scene reporter in Seabrook, where a man had been shot dead in what preliminary reports indicated to be a domestic dispute outside the home. A dozen yards beyond yellow crime scene tape, Alana's car remained in the driveway and beyond it, Toby's truck, its outline dimly visible. *The reporter must live in the area*, Dan thought, *to be on the scene so quickly*. EMS personnel labored where Dan knew Toby lay. Flashing red lights illuminated the reporter's face. He turned the TV off. He had seen enough.

Once in bed, he stared at the ceiling, wondering if his tires had left any identifiable trace in Alana's driveway. Near dawn, after a night of wild imaginings about anything that could draw him further into what felt like quicksand, he fell asleep.

# CHAPTER 27

# Never Mention

To feel anxious in his own courtroom was not something Judge Borders had experienced, but on the morning after Toby Morgan's death, a sense of dread surrounded him as surely as his black robe covered him. He had spent the better part of the night running through every imaginable scenario, and in none of them did he take even a modicum of comfort. The newspaper delivered to his mailbox that morning had been printed too early to recite any details, and the morning news channels reported essentially what had been reported the night before, with one exception; the incident was under investigation, and no charges had been filed.

A full docket promised welcome distraction. Witnesses in a civil trial came and went as he forced himself to focus. Lawyers made motions, argued them, and in several cases got no ruling, hearing instead that Judge Borders was "taking it under advisement" and would notify them of his decision. One of those lawyers, a regular in the judge's courtroom, commented to the clerk that he couldn't recall even a single occasion on which Judge Borders had deferred a ruling.

Court recessed for a short break for lunch, but only out of

consideration for the court personnel's need to eat. The judge had no appetite. During a lengthy hearing that consumed most of the afternoon, he pondered how he might contact Alana to learn what had happened after he left. He couldn't fathom spending another night in his present uncertainty.

He didn't have to. As his car was about to exit the parking lot to begin the drive home, a car he at once recognized as Alana's pulled in front of him. With her right hand positioned beneath her rearview mirror, she motioned for him to follow. Minutes later, she turned onto a poorly maintained road leading to the river. A quarter mile from the main road, they stopped. She got out, came to his passenger door, and opened it. "We have to talk." she said. Her hair in disarray, eyes hollowed out like she had less sleep than Dan, she climbed in before he could respond.

"I know you said we need to keep our distance, so I'll make this quick," she said. "I had no choice about shooting him. Sooner or later, he would have killed me or Holly or both of us in one of his drunken rants. You saw how crazy and out of control he was. When he handed over the gun, something came over me. It was like someone else squeezing the trigger." She stared straight ahead, as if in a trance, pausing for several seconds before saying, "Like you said, I had to give a statement."

"To whom?"

"I can't remember. Russell . . . Robertson . . ."

"Rutherford. He's SLED's investigator."

"SLED?"

"State Law Enforcement Division."

"That's it. Rutherford. Anyway, I told him about talking Toby out of the gun. When he turned and started back at me screaming, I was sure he was going to kill me, so I shot him."

"So far so good. What else?"

"He asked me where I was last night. I lied because I didn't want you involved in this mess. I told him I went to see a house that is for sale. I actually looked at it last week. It's out in the country—down the road we're on now—and so much closer to the school that Holly would be able to do after-school things she can't do now. So, I told the deputy I was walking around the property when Holly's call came and I dashed home. Your name never came up."

Dan stared straight ahead, out the same windshield and down the same road that held her gaze. In a relationship that fed on eye contact, they couldn't see each other in that moment.

After a long silence, she turned to him. "I am so sorry. You have been nothing but nice to me, and I repay you by dragging you into my war with my ex-husband."

"I'm a grown man," he said. "I'm responsible for my choices. If you dragged me, I willingly went along. Neither of us could have anticipated it would become so . . . messy. Tragic."

"Yes, but it is mainly my mess, and I would like you as far away from it as you can get. I read the papers, and I know how close you may be to this supreme court seat. You can't afford to get mixed up in this."

He turned to face her. "You're right. I can't. But it may be unavoidable. Let's hope no charges are filed, for both our sakes."

"Who decides that? Whether to bring charges."

"Jillian Pillai, the solicitor. Sometimes they take a case to a grand jury, but those usually rubber stamp whatever charges the prosecutor recommends."

Alana nodded. "The Indian woman? I remember her from the Lopez hearing. She's a smart lady."

"Very bright," he agreed, "and not too happy with me after my Lopez ruling."

He thought for a moment that she was reaching for his hand, and perhaps she was, but she placed it on the seat.

"I want to promise you something," she said, her voice a blend of intimacy and authority. "I swear to you that I will never mention your name, no matter what happens. I took a risk by seeing you today, and I'm smart enough to know we won't be able to talk, but believe me, I will keep my word."

"I'll have to think this through, but I appreciate your wish to keep me out of it. I'm not sure it can be done. So much depends on what happens now." He hesitated before asking, "Did we ever speak on the phone?"

"Never," she said.

He nodded. "That's my recollection, too."

"I'm scared. What's the worst they can do to me?"

"Theoretically, convict you of murder if they don't believe you acted in self-defense. A more likely outcome is manslaughter, but I don't think you should panic about that either. Remember what I promised you last night. I'm one of only two judges in the county who can try you. I'll make sure that any case against you is steered into my court. If you keep me out of this, you won't be convicted of anything."

"I should go," she said. "There's one more thing I should tell you. The prosecutor called. She wants to interview me."

Dan drew in a breath and said, "That doesn't surprise me. Standard procedure when someone dies in violent circumstances. Just tell her exactly what you told the investigator and stress how terrified you were."

She opened the door, got out, and closed it with more force than required, but then the days ahead promised complications unseen twenty-four hours earlier. Her last forlorn look at him through the passenger window seemed to say, *The other men in my life have all let me down. If you do, I'm lost.*

She turned her car around toward the main road, dust kicking up behind her. Dan sat contemplating just how much he had riding on her promise to never reveal his presence at Toby's shooting. *Can I trust her?* He thought back to that Saturday morning, when he walked home with Andy. He was reasonably sure it was her car he saw drive by his house, and probably her daughter staring from the passenger seat, but he couldn't be positive. They were too far away, at least fifty yards. She had denied it. Why would she lie about something so innocent, so trivial? And just last night, as they were having dinner on the boat, she had said, in an offhand manner, that she hadn't had a date since her divorce. Yet a couple of weeks earlier, in the late afternoon, he had seen her riding shotgun in a convertible driven by a uniformed Marine, and this time, there could be no doubt it was her. He remembered the pang of jealousy at seeing them together. Holly's call was the only thing that prevented him from asking about that Marine at dinner. *Was that a date? Can I trust her? Now I have no choice*, he thought bitterly.

After several minutes, he drove straight, looking right and left for the house she mentioned. *Is there such a house?* After three miles of pock-marked road, he saw a farmhouse with a *For Sale* sign. *The old Elkhart place*, Dan remembered. He had hunted turkey on it as a boy. What had once been a three-hundred-acre farm was mostly sold off by Elkhart's children, who left the old man a life estate for his final years. The house, set well off the road, with peeling paint, shutters askew and perched on a thin ledge between fix-it-up and tear-it-down, stood surrounded by fallow land. This must have been the house she visited. He parked in the driveway and got out. Walking toward the house, he paused, stretched, and yawned, a reminder of the little sleep he had and a foreshadow of the night ahead. Late afternoon stillness settled over the house and fields. For a moment, he was able to recall a turkey hunt here with his father, a memory overtaken by the conversation he had just had with Alana.

☉ ☉ ☉

On the surface, her case for self-defense looked cast-iron. Properly presented, Toby charged her in a drunken rage that would have terrified anyone. He could have taken the gun back and killed her in her own yard. She feared for her life. He knew from what he had come to think of as their monument conversations, when they drifted from the business of the meetings into personal revelations, that the sheriff's department had responded to several 911 calls when Toby showed up drunk and belligerent. They would have records of those. Deputies sent to investigate likely thought Toby a train wreck in progress, as Alana herself viewed him, and it was just a matter of time before he went off the rails. And now he had. A prosecutor had to see it that way. Alana would not be charged, and his presence at the scene would remain a secret. Dan took a moment's comfort in Alana's near-certain vindication and his own narrow escape.

She had lied to protect him. Making a false report to a law enforcement official was itself a crime, though not a major one. As he turned around and drove back to the main road leading home, his hope, his prayerful hope, was that Jillian Pillai would see it as a classic case of self-defense, no charges would be filed, and that the entire matter would be allowed to die peacefully. Unlike Toby.

# CHAPTER 28

# A Peeping Max

Jillian Pillai lived alone in Eagle Retreat, one of the few modern, upscale townhouse complexes in the county. Her neighbors greeted her pleasantly, both because she spoke first and because, as they well knew, her presence in the community assured constant vigilance by the sheriff's office. One deputy received a rental supplement from the county to live there as extra protection. Jillian had recently found a terse note in her mailbox, *I cut your throat, bitch.* And while such threats occasioned not much more than a sleepless night or two, someone out there who did not wish her well knew where she lived. Law enforcement protected their own, and Jillian remained on the top rung of the law enforcement ladder.

She had been drawn to the place, sold on it, really, by the skylight in the bedroom and a patio that waited in stark simplicity for whatever botanical inspiration seized her. In law school, she had speculated that such a house might be within her economic grasp by age forty, but the truth was she now earned, thanks to Frank Walthall's untimely death, more than the bottom rung of her professors and far more than fellow top-tier classmates.

Waist-high stucco walls enclosed the patio, and against these, she set small trellises to support ivy, which was certain to thrive, and bougainvillea, which was certain to die in winter, but she couldn't help herself, having fallen in love with it during a backpacking trip in central Mexico. Replanting it each year was a small price to pay for even a few blooms. Large clay pots, also Mexico-inspired, held rosemary, wisteria, and purple rhododendron. She kept her small yard tidy. On weekends, she enjoyed reading among her plants as Eagle Retreat's resident voyeur, Max Ritter, peered through blinds to spy on her. She strung multicolored lights for Christmas and took them down on New Year's Day. On her front door, next to the knocker, a bumper sticker in splashy yellow and Caribbean blue proclaimed *Jillian* in a bold font, while underneath appeared *For Solicitor.*

In temperate weather, from an open window in the kitchen, wafted the aroma of curry blended with the highs and lows of an Adele album faintly audible in the background. Jillian's parents stopped in from time to time, usually at the dinner hour. Regardless of the time, she walked them to their car when they left. On her way back, she stole a glance at Max Ritter's unit, where the blinds parted just enough to accommodate his prying eyes. Everyone in the building complex knew her, but no one knew her well. If there was a man in her life, no one knew him either. Not even Max.

Max's surveillance annoyed her. It began the day she moved in. Stephanie, the gum-chewing resident manager, warned her that he used binoculars to scope out women in and around the swimming pool. "There's nothing we can do about it," Stephanie said. "Just be aware."

"What's he like?" Jillian asked.

"Let's start with weird. And here's the thing. No one has ever actually seen him. He's a hermit. His sister came in to sign the lease, and she pays the rent. She registered this maroon Fiat that hardly ever leaves the property and then only at weird hours at night. If he walked in now, I wouldn't know him, or maybe I would because I imagine him with Spock ears and one eye in his forehead." She popped a small bubble for emphasis.

Jillian, absorbed in furnishing her place, changing her address, registering her car, and the other tasks demanded by a move, gave Max no further thought. But after she settled in, leaving for work early, she noticed the blinds in Max's unit part as she walked to her car. When she returned, the same thing happened and, as time went on, like a pebble in her shoe, it grew gradually more irritating. *Does he spend all day watching?* she wondered. On the occasions Jillian returned at night, a flicker of light would escape the blinds as Max took up his vigil. She returned to the property management office, where Stephanie again pleaded helplessness. "As long as he stays in his own unit, we've been told there is nothing we can do. If you can find a way to make him stop, we'd love it." Pop went the gum.

Almost every car in the complex parking lot sported a *Jillian* bumper sticker. Not only did she visit every unit (except Max's) to campaign in her soft-sell style, but she also returned to thank them for the bumper sticker they displayed. Jerry Higginson, her opponent in the upcoming special election, didn't waste his time stumping in Eagle Retreat—until that nolle pross of Rodrigo Lopez. And while none of Jillian's neighbors wished to be seen removing their bumper stickers, several expressed to Higginson their fresh doubts about her.

# CHAPTER 29

# As Simple as That

If Jillian had any doubts about herself, she didn't let them show. With the election still several months away, she focused on a heavy caseload that now included the death of Toby Morgan. The first reports coming to her suggested self-defense—but with a twist. The one who showed up with a gun was the one who ended up dead. She needed a better explanation of how that happened before closing the case. A background check on Toby confirmed habits likely to lead him to an early appointment in the morgue. He drank too much, fought on slight provocation or none at all, mouthed off to the wrong people, always kept a gun close at hand, and treated women the way he treated Alana as she recited in her divorce deposition. He had few friends. It took a week for a family member to claim his body. Still, he was a human being, and Jillian's job didn't allow her to make value judgments on the worth of a victim. In the unlikely event it wasn't self-defense, it was murder or manslaughter, making it Jillian's business.

Doubt about what had actually happened was confirmed in the medical examiner's report, detailing a shot in the back near the right shoulder. How did that come about? She should put that question to Alana Morgan. Jillian's review of the toxicology report documented Toby's intoxication. His blood alcohol level was over three times the legal limit to be driving. Trace amounts of cocaine were also present.

SLED agent Ben Rutherford worked the crime scene on the night of the shooting. Tall, rangy, with arms like the basketball player he was, Rutherford met Jillian at Alana's former home in Seabrook, now vacant until the new owners moved in. A realtor sign by the road proclaimed it *SOLD* on a banner hastily splashed across the sign, creating an impression of hurried disposition. Azaleas past their peak dotted the lot, and sited among them a modest rancher with aluminum siding recently power-washed for maximum buyer appeal.

"Not much to see with all the furniture gone," Rutherford told Jillian as they walked through the echoing rooms. He carried a clipboard he raised to waist level. "House was neat the night I arrived. Clean. In my business, people whose lives are a wreck usually live in shabby homes. Not hers." Their footsteps echoed on the wooden floors. "Back here is the bathroom where I found the girl. She heard shots, but fortunately stayed here like her mother told her and wouldn't come out until her mom came to get her. Poor kid. At least she didn't have to witness her father getting shot."

"Your report mentions some empty shell casings," Jillian said.

"Yeah, that was interesting. Let's go out back."

A line of trees bordered the rear of the lot, and beyond them, woods filled with pines, the trunks of which bore charred evidence of a fire several years before. Rutherford led her into the woods far enough to shield the house from view. "The power company owns this property. They cut the timber every couple of decades." He swept his arm in a downward arc. "This is the area I found the shell casings. I forget how many, but quite a few."

"Your report states fifty-three."

"That sounds right. Took me a while to pick them up, and I may have missed a few."

"Look there," Jillian said, pointing.

"I know. A cardboard dummy. Someone took some serious target practice back here."

Jillian walked to the spot where the dummy rested against a tree. "Judging by the shot pattern, they needed it. Did she do the shooting?"

"I didn't get a chance to ask because I found this the following day when I came back in daylight."

"When she comes to my office later this morning, I'll find out. How did she seem to you when you took her statement? Scared? Angry?"

Rutherford raised his clipboard. "Not scared, not angry. She was nervous and talkative. Seemed like she wanted me to know every detail she knew. Didn't hide anything from me as far as I could tell. She repeated several times that her daughter knew nothing and pleaded with me not to interview her. 'Course I had to, but momma was right. She heard some yelling but couldn't make out what was being said. She heard shots but can't remember how many or anything about time and sequence."

Jillian turned slowly in a complete circle, taking in the woods, the lack of neighbors on either side of the house, the lonely road leading to it. The place was indeed isolated. Any single mother living here would want a weapon, especially with a menacing ex-husband lurking. *Does she own a gun?*

The prosecutor turned back to Rutherford. "You've seen a few of these domestic brawls. What do you think happened?"

"Her story makes sense if that's what you are asking. A bit odd that she was able to talk him into handing over the gun, but that could mean he wasn't worried about getting shot. As I said in the report, after he gave it to her, he walked away. I asked what made him turn around and charge at her, and she said he must have figured out she lied about wanting to talk. One minute he was walking toward his truck like he was leaving and the next minute he's coming for her like he wants to kill her. She said he's nuts, and it might be as simple as that. I've worked enough of these to know how raw nerves get when a marriage goes south. Maybe she pushed the wrong button at just the wrong time. It would explain his sudden turnaround. Either way, I wouldn't spend a lot of time on this one if I were you."

"Let's see if your opinion changes after we meet with her."

# CHAPTER 30

# A Warning Shot

Prior to Alana's arrival for their scheduled interview, Jillian read again her statement. Agent Rutherford sat nearby, his legs extending out to the middle of the small office. He held his copy in his lap.

From her chair, Jillian could see Alana walking down the hall toward her office. She appeared neither anxious nor apprehensive, striding at a purposeful pace. Jillian gave a subtle nod to Rutherford, a momentary "here she is now" alert. Jillian waved her in, and both stood as she entered. "I believe you've met Agent Rutherford," Jillian said as Alana extended her hand to him.

"We meet again," said Alana. "Your first impression must have been terrible."

"You were under great stress that night," he said. "Anyone in your situation would have been."

She impressed Jillian, appearing precisely on time and professionally dressed. When seated, Alana handed across the desk the copy of her divorce decree Jillian had requested she bring with her.

"Thank you for bringing this," Jillian said. "Give me a moment to look it over."

While Jillian read, Alana gazed around the office, her attention drawn to a photo on an austere credenza showing Jillian in cap-and-gown graduation attire, flanked by what must be her parents and siblings. A happy, proud, well-adjusted family, so unlike Alana's own.

After assuring Alana that such interviews were routine, she asked if Rutherford had read her Miranda rights on the night of the shooting. Alana nodded. "Again," Jillian said, "this is just routine, but I'm going to read them to you. You have the right to remain silent. Anything you tell me can and will be used against you in a court of law. You have a right to an attorney, and if you cannot afford one, the state will provide one at no expense to you. Having been so advised, do you still wish to speak with me?"

Alana shrugged. "I have nothing to hide."

After getting her to acknowledge that their interview was being recorded, Jillian confirmed what she considered the most salient facts. Alana's daughter, locked in a bathroom pursuant to her mother's instructions by phone, had seen none of the ensuing fight between her parents, nor were there any witnesses. Toby had accosted Alana as soon as she stepped from her car that night.

"He fired a shot at me," Alana said. "He aimed high, and maybe he was just trying to scare me, and if he was, it worked."

Jillian threw a furtive glance at Rutherford as she flipped pages in the report resting on her desk. "Wait. Are you telling me he fired a shot before handing over the gun? Maybe I missed it, but I don't recall you telling Agent Rutherford about that." She looked at Rutherford, who nodded in confirmation.

"I was so nervous, I don't know what I said. I had just killed him not half an hour earlier and was in total shock. Maybe I forgot to mention that shot. I've replayed it over and over in my mind."

"This shot was fired into the air? How close would you say it was?"

"Not straight up if that's what you mean. More at an angle over my head. The bullet may have hit some tree behind me. Across the road behind me."

"Okay, then. Can you tell me how you ended up with his gun?"

"Typical Toby," Alana said in a wistful tone, like she'd seen it all before. "He fires the gun to scare me to death, then he staggers over real close. He was so drunk, I thought about trying to grab the gun, but that seemed risky with the condition he was in."

"I would think so," Jillian said sympathetically. She glanced down at the report on her desk. "Didn't you tell Agent Rutherford that you talked him into giving you his gun? You aren't saying there was a struggle for it, are you?"

"I said he staggered over, and for a second, I was tempted to try to grab it."

"Yes, that part I got. What happened then?"

"We talked some. He wanted to get back together, but he talks like that when he's drunk. I was trying to humor him because at that point he's still holding the gun a couple of feet from me. I didn't want to make him mad. So, when I promised him we'd talk things over if he'd get the gun out of my face, he calmed down a little."

"Okay. And then what happened?" Jillian asked.

"Like I say, he calmed down some after I promised we'd talk. He didn't act like he believed me because he kept saying, 'You're sure we're gonna talk. You promise we're gonna talk.' He was right to be skeptical because I had no intention of standing in the yard talking to a drunk in pointless conversation while my daughter remained locked in a bathroom. But I had to put on an act to get the gun. I should maybe get an Academy Award because he handed it over butt-end first. My hand was shaking, but I took it."

"Was he still calm?"

"It didn't last long. He said he needed some whiskey from his truck, so he turned his back on me and started toward it. That's when I told him he might as well get in the truck and keep going because I was calling 911. He said I lied to him, so I said you're damn right I lied, and I leveled it at his head and told him I'd shoot him if he didn't get in his truck and leave. I guess he figured out he'd been tricked because he screamed and came back at me like a raging bull, so I shot. I was so scared, so I shot again."

"How long between shots?"

"A second or two. I panicked."

"How far was he from you when you fired the gun?"

"I guess ten feet, fifteen at the most."

"And the first shot hit him in the chest?"

Alana nodded. "It must have. That's all I can figure. All I know for certain is that it stopped his charge."

Jillian stared at her statement, tapping a ballpoint as she considered her next question. "How do you explain the bullet found in his shoulder? The entry wound suggests it came from behind him."

Alana extended her hands in a pleading gesture. "It all happened so fast. I guess the first shot turned him as he was falling."

"But he was found supine. Face up."

"When he didn't move, I walked over to him. He lay facedown. I pointed the gun at his head just in case he tried something. I turned him over with my foot. He wasn't moving."

"So let me make sure I have this straight," Jillian said with an air of authority. "You had just stepped out of your car when he fired a shot somewhere over your head. He approached you holding the gun. There were words exchanged, and you promised you'd talk about your relationship. He handed you the gun. As he returned to his truck for whiskey, you threatened to call 911. He turned and came at you. You shot him in the chest, and as he turned, you shot again, and he fell facedown. You walked to where he lay, turned him over with your foot, and that's where the sheriff found him. You didn't touch him or move the body."

"I may have touched his hand when I got the gun, but not after that. And no, I didn't move his body except to turn him over."

Jillian shifted in her chair. "And it says here that you were looking at some property. At that time of day?" she asked, obviously skeptical. She lifted her eyes to Alana's for the answer.

"I teach during the day, as you know. By the time I get home and make dinner, there is so little time, and I'd seen an ad for this property for sale. It sounded like just what I had been looking for, and I had to see it. I couldn't get inside, of course, but I was able to look in windows and walk around the yard. It's quite big, and I love it. I closed on it a few days ago."

Jillian nodded. "I saw the deed in the clerk's office." She asked for the new address and noted it on a legal pad beside the file. Pausing, she stared into space above Alana's head, which Alana or Rutherford might have taken as a meandering of her mind to other subjects, other cases. It was anything but. "In your divorce decree, your husband was ordered by the court to carry life insurance until your daughter reached eighteen. Did he take out a policy?"

"He did, at least at first. I know he paid the premiums for a while. Then he lost his job, and who knows after that."

"The amount?"

"Fifty thousand, I think. He couldn't afford any more. I always figured he'd let it lapse. When I got my teaching job, I took out a policy on myself so Holly would have something if the worst happened, and it nearly did."

Jillian looked down at her notes. "You bought a gun about a month before all this happened."

"I'm telling you Toby was acting crazier than ever. I'd pull out of the school parking lot, and there he was, sitting in his truck, just waiting in that vacant lot across the street. He followed me a few cars back until we got to the two-lane leading to the house. Then he gunned it to within a couple of feet of my bumper." She closed her eyes until they were mere slits, as if bracing for impact from behind. "Something had to give."

"The shell casings found behind your old house were yours?"

Alana nodded. "I'd never shot anything in my life, so I figured it made sense to practice just in case. I could shoot in those woods without worrying about hitting anyone, and practice might make perfect, like they say, but not for me with a gun." A subtle laugh seemed aimed at her own ineptitude.

"Did you have the gun with you that night?"

"It was in the house, locked in a drawer."

Jillian set the file aside and stood. "Thank you for coming in today. I can appreciate that this hasn't been easy for you or your daughter."

Alana, now standing, teared up. "I loved him once. I can't believe I did, but I did."

"Love and war," Jillian replied, putting her hand gently on Alana's shoulder. "Both are equally unpredictable."

Jillian closed her door and turned to Rutherford. "So, what do you think?"

"Her story pretty much matches what she told me that night. A few minor discrepancies. My notes show Toby called her a lying bitch as he charged her, and she said nothing about that today. And just now she said he handed her the gun butt-end first, and that night she just said he handed it over. The biggest difference was the first shot. That just doesn't seem like a detail you're likely to forget, even if you're traumatized."

"Agreed," said Jillian, and thanked him for coming. In the privacy of her sparsely furnished office, she debated closing the Toby Morgan file. Alana struck her as credible, earnest, and sympathetic. In a coldly dispassionate way, Toby's death simplified Alana's life, already challenged by the demands of a full-time job and a young daughter. Alana had confirmed that Toby paid no child or spousal support, so the family's income wouldn't suffer. That life insurance policy he was ordered to carry most likely lapsed. She made a note to follow up.

Weighing the rationale for closing the file brought a tiny jolt of adrenalin. Her job required decisions that truly mattered, which was what she loved about her work. She had the power to close the file and thereby, in essence, close the book on Toby Morgan's life. Alana and her daughter would also benefit from whatever solace they could take from putting the matter behind them. They could begin to experience closure.

Still, there was the issue of the shots. Her now-dead ex fires a warning shot over her head, and she fails to mention it to the investigator a half-hour later? Maybe shock explained that, or maybe not. Jillian knew enough forensics to know that the force of a gunshot could turn a victim in an unpredictable direction, so it was entirely possible that the fatal shot to the chest turned Toby in the manner Alana described. But perhaps she should investigate that before making a final decision, and she knew just the person to call. In fact, she had been looking for weeks for an excuse to call him, and now, thanks to Alana Morgan, she had one.

Also, the cell phone service provider would have records of the calls that day. Those would likely turn up nothing of value, but it was simple enough to subpoena them, which she did before leaving for the day.

# CHAPTER 31

# Powwow

Brock Jamerson's fondness for The Grotto bar in Columbia grew out of the two things that brought him the most pleasure— political insider gossip and single women out for a good time. Jane Magette, the nurse he lived with, worked nights at the Lexington Medical Center, giving Jamerson what he considered a license to roam.

On this summer evening, the crowd in The Grotto showed promise, packed with regulars like Jamerson and tourists seeking its stellar air-conditioning. The legislature wasn't in town, so buying a round or two for a committee chairman was less likely. Jamerson walked down the steps and paused, both to let his eyes adjust to the light and to survey the social scene. He spotted an empty stool next to three women at the bar.

"Evenin' girls, how we doin'?" he said in the friendliest of voices. A decade earlier, he would have called them gals, but he had evolved, or so he told himself. Each woman appeared to be drinking a margarita, and uncollected empty glasses confirmed it wasn't their first. All three greeted him. The one next to him, Kate, asked his name. Before he could answer, Jake the bartender, a USC student, said, "What will you have, Brock? The usual?"

"So, I guess your name is Brock?"

After telling Jake to bring him a double bourbon on the rocks, he said, "I can't deny they know me here. Where are you girls from?"

"Evanston. Outside Chicago," Kate said. She introduced her companions as Elaine and Margo. "We've heard so much about Southern charm, we decided to search for some."

"And to get away from the kids?" he asked, pretty sure that what children there were would be grown, but he'd never found underestimating a woman's age to be a mistake in this setting.

Kate took a sip of her margarita. "We're all empty nesters." She looked at her companions and raised her glass in toast.

"Get out of town," he said, aping surprise, and everyone laughed. "I guess you heard Sherman burned us out a few years back."

Elaine, seated beside Kate, leaned toward him and said, "We read all about that today at your state museum. He really did a number on Columbia. I understand better why the South lost the war."

"Did we lose?" Jamerson asked. "I thought it was still going on."

"Let's not get into politics," Kate said. "We came here to get away from all that. So what do you do, Brock?"

"Newspaper reporter. I cover the courts, mostly."

"How very serious."

"It can be," he acknowledged. "We take justice seriously in South Carolina. Not like Illinois."

Elaine again leaned in. "You're confusing us with Ohio. It seems like everyone elected governor of our state ends up in prison. I'd call that serious. Are you here tonight working on a story?"

He couldn't suppress a grin. "I've told a few stories in here."

The women laughed. "I'll bet you have," Kate said. "Possibly to ladies from out of town?"

"Well, possibly. And to some in town." He broke eye contact to look toward the end of the bar. "See that guy who just sat down?"

The women turned their heads to follow his gaze.

"He owes me money. I need to see him about it. Excuse me for a minute." Jamerson picked up his drink and joined Peter Wolfe.

As he approached, Wolfe eyed him warily, but with a hint of humor. "Do you sleep here?" Wolfe asked.

Jamerson set his drink on the bar and eased onto the stool next to him. "You see those three lovelies I was just talking to? I told them you owe me money." He raised his glass in the direction of the women, and they raised theirs in return.

"What a joke!" Wolfe said. He reached into his pocket, pulled out a one-dollar bill, and waved it at the three women before handing it to Jamerson. "I want that back. Any action with those ladies? The one in the middle looks pretty cute."

"That's Elaine. She's a possibility, but she seems glued to the pack. We'll see. So what's new across the street?"

"Tom had a visitor last week," Tom being Thomas Wentworth, the senator for whom Wolfe worked and the chairman of the Judiciary Committee. "Sidney Callahan." Wolfe raised the toothpick from his martini and bit off an olive. "You'll never guess what he wanted."

"You mean Supreme Court Chief Justice Callahan?"

"That's the one."

"Has he got the votes?"

"Well, off the record, he doesn't have Tom's yet, which isn't to say he won't get it. He's pretty persistent, and he helped Tom out on a redistricting issue a few years back, so there's the IOU factor. Plus, Tom likes to be in synch with his committee, so there's that, too."

Jamerson placed an avuncular hand on Wolfe's shoulder. "In synch with his committee? Is that what we're now calling a moist finger held to the political winds?"

Wolfe laughed. "Come on, Brock, you know Tom's a statesman above petty politics. But seriously, I don't think he's made up his mind yet."

Jamerson removed his hand. "You've mentioned the redistricting IOU and the committee, but you haven't said anything about Tom's view of Callahan's ability. High, low, mediocre?"

"I'd say just north of mediocre. It's no secret Callahan's wife, who Tom dislikes intensely along with ninety-five percent of his colleagues, pushed him into elective politics and that she funded his campaigns."

"Which doesn't make him a bad justice."

"No, but his fondness for the bottle might. I hear from others—not Tom—that Callahan has developed a real problem since he left the legislature."

"Yeah, I've heard that, too." Jamerson sipped his drink while drumming his fingers on the bar. "What about Dan Borders? You hear any chatter about him?"

"Quite a bit. If I were a betting man and didn't owe you so much money," he said, scoffing, "I'd wager on him. Do you know him?"

Jamerson shook his head. "I saw him a few weeks back down in Beaufort. A preliminary motion in a murder case. I later heard the guy got off. Borders is impressive. I need to do some more research before I interview him."

"You mean the kind of research you're doing in here tonight?"

Jamerson laughed. "If you haven't noticed, I take my work seriously. This?" He raised his arm and swept it in a semicircle that took in the bar. "This is all play."

Wolfe turned his head toward the end of the bar. "I noticed that

Elaine, the new love of your life for at least tonight, just ordered another round."

Jamerson rolled his eyes. "All three will be hammered by nine o'clock. I hope their hotel is close by." He paused before asking, "Do you expect a courtesy call from Borders one of these days?"

"Funny you should ask," replied Wolfe, his tone matching the seriousness of the question. "Tom told me to reach out to him, suggest he stop by the next time he's in town, that kind of thing. It's on my to-do list."

"Do me a favor," Jamerson asked.

"If it's lending you more money, forget it."

"I'm serious. If Tom meets with Borders, how about letting me know? That way I can drop by the state house and see if Tom will talk with me about Callahan and Borders. I'd be interested in Tom's take on them."

"I'll let you know."

"Thanks. I need to roll."

"Back down the bar to your bevy of beauties?"

He grinned and shook his head. "Not feeling it tonight. Their loss."

◉ ◉ ◉

Several days later, Wolfe fulfilled his promise to call Jamerson.

"Peter, what's up?"

"Wentworth-Borders powwow yesterday. I sat in on the meeting at Tom's request. You were right about Borders being impressive."

"So, has he got it locked up?"

"Not if he was listening to what Tom was telling him. He suggested, in the nicest way possible, that Borders lower his expectations. His committee isn't on board, or at least some of them aren't. Callahan has been working overtime on them, and it seems to be paying off. I think Tom himself is with Borders, but he's only one vote and he is rarely out of step with his committee."

"How did Borders take it?"

"He's a grown-up. Couldn't have been more gracious. Thanked Tom for the chance to meet."

"Figures," Brock said. "Thanks for the info."

"Will I see you at The Grotto anytime soon?"

"Does the sun rise in the east?"

"Save me a place at the bar."

"You got it, buddy. Later."

# CHAPTER 32

# Long-Distance Love

Jillian's work ethic had been shaped by a mantra her parents repeated on an almost daily basis—work and education lead to success, and there are no shortcuts. At sixteen, she took a job cashiering at a local grocery store, working after school and preserving her straight-A average. By the end of her junior year, she had saved enough to pay cash for a used Ford she named Matt after a Hollywood crush. Within weeks of being voted most likely to succeed by her senior class, she smoked her first joint at a party busted up by three cops. Luckily for her, the lead cop was a rookie who had graduated in the class ahead of her. He called her into the kitchen and told her to leave by the back door. She walked the two miles home to clear her head, vowing never again. She returned for Matt the next morning.

Through three years at Wofford (she graduated early with high honors), she dated sparingly while focused on her studies. An Indian date was a little too progressive for the BMOCs, and her intellect intimidated them. One who wasn't was Connor Nalley, a star soccer player and future orthopedic surgeon. They met in an organic chemistry class. When he suggested she come to a home game that weekend to watch him play, she said she didn't care for soccer, but if he played cricket, she would never miss a match. "I'm joking," she said, touching him lightly on the arm. "Of course, I'll come. Besides, I don't know the first thing about cricket." When Connor, as if on cue, scored the first two goals that Saturday, he pointed to her in the stands. His Mediterranean complexion was only a shade lighter than hers. His eyes reminded her of an eagle's or falcon's, seeing all and missing nothing.

They had been dating steadily for a few months when he announced he had been accepted at Yale's medical school for the following fall.

"Oh?" she said in disbelief. "You didn't mention applying there."

"Wanted to surprise you."

"Mission accomplished."

"You come, too," he said. "New Haven is a great town, and we'll fit right in."

"But I don't want to go to Yale Law. I didn't even apply."

"So what? We'll be together. Isn't that what matters?"

"Of course, it matters, but that's not *all* that matters."

"Nice little apartment. Bike trails. Yoga classes. You'll love it."

"I won't love it because I'm going to law school. At USC in Columbia."

"Bad idea," he said. "Long-distance love doesn't appeal to me." His tone suggested the subject was closed.

"Really? You're serious? Because there is an easy solution to this. I can go to USC Law, and you can go to MUSC two hours down I-26. Charleston in springtime. Bike trails. Sushi. Yoga. You'll love it."

"Very funny."

"Why is that funny? Help me see the humor."

"We can talk about it later. I've got to go to class."

Having accepted the offer from Yale, there was nothing for Connor to discuss. Long-distance love didn't appeal to Jillian either and, gradually, neither did he as she began to sense her place in his universe. She had been seduced by the macho swagger he brought to soccer and by the intensity of his intellectual curiosity, but after their Yale confrontation, she noticed things she had previously either not seen or minimized. For example, his occasional criticism of their classmates, cutting and often very funny, grew less so when she realized how frequently it was directed at women. She chided herself for tolerating it. In the weeks before graduation, each pleaded exams and workload as a way of avoiding what couldn't be fixed. Diploma in hand, he sought her out to assure her he would send a forwarding address. She thanked him, smiled, and mumbled, "Whatever."

◉ ◉ ◉

During that summer between college and law school, Jillian lived in Myrtle Beach with Rachel, a Wofford classmate. Rachel worked for a software company, an entry-level position in her chosen field, while Jillian tended bar at night and spent long hours at the beach during the day. She missed Connor, a feeling that left her both sad and frustrated. Maybe she had overreacted to his chauvinism. She could have tried harder to keep him in her life, as guys like him were surely rare. But, she told herself, she was rare, too, a fact he didn't seem to appreciate, and in the end, she didn't like the way she felt about being undervalued. As the summer sun beat down, it seemed to bleach out her memory of Connor. By the time the fall semester began, she hungered for the next challenge.

# CHAPTER 33

# A Savage Man

A courtroom drama Jillian witnessed in her first year at USC
Law School set her feet on the prosecutorial path. A man arrested
for the rape and strangulation of the night manager at a local hotel
went on trial in nearby Lexington. She joined fellow law students
in packing the courtroom. She had arrived at the campus with no
leaning toward criminal law as a course of study, but the gruesome
crime and the headlines it generated made a seat at ringside
irresistible. Seated in the first row of spectators, she studied the
defendant a few feet from her, a man thought to be capable of such
heinous acts, and a lawyer whose job it was to keep him from a
date with the electric chair. High drama with life-and-death stakes.
What more could she want?

The judge, snowy-haired with pudgy, florid cheeks and a
deep drawl, orchestrated jury selection with the casual tone of a man
tending bar at the local VFW. A few months short of retirement,
His Honor had seen it all in his twenty years on the circuit court.
If he'd ever feared reversal on appeal, he didn't now. When the
pace slowed, he told both lawyers to "Move along, gentlemen,"

words that sounded like they came from the bottom of a well.

When the defendant, a man ironically named Savage, turned toward the spectators, Jillian suffered a moment of terror as his gaze fell directly on her. His face was pocked, likely a result of untreated acne, and dark, deep-set eyes stared out from under prominent brows. A tattoo of linked chain at his neck evoked bondage, domination, control. *That poor night manager,* she thought.

Her doubts about the prosecutor, Wayne Armistead, began when he addressed the jury for the first time. A nervous, bespectacled man who looked to be in his early forties, Armistead's opening statement, delivered just above a whisper, rambled as he shuffled notes. Previewing the coroner's testimony, he stopped to search for the reported time of death. For what Jillian estimated to be a full minute, the only sound heard was paper sluffing from one haphazard pile to another while everyone in the courtroom grew increasingly uneasy, as they might have watching an actor who forgot his lines. When at last he resumed, it was only to assure the jury that he had the time of death "somewhere." Bad got worse when the judge refused to admit evidence offered by Armistead because the chain of custody had been broken in Armistead's office, and worse went to catastrophic when the one witness who had picked Savage out of a lineup hesitated when asked if the man she saw leaving the motel that night was seated in the courtroom. As Jillian left court after the prosecution rested, she asked a girlfriend, only half in jest, if the law school had put the whole thing on as a lesson in how not to try a case. She fully expected the not guilty verdict returned by the jury a day later. Savage walked out a free man.

Which meant that he was out there somewhere when Jillian left the dorm, walked across campus, or strolled Greene Street. The terror she felt when he turned to her that first day had not fully dissipated. She found herself for the first time jumpy when rounding blind corners or quickening her pace when footsteps approached from behind. Her fears were well founded. A month later, Savage was arrested for a similar crime in Dentsville, where a female Army private died needlessly, in Jillian's opinion, due to a prosecutor's incompetence.

Near the end of her first year, she found herself in Wayne Armistead's office interviewing for a summer internship. If asked about the Savage fiasco, how would she respond? She had worried about that on the night before the interview. Armistead proved to be polite, attentive, and enthused over her resume, while between them his desk gave ample evidence of his disorganization. Paper escaped from files that not only covered the surface of the desk but littered the floor in what appeared to be haphazard stacks. Jillian wondered if he was one of those people who knew where things were, despite the chaos, then thought back to his search for the time of death in the Savage case and decided, no, he was simply inept.

"I'll be honest," Armistead said. "We could use some help here."

Jillian's instinctive response, *"No kidding,"* gave way to a more diplomatic reply. "I like things neatly arranged, and I'm good at it," she said, which was not just true but what Armistead hoped to hear. She spent that summer, unpaid, bringing order out of chaos. By the time fall semester began, Armistead's office had been transformed into a professional setting. Had her duties been limited to organization, the summer would have been just marking time, but as the clutter evaporated, he began asking her opinion on various cases. She researched, wrote memos, and on a few occasions, accompanied him to court. She returned the following summer.

By the time she approached Frank Walthall for a job, her qualifications included not only six months of internship in a prosecutor's office but top grades in criminal law and procedure, Constitutional law, indigent representation, and a seminar on the Nuremberg trials. Small wonder, then, that Walthall offered her a job in less time than he usually spent at lunch.

# CHAPTER 34

# Averted Glances

Shortly after Jillian came to Beaufort as Walthall's assistant, he needed a ballistics expert to convict a suspect of assault. He hired Glen Coleman, a brash, thirty-six-year-old former FBI agent with a crop of boyish blond hair that made him look like a surfer, even in a suit. Walthall insisted Jillian sit in on Glen's witness preparation. "We call it taking 'em to the woodshed. The trouble with experts is they want to tell you everything they know about whatever it is they're experts in. In the woodshed, we rap their knuckles until they say what we want 'em to say and not a word more. Most cases come down to one or two critical points, and your expert needs to know exactly where those are. Think of it like a minefield. If he knows where to step, he can cross it and keep his legs attached to his body and keep your case from blowing up."

Jillian looked on and took notes. Having never experienced an expert witness woodshedding, her concentration bordered on manic. She wanted to know everything. She focused on Walthall's posture, tone in asking questions, facial expressions at the answers, coaxing when he thought they might have been stronger, insistence on clarification when a detail dangled like a loose tooth or when a juror might struggle with a technical term or concept. As she scribbled, her head bobbed down at the notepad, up at Walthall or Glen. Because she was so preoccupied, it took time for her to sense Glen's repeated glances. When they registered, she couldn't be sure of what they meant, if anything. The moment her gaze lifted from her notes to find him staring, he looked away, at times back at Frank and at other times at the wall behind her.

*Does he find me strange?* she wondered. *Has he never seen an Indian woman at such close range? Is my presence an unwelcome intrusion on a process Frank had said was usually one-on-one?* She wasn't sure what those averted glances meant, but they distracted her. She shifted in her chair to sharpen the angle of his line of sight while making a mental note to ask Frank about it after the session. When she did, he acted like he expected her curiosity. "Yeah, I noticed that, too," he said. "I think he was paying you a compliment. But his mind was on the case. He's a pro. You'll see that when he testifies."

And she did. For two hours, the defendant's lawyer cross-examined Glen in a tone of skepticism designed to challenge his expert conclusions and undercut his credibility with jurors. He responded with patient forbearance. His time in the woodshed had prepared him well for the lawyer's line of attack. As the questions grew shriller, his answers came in reasoned calm, justifying his opinions. His voice, a natural baritone, carried the same authority. As he testified, his congenitally friendly eyes and mouth signaled an urge to cooperate, to help his interrogator get to the truth while simultaneously holding his ground where his opinions conflicted with the lawyer's version of that truth. It was, as Walthall had forecast, a professional performance.

Jillian watched from the chair next to Walthall's. She admired the way Glen addressed the jurors as equals, explaining his opinions and how he arrived at them. After a time, she noticed something else. Not once did he look at her, though he shot an occasional glance at Walthall during cross-examination. She was surprised to find herself slightly annoyed at Glen's seeming indifference. *Maybe,* she thought, *I really am just an East Asian curiosity to him, like a fish caught out of season.* Or, like Connor Nalley, perhaps Glen viewed her as ancillary to some process better suited to men.

When the trial ended, Glen approached her as she stayed to collect the state's exhibits.

"So, how did I do?" he wanted to know. His curiosity struck her as genuine as she felt a flush of satisfaction at being asked.

"We won, so I'd say you did okay."

"Just okay?"

"Fine, then. Really professional job." Something inside told her not to gush.

"Thanks again for your help in the prep."

"But all I did was listen and take notes."

"Sometimes that's enough."

She wasn't sure what that meant. She busied herself with the exhibits, expecting him to move on, but instead, he said, "I have to catch a flight in a couple of hours. When I come back, any chance for dinner?"

She thought she detected nervousness as he awaited her response, odd for a man who had spent the better part of the afternoon confidently testifying under oath.

"Maybe," she said.

"If you're involved with someone, I get it, but Frank said that as far as he knew, you weren't."

"He's my boss, so he would know. Sure. Dinner sounds nice."

# CHAPTER 35

# A Favor

Jillian watched Glen leave the courtroom, mildly curious that he would have bothered to check with Walthall about her dating status. *Maybe I should check on his.* But she thought it unlikely she would hear from him again. What were the odds he would be coming back anytime soon, or ever? For all she knew, he came on to lots of women, though that didn't feel right either, because for all his confident competence as an expert, he seemed nervous and vulnerable in asking her about his testimony.

Months had passed since that trial. He had called a few times, always from a different city and usually on his way to or from an airport. He spoke about his cases and asked about hers. Conversations teetered between professional and personal, though she sensed he wanted more of the latter. His telephone voice softened from the tone he used to testify. He sounded sincerely interested, hardly patiently forbearing, and as time passed, she looked forward to his calls.

Ballistic issues raised in the medical examiner's report on Toby Morgan's death presented an opportunity Jillian had been looking for.

"Where are you?" she asked when he answered on the second ring.

"Dallas," he said. "It's nice to hear your voice again. Please tell me you are also in Dallas."

"No such luck. Still stuck in little old Beaufort, where you last saw me. But there have been some changes here. Frank Walthall died suddenly, making me the acting solicitor."

"For real? Congratulations. But I'm sorry to hear about Frank. I really liked that guy."

"You and almost everyone else. Will you be coming my way anytime soon?"

"I've been a jerk by not coming back there."

"Well, you're my favorite expert witness jerk, so I need a favor."

"Shoot."

"Is that a pun, because that's why I'm calling?"

He laughed. "I'll claim it though it never entered my mind. You don't miss much, do you?"

"We've had a shooting here and it looks like self-defense, but there's an outside chance it wasn't, so I need some help sorting it out."

"A he-said, she-said?"

"He can't say much since he died at the scene. So it's just she-said."

"My favorite kind of case. The gun?"

"A .38 Smith & Wesson. Fatal shot to the chest, but also a shot to the shoulder. From behind."

"Hmm. Front and back trauma?"

"Yep. I'm leaning toward closing the file, partly because she's a schoolteacher and he was a worthless bag of garbage, but before I do, I want another set of eyes on her explanation. If I send you the medical examiner's report and photos, could you tell me what you think?"

"Can I tell you in person?"

"Promises, promises."

"Will my opinion prevent you from having dinner with me?"

"Highly unlikely this case is going anywhere, and I'd love to do dinner."

His voice abruptly turned professional, reverting closer to his expert witness tone. "I'll need more information than a report and a few photos. I assume you have the gun?"

"We do." Jillian sighed. "I'll be honest. Now that Frank's gone, I have to worry about things like budgets, and there isn't enough money to retain you. Like I said, I need a favor."

"Understood. When this trial ends, I'll see what I can do. What else is new in your life?"

"Other than facing a special election in the fall that odds say I will lose, not much."

"You're not a loser. There's something wrong with that picture."

"It's complicated. I'll explain over dinner."

She hung up thinking not of the Morgan case but of how good it had been to hear Glen's voice again. Aside from blue eyes she found appealing, he combined competence with personality, making her wonder how, at thirty-six, he had managed to stay single. And he was single; she had checked. Perhaps his constant travel explained it. When her mind returned to the Morgan file, she asked herself if the prospect of dinner with Glen could be the one thing keeping her from closing it. She didn't like the answer.

But before Glen returned to Beaufort another variable arose in her prosecutorial calculus. Alana left in Jillian's office her final divorce decree, which she had brought to the interview at Jillian's request. Jillian had it copied for her records, then summoned a sheriff's deputy to return the original.

Victor Blasingame came to her office. He arrived in his usual state of dishevelment, wrinkled pants, stained shirt, and badge at a forty-five-degree angle. The sheriff tolerated him because Blasingame had lost his wife several years back, lived alone, and was his most reliable deputy, never missed work, and always carried out assignments. He wore his nickname, Soapy, as an honor, though no one could remember its origin, including him. Had he been years younger, he could have served as the sheriff's department's mascot.

"Good morning, Soapy," Jillian said when he knocked at her door.

"Mornin', Miss Jillian, how can I help you? Sheriff says you need a favor."

She handed him the divorce decree, sealed in a manilla envelope. "This belongs to a woman named Alana Morgan. She recently moved into the old Elkhart place. You know it? No rush, but give it to her the next time you're out that way."

He returned that afternoon, clutching the manilla envelope. "That woman's got a real fix-up project on her hands. I hope she knows how to paint and use power tools 'cause she's gonna need 'em. But there weren't nobody home, and I didn't know what was in this, so I thought maybe you didn't want me to just leave it."

"Oh. It was okay to leave it. You should have called."

"I tried. No cell service that far out."

Jillian's eyebrows went up. "No cell service?"

"Folks down there have to drive a ways to get a signal. Two, three miles."

*But*, thought Jillian, *Alana Morgan was there when she received the call from her daughter. Or was she?*

# CHAPTER 36

# Woodpecker Sighting

On a Saturday, Dan surprised Claire with the suggestion that they take a day trip to the lake. "The T-bird, with the top down," he insisted. If he had a prized possession, it was his always-garaged, seldom-driven 1958 throwback. He had bought it on a whim, and because whims were as foreign to his nature as singing soprano, it became a stand-in for the frivolous years he never experienced but sometimes dreamed about. When his fraternity brothers packed a trunk with cases of cheap beer for a weekend at the beach, he headed for the library. *Someday,* he told himself, but that day never came.

Their last conversation about the lake house had been weeks before, when Claire told him she couldn't bear to think about it, and when she did, elevators and access ramps crowded out any pleasure in the sunsets she dreamed she would own.

Claire gushed. "My, my, Judge Borders, that may be the best idea you've had in ages. I need to get out of this house. Can you get me a scarf?"

On the road, music from the '60s swept past them as it had before Christina and Ethan rooted them to domesticity. Wind and music made conversation difficult, but wasn't that the sheer joy of an open road? Painted white, the car evoked in Dan the image of a rocket, with its distinctive fins and missile trim equipoised over the rear wheels. He felt he could pull back on the wheel and fly. When John Denver's "Take Me Home, Country Roads" came on, they sang words they had forgotten they knew, and even though neither could hear the other, sideways glances made it a duet.

At the lake, they walked their property in silence. Careful where she stepped, Claire made steady, if slow, progress. He strayed no more than a step or two away, alert to any stumble or trip that could require his support. But she managed nicely, and *Maybe*, he thought, *the dream of a house here wasn't so remote.* For someone who couldn't bear to think about it, here she was. He guessed she was mentally going over the last design she and that architect had agreed upon. *Where did she put those drawings?* Perhaps that was exactly what Claire needed now—more than her church, her bridge club, her monthly appointment with her hairdresser. She needed total immersion in a building project that would keep her mind off the very thing that she perceived would inhibit her.

And at that precise moment, Dan had his first subversive thought of the day. Building a lake house might channel Claire's energy and frustrations, but it would also guarantee she spent more time at the lake. Time he might carve out at home with Alana. That thought, momentary as it was, startled him. *Absurd!* He reminded himself that Alana was a fantasy and always had been, an infatuation perhaps understandable in a man his age, at his stage of life, enduring the borderline celibacy imposed by Claire's illness. Had he not met a flesh-and-blood Alana, he would have needed to invent her. Perhaps he had invented her, or at least projected onto her the charms found in dreams. Alana, real or imagined, represented sweets a diet didn't permit, a drink recovery from alcoholism forbade, a monster bet when the house holds all the cards. And now, if that weren't quite enough, his destiny and that of this half-vision, half-woman hinged on and were forever bound together by the tragic events of the night Toby died. Like two drowning souls clinging to each other, both might still slip below the water in a fatal embrace.

Yet, for all the illogic Alana represented, he couldn't completely banish the fantasy. It was about sex but also about power, the testosterone rush begun by his Jury of One idea and fueled by that looming supreme court seat.

They spread a blanket near the shore, at a spot that would have been just below the main deck Claire had designed. She unpacked sandwiches and, to his mild surprise, a bottle of wine. "Would you get my chair?" she asked. "I'm afraid if I sit on the ground, I won't be able to get up."

Between bites of a pimento cheese dip, Claire reminisced about his birthday weekend. "I laughed and cried at Ethan's stories like we all did, but my God, that place sounds dismal."

"Yes, and a few hundred miles from the richest nation on earth. He's making a contribution to people who need it," Dan said. "I'm proud of him. And if he ever gets the urge to leave, I hope he'll return to Europe before that youthful window closes."

"My junior year abroad did wonders," she said. "You never got to go, did you?"

He shook his head. "Back then, it was an issue of money, and I must have lacked Ethan's wanderlust. One of my regrets."

"Am I another one?"

"Don't be silly. You've been a perfect companion."

"Banjo is also a perfect companion." Then she laughed. "I'm only teasing."

A woodpecker began a persistent assault high in a tree Dan looked for but couldn't pick out. Its hammering jabs echoed through the woods. "But since we're on the subject of children," he said, still scanning the trees behind her for the bird, "what's the latest with Christina? Do we need to start planning a wedding?" From across the lake, a breeze rippled the shoreline.

"I want to meet him. She promised to bring him on her next trip home. He's a handsome boy judging by his picture. Did she show those to you? And he graduated from Brown. We just learned that. Somewhere I got the impression he was a street artist, but that is hardly the case."

"It sounded to me from what she said that Chad hopes to make a living at his art. If so, I hope he's good. Marrying an artist would be difficult enough, but a bad artist?"

Claire cocked her head, as if visualizing one of Chad's paintings. "A bit modern for my taste, but not too bad. He does seem nice enough, and he's crazy about Christina. I'm not supposed to tell you, but he asked her to move in with him. Don't worry . . . she said no. Or at least not yet.'"

"That's a relief."

"She asked me to reassure you she's being sensible in what she called 'all things Chad.' Kind of poetic, don't you think?"

He scoffed. "A poet and an artist. I smell trouble. But they're both old enough to make their own decisions. Let's agree now that if we ever build a house here, and if she stays with the guy, we won't hang some dreadful Martian landscape over the fireplace."

"Those are a couple of big ifs, wouldn't you say?"

"There is another one," he said, shifting his gaze across the lake. "This supreme court business. Kennedy tells me I have a real shot at it. Sidney Callahan may not have the strength in the legislature he thinks he has."

"Do you know Callahan?"

"Met him a couple of times. Seems like a nice enough fellow. By all accounts, his wife runs the show. I've met her, too. One of those people who can't resist telling you just how rich they are. You know the type. If a supreme court seat can be bought, she'll be standing there with her checkbook."

"That's not the way we do things in South Carolina, is it?

"Not yet, but campaigns are becoming so expensive that big donors like Isabell Callahan draw a lot of water. Kennedy tells me he spends half his time raising money."

"Aside from his legislative contacts and a wealthy wife, is Callahan even qualified for the court?"

"He had a decent trial practice at one time, so that's a plus. I doubt he's been inside a courtroom in years. I'm told now he just steers clients to his law firm in Aiken. They do the work, and he cashes the checks."

Claire sipped her wine. "You say so little about it these days— the selection, I mean—I was beginning to wonder if you wanted it. You've been very distant lately, like you have something heavy on your mind."

Dan turned his gaze from the lake to her. Her last comment was unexpected and not one she was likely to have made. *Does she suspect something?* Had he talked in his sleep? Had she picked up some rumor from her bridge club or at church? "Trying not to get my hopes up, that's all. Did you know there has never been a judge from Beaufort County on the high court? In all this time."

"Would we have to move?"

He dipped a cracker into the last of the cheese spread. "Nope. I can work from home and commute when I need to be in Columbia. And the spot we're on now is closer, so that is another reason we should consider building here."

Silence settled in as the breeze died and the lake calmed. From her chair, Claire looked down on him, seated on the blanket. "I'll make you a deal," she said. "If you're selected for the court, we'll build the house here. I've been thinking about it since the night we watched that old Paul Newman movie. I should move forward with things."

He looked up at her. "That's the spirit," he said, reminded that Claire was still the lovely woman he had married. "What if the court appointment doesn't come?"

"You know it will."

"Where politics are involved, you don't know anything until it's done. And this is politics." Even as he said it, he knew his odds were improving, but that assumed Alana keeping her oath of silence.

"If the appointment went to someone else, I'd still have my day job. And one day, there will be another appellate seat opening, and maybe I'd have better luck. But let's get back to you. Were you serious about reviving the lake house idea?"

"This trip today has made me serious. I'm remembering how much I love it up here, even with that woodpecker destroying one of our trees as we eat lunch."

"What's the next step?"

"I'll dig out the plans and call that architect. I promised I'd work with her if we ever put the project back on track . . . and if I stay healthy."

His mind drifted to his own *ifs*. If the legislature selected him, and if Toby Morgan's death was confirmed as self-defense, and if Alana honored her pledge, he could see himself writing supreme court opinions in the library of a lake house to be built. If . . .

CHAPTER 37

# Party Pants

Jillian could not postpone another meeting with Harper Kline, head of her one-person campaign finance committee. Asking people for money made Jillian physically ill, but Harper liked it and earned far beyond her pay, which was exactly zero. "I believe in you," Harper had said when she signed on. "Besides, Jerry Higginson hits on me every time he sees me in the Riff-Raft. We don't want him as our solicitor."

Jillian met Harper Kline, age forty-two, in a jazzercise class shortly after moving to Eagle Retreat. Her first impression was of someone with whom she would have zero in common. Harper's workout garb said much about her personality. Harper wore cropped leggings and a tank top without a sports bra, bulging from places most others in the class covered. In fact, Harper disliked bras generally, and on all but the most solemn occasions refused to wear them, calling them a nuisance. "And besides," she said with a quip Jillian would come to think of as typical, "why make the boys work harder?" With hair splayed out as if she just got out of bed and sneakers that might have been the first pair she ever owned, Harper flounced around the mats in her own world. Jillian thought the expression "dance like no one is watching" should be her motto, though her wild gyrations ensured everyone noticed. After two sessions, Jillian concluded that Harper was one of the most unusual and entertaining people she had ever been around.

At one instructor who insisted on music too upbeat for Harper's breathing, she muttered a stream of profane invective that had everyone within earshot laughing. In mid-routine, Jillian bent at the waist, hands on her thighs, laughing and pleading with Harper to stop. The oblivious instructor kept going, as did Harper.

"You need to stay out of the Riff-Raft," Jillian cautioned. "We prosecute a case a week from that dive." The Riff-Raft had earned its reputation for trouble. It owed its existence to a local good ole boy who purchased a huge barge and cemented it in place on the river. Working largely by himself, he built a structure on top, complete with a small kitchen and long bar. To all who predicted he would never get a liquor license for such a joint, he'd smile and spit tobacco, saying he just might. And he did. Getting thrown into the river from the Riff-Raft's deck became a rite of passage for area rednecks, and a badge of honor for the boys doing the throwing.

"I know, but where else can you go around here? Sure, the guys get drunk, but I leave early, right after I take a couple of them at pool." Harper, who was and always had been single, smiled her sassy smile.

"So," said Jillian, "how's our war chest?"

"About where I thought we'd be, which was enough to win."

"Was?"

"Jillian, hello? Jerry's getting traction. His recent filing showed a big money surge."

"We can thank Judge Borders for that. The Hazel Hudgins case."

"Yep. If one more person mentions it, I'll choke them. You need to go on the attack. Plant some rumors Higginson's a child molester, beats his wife, that kind of thing."

Jillian laughed. "Not my style."

"You're right. That's my style. Let me know when it's time to unleash the hounds."

Jillian walked around her desk and leaned against the front edge. Case folders stacked neatly behind her signaled an organized, methodical approach to her job. She folded her arms and said to Harper, "I'm going to win this thing."

"Love that positive attitude, but you're a rookie when it comes to elections. This isn't like being elected homecoming queen."

"I was certainly never that."

"I was," Harper shot back. "Look, let me take care of the money, and you just make yourself available for some meet-and-greets. We've got time before folks vote. And get yourself in the newspaper and on the internet every chance you get. Maybe a big case like Hazel Hudgins that shows off your talents. Anything like that in the hopper?"

"It's all pretty routine at this point. Lopez cases don't come along very often."

Harper stood to leave. "Then put on your party pants some night and come with me to the Riff-Raft. Work the crowd. You hit 'em up for votes and I'll hit 'em up for cash and we'll leave winners."

Jillian smiled. "You're the best."

# CHAPTER 38

# Go Redskins

With Harper Kline's departure, Jillian returned to the file on top of her stack—Toby Morgan. For the first time since Alana's subpoenaed phone records had come in, she sat down to study them. Calls from Toby's number predominated in the months leading up to his death. Most were less than twenty seconds, with a few longer ones likely sent to voicemail. No calls to Toby registered on her phone. At 8:10 on the night he died, a call came into Alana's cell from her home number, just as she had said in her interview. When asked how long Holly's panicked call had been, Alana estimated "maybe a minute." The record showed it to have been forty-nine seconds. As Jillian expected, nothing unexpected or puzzling except Alana's location when the call came in.

Jillian left her office early. Glen was in town, and she needed a few extra minutes to ready herself for the dinner date she had promised him in exchange for his ballistics expertise. He arrived promptly, dressed for Texas. She couldn't recall the last time she saw a man wearing boots and a string tie held together with a steer's head clasp. But he was as handsome as she remembered, about five-ten, with the soft blue eyes of a priest about to forgive a penitent. They drove to Edisto for seafood.

Conversation over dinner omitted any discussion of Toby Morgan's death and instead followed the arc of their telephone chats—his travels and assignments of interest, her caseload and battles with defendants' lawyers. Jillian sensed they continued to walk the line between the personal and professional. The exchanges impressed her as remarkably balanced, each interested in the other's contribution, leading her to heightened curiosity about his private life. She found his modesty enticing and his lack of ego downright sexy. The longer they talked, the more she looked for an opening to probe.

Seated in his rental car back at Eagle Retreat, he told her how much he had looked forward to seeing her. Into the awkward silence that followed, she said, "Yes, but you mentioned at dinner you are a Dallas Cowboys fan."

"Hey, I'm from Texas. Of course, I'm a Cowboys fan. Uh-oh, you're originally from Virginia. Don't tell me—"

"Yep! Redskins rule forever. Well, not lately, of course."

Glen had evidently been looking for the same avenue into the personal that she had been seeking because, in a gesture that struck her as spontaneous, he reached for her hand. "You won't remember the night I almost became a Redskins fan because it happened before you were born. The night John Riggins told Sandra Day O'Conner to 'loosen up, Sandy baby.' I loved the guy from that night on."

She returned the squeeze. "That was 1985, and even though I was only two years old, I heard the story so many times, I felt I was there. I grew up with that legend." She smiled with the recollection. "My parents said we had a duty to support the team closest to our home, but I always thought part of their obsession was the fact that the Redskins had an Indian mascot, even though those

Indians were no more related to us than a cow is related to a duck."

Glen laughed, pulling her close and kissing her. He whispered, "Did you see that coming?"

"I did. Do it again. Go Redskins."

In an alcove shielded from the view of Max Ritter and other residents, he kissed her at the door. She sensed he hoped for more but received only her promise to see him again.

The next morning, she bristled over a news article reporting comments made by Jerry Higginson to a local Kiwanis club. "She's over her head as solicitor," he was quoted as saying. "Too young, too inexperienced. Crime in this county demands a veteran trial attorney, which she may one day be but isn't yet." The "over her head" mantra was becoming a theme of Higginson's campaign, his message consistently reinforced by a recitation of her failed Hazel Hudgins prosecution.

# CHAPTER 39

# No Charge

The restaurant Jillian chose for her next dinner date with Glen, inspired by his Lone Star look on the day he arrived, served Tex-Mex. "Order the ginger margarita," she suggested. Mariachi music blared through and around Latin waiters bussing tables arranged under piñatas suspended from the ceiling. Jillian had romance on her mind but figured this setting would be the least likely to telegraph it. A perky waitress in a floral apron who looked young enough to have just celebrated her quinceañera, took their drink orders.

"Thanks for the copy of the autopsy report and the Morgan woman's account of how it happened. I suppose it could have been self-defense," he said, jumping straight to the business at hand.

"You sound doubtful."

He shrugged. "Too soon to draw any conclusions. The photos weren't bad, but they could have been better. This is one of those cases when I'd love to examine the body myself."

"If he wasn't cremated, maybe we could get him exhumed," she said, stirring a margarita set before her along with chips and guacamole and still irked by Jerry Higginson's snipe at her record.

"How did you know I like Mexican?" he asked.

"Lucky guess, though the string tie and steer head were hints. And in all honesty, the choices are pretty limited here once you get past seafood and pizza."

"Any Indian restaurants?"

"No, but if you like that cuisine, you've hit the jackpot. I happen to be a fair cook, thanks to my mother. Do you cook?"

He shook his head. "I have a kitchen but no time to spend in it."

"Tell me about your house."

"Do you want to order? This may take a while."

Jillian scanned a menu. "I don't think I'll order mole. They ruin your lawn. Gross."

He laughed. "Not mole, as in the blind critter. *Mo-lay.* Two syllables. Chocolate sauce with chiles. Delicious. You should try it. Let me order for you. This guacamole tells me this place is more Mex than Tex."

Jillian prompted him about his house.

"I was born and grew up in Dallas in the same house I live in now." As he described the house, she studied him. She liked his hands, with their neatly trimmed nails. As he dipped chips in guacamole, he kept one hand in his lap, and she liked that too because her parents had taught her that as part of good table manners. His eye contact, steady and unforced, pleased her as much as last night's kissing. She sensed in it that unspoken connection she had never found with hawkeyed Connor Nalley.

"You live with your parents?"

When he dropped his head, she braced for embarrassment, but when he lifted it, she saw hurt.

"They were both killed in a car wreck my senior year at Texas A&M. Drunk driver with two prior DUIs. I inherited the family homestead."

"I'm so sorry," she said. "What a blow! How did you end up in the FBI?"

"They came to A&M to recruit. I majored in English and had never considered a career in law enforcement, but after I lost my folks in such a senseless tragedy, I was open to their pitch."

"Can you talk about your parents?"

"I want to talk about them. Great people. Best parents ever. Dad was a State Farm agent and Mom taught high school. I have two older brothers, one on the East Coast and the other on the West, and neither wanted to live in Dallas, so I got the house."

"Any college girlfriends out there I should be jealous of?"

"Several. Most are married with kids by now." He smiled, then asked about her college boyfriends.

"Like you with cooking," she said. "Not much time for that. Have you noticed my nose? A bit pug, don't you think? That's from the grindstone that wore it down. Though, in my senior year at Wofford, there was one boy—"

"I knew it! There had to be. Give me his name so I can do a background check."

"His name is Connor Nalley, and you need not bother. I've had no contact with him for several years. He's too busy saving his patients' knees and shoulders and reminding some poor woman or women how great he is."

"But you loved this guy, or is that too personal?"

She squinted. "I thought I did, but now I realize I loved the idea of him more than the person."

"What does it mean to love the idea of him?"

"You know, when someone is attractive and smart and ambitious, you begin to picture yourself as a fit for that person, and then you learn he just isn't. Haven't you known couples that seemed mismatched but were happy? That's my idea of loving the person more than the idea."

"Are you saying you want to love someone in spite of who they are?"

"Well," she said with a smirk, "I wouldn't go that far. And who said I wanted to love anyone? Maybe I want to stay single like my friend Harper Kline. She's about the happiest person I know, and the most fun. I'll introduce you sometime."

"For the record, you have a lovely nose, and a lovely face to go with it. And when can I meet this Harper Kline?"

"If your seatbelt is buckled and your helmet is a good fit, soon."

Their perky waitress returned, setting before them fresh tortillas wrapped in cloth nestled into a wicker basket. The earthy smell of baked wheat sharpened their appetites.

After her second bite of mole, Jillian pronounced herself a fan. With dinner over and a glass of wine half consumed, she revisited Toby Morgan. "Are we wasting our time on that creep? Sorry, that victim who happens to have been a creep."

"Maybe not," Glen said, slipping into his expert testimony voice. "A shot to the front and back of the same victim is pretty rare. I guess it's possible that the impact of the chest bullet turned him in a way that exposed the right shoulder, but I've never seen it. If I had to bet, I'd say she shot him in the back and the force of that bullet turned him toward the fatal shot. If I had to bet."

"In which case, he should have been faceup when they found him, which he was, but she says she turned him that way with her foot."

"She would say that, wouldn't she? To shoot an unarmed man in the back is murder. Manslaughter at a minimum. Her case for self-defense depends on his charging at her, putting her in fear of her life. Do you happen to know if the driveway was paved?"

"It wasn't. Gravel and dirt, as I recall. Why does it matter?"

"If it happened as she claimed, and the shoulder shot was the second shot, so he hit the ground prone, he should have had some residue from the driveway on his face or the front of his clothes. I didn't see anything like that noted in the report. I should examine his clothes."

"So, based on what we know now, your expert opinion would be—"

"Whoa, girl, we're a stretch away from an opinion. Sorry. I'll need more than I've seen so far. I could do some ballistics tests, angle of bullet entry, that sort of thing. Between those and some additional information from the medical examiner, maybe, but not today. I should also mention that I've been doing some work with computer modeling, three-dimensional stuff, reconstructing shootings so juries get a better picture. I brought a couple with me I could show you if you're interested."

"Fascinated would be closer. I must see them."

"Pretty impressive technology," he admitted. "As you might guess, defense attorneys love it when it shows the result they paid to get."

"Are you suggesting—"

"Okay, that was a bit cynical. What I meant was that prosecutors haven't been as quick to take advantage of this as the lawyers on the other side."

"It sounds like sophisticated stuff I can't afford." She pouted, more in flirtation than disappointment.

"No charge," he said, grinning. "If I can form an opinion, a real opinion instead of betting like I'm at a horse race, and you decide to bring the case, we can discuss a fee. Believe me when I tell you how low I can make it. Happy now?"

"Very," she said, returning her warmest smile. An instant later, it was replaced by doubt.

"What's the matter?"

"Nothing."

"As the expression goes, that dog won't hunt. Something is wrong."

She glanced away, blushing faintly. "I'm on what Frank Walthall would have called the horns of a dilemma. If I close the file, I won't need your testimony, so I may never see you again, and if I go to trial, I'll . . . how can I put this . . . need to be on my best behavior."

"Let me help you there. You'll never get rid of me by something as simple as closing a file, and as to your behavior, I can wait."

The smile she sent across the table registered not a speck of doubt.

# CHAPTER 40

# Neither Priest nor Pope

On the night before his appearance before the Senate Judiciary Committee, Dan traveled to Columbia. He checked into his hotel, ate a light dinner, then retired to his room to face the night ahead. In the closet hung the suit, shirt, and tie he would wear the next day, and in his carry bag rested the flask he would need that night. After a trip down the hall to the icemaker, he poured himself a stiff bourbon. Before that awful night in Seabrook, booze tended to keep him awake, whereas now he couldn't fall asleep without it. He knew the risks of one, then two, and promised himself he'd return to the old ways once he was sure Alana was out of legal jeopardy. On this night, he thrashed fitfully until 5:00 a.m., when he gave it up.

His closest contacts in the state legislature assured him of a hospitable welcome. Kennedy Mosby, his state senator, though not a member of the committee, had met privately with its chairman, as had William Reynolds, general counsel. Mosby, scheduled to pick him up at the Hotel Jackson a half-hour early, canceled due to some office emergency, so Dan drove to the state capitol, parking several blocks away to walk in what had turned out to be perfect weather.

Heads turned as Circuit Court Judge Daniel Borders walked into the crowded hearing room. One of those belonged to Brock Jamerson, who attended all such vettings. He had yet to meet Judge Borders, having spent only one day in Beaufort, the day the judge ruled that the knife in the Lopez case could not be admitted into evidence. Jamerson hoped to meet with him after today's grilling.

Senator Thomas Wentworth, a Republican from Pendleton, chaired the committee. At the center of an arced table, he sat Buddha-like, with a ginger complexion and the jowls of a bulldog. A slight tremor in his hands, rumored to be early Parkinson's, could be seen when he raised them. He called the hearing to order and asked Judge Borders to stand to be sworn in, and then be seated.

"Judge Borders," Wentworth intoned, "we are here today to determine your suitability to sit on the state's highest court as its chief justice. It is nice to see you again. Thank you for coming. We have your résumé, which I must say is impressive. The floor is yours for an opening statement."

The judge thanked the chairman and the committee members before expressing his appreciation for both the honor and the responsibility he would feel if selected. He kept it short and general, then invited questions.

Chairman Wentworth spoke first. Looking over half-rim glasses, his index finger quivering as he pointed, he asked, "Do you think you would be sitting here today without that intriguing Jury of One idea you wrote about?" He had asked the same question in his private meeting with Dan attended by Peter Wolfe, and evidently wanted his entire committee to hear Dan's response.

Judge Borders scanned the committee members in a sweeping glance before returning his focus to the chairman. "In all candor, probably not. There is no question that the publicity surrounding the proposal has given me some status I wouldn't have otherwise

had. Those of us"—and here, Dan could not suppress a wry smile—
"who labor in the vineyards of rural counties don't usually receive
that kind of notice."

Wentworth returned the wry smile. "I remind you, Judge, that
as a native of Pendleton, I am well aware of the realities of rural
counties." Laughter among the committee members and in the
audience dispelled a certain tension that had prevailed until that
moment.

"If I felt that my idea, which you generously characterized as
intriguing, was my sole qualification for this position, I'd like to
think I'd withdraw my name from consideration. But, as strongly
as I feel about the Jury of One concept, I feel just as strongly about
other strengths I could bring." He listed those, with nodding heads
confirming his optimism that the hearing was going well.

The tone changed when Cecily Whitt, a recently elected senator
from Florence, began her allotted time. Whitt had been propelled
into the senate largely through the efforts of parishioners of her
megachurch. "For all your strengths, Judge, I find your support for
suicide distressing. Even immoral."

"Then you mistake me, Senator. I never said I favored suicide,
nor do I. For all but an infinitesimal number of people, it is wrong.
Certainly, people of faith condemn it on religious grounds, and I
respect their faith."

"Sounds to me like you lack that faith," Whitt said.

"I'm neither priest nor pope, Senator, just a judge facing a
defendant named Otis Hazzard who committed a heinous crime
and fully deserved the sentence he received. I remind you that
everyone here today, including me, has the option of suicide at any
time for any reason, and the exercise of that option is as near as the
tall building we are in or the pharmacy down the street. It is called
free will. Ironically, Hazzard does not have that option. His prison
will deprive him of the means to do what you and I can, and if he
expresses the desire to die rather than rot in a cell for decades, they

will put him on suicide watch to reduce the chances he can carry out his preferred path."

Whitt appeared to change tactics. "We've read accounts of some mental health counselors who fear the mere presence of your death chamber will encourage its use."

"I doubt that. Death row inmates already have a death chamber just down the hall. They know they may be forced to take that final walk when their last appeal fails. At that point, they lose all choice in the matter and all hope. Experts with whom I've spoken have said that hope is the single most important component of this Jury of One concept. Consider the dilemma of two life-without-hope-of-parole inmates. Prisoner A is guilty. He knows he is guilty, and he knows the evidence against him proves that guilt. Prisoner B is innocent. He knows he did not commit the crime that put him there. He knows to a certainty that a mistake has been made, either in the evidence relied on to convict him or the lawyer who represented him or perhaps the judge who presided over his trial. Is Prisoner B going to opt for my death chamber when he still has hope that one day an injustice will be discovered? That something like The Innocence Project, which has freed dozens of condemned men, will show that his confession was coerced, that the eyewitness who doomed him made a mistake, that the rapist's DNA does not match his? Hope will keep Prisoner B from using my death chamber. But Prisoner A? He lives without such hope, and for him, the choice between life and death is real. If he prefers death to decades in a cell before dying in that cell of old age, who among us could call that an irrational decision? It is analogous to someone with a terminal illness in unrelenting pain. That is why a number of countries, and a handful of our states, have legalized assisted suicide. My death chamber is a form of assisted suicide for those who choose it in circumstances most of us would agree are comparable to a terminal illness. The psychological pain of life without hope of parole makes it comparable."

"How do you address the slippery slope argument?" Whitt wanted to know. "That the adoption of your idea will lead inevitably to suicide becoming more acceptable."

The judge adjusted his microphone to bring it closer. "I've heard those arguments and I don't accept them. Suicide has been on the rise generally in the US, and that increase can hardly be blamed on my idea since it is only that, an idea. What explains this increase in suicides? Consider the differences between people in the free population, like you and me, and a life-without-hope-of-parole inmate. Take, for example, someone in the free population pressured by family, or by themselves, to end their life to avoid becoming a burden on their loved ones, either financial or caregiving. This is a common concern according to studies in the few places where assisted suicide is legal. A death row inmate is a burden only upon the state and its resources. Whatever pressure that inmate feels is self-imposed.

"Loss of personal dignity, a fear understandable to those of us who cannot imagine ourselves relying on others to help us in our most basic needs, also explains why some may view suicide as desirable. But prison is by its very nature undignified, with close quarters, communal existence, security cameras, armed guards, and privacy all but eliminated in the name of safety to other inmates and prison personnel. To put it bluntly, a prisoner has already forfeited his right to dignity by the crime he or she committed, and the loss of what has already been forfeited is no great loss."

The judge held eye contact with Senator Whitt, who adjusted her glasses, which had slipped during his remarks. "Are you familiar, Judge Borders, with studies in what has been called choice architecture?"

"I am not."

"The basic precept is that our choices in life can be strongly influenced, even decided, by how those choices are presented.

An example would be a survey that contains a default response, and that response differs dramatically from the results in surveys where there is no default, or a different default."

"I'm not clear."

"One study in particular drew my interest as it relates to a Jury of One. Terminally ill patients were asked to decide whether they preferred comfort care, essentially hospice, or whether they wanted their lives prolonged by the magic of modern medicine."

"In other words, death versus extended misery."

"Correct. And like the survey I mentioned, results correlated to a high degree with the default option. Where the default option was hospice, patients opted for it at a higher rate than in surveys where the default was prolongation or no default, which suggests they were content to let others make such a choice for them. Imagine your choice of how and when to die made by a form. The point is that life or death decisions can be influenced by factors beyond the control of and maybe even beyond the comprehension of the decider."

"Interesting," the judge said, reflectively. "If you can point me to those studies, I'd like to read them."

"And I," said Senator Whitt, "would like to know your views on them. Because I think our prison system would bring all kinds of pressures—some subtle, some not so subtle—to drive these inmates into that chamber of yours."

For a moment, Judge Borders dropped his head like a man defeated, but then he lifted it to focus a controlled indignation at Whitt. "Before coming here today, Senator, I had resolved not to mention what I'm about to say, but since a Jury of One has become such a focus of this hearing, I'll share it. Otis Hazzard, the man I sentenced to death, and the man who inspired the Jury of One concept, has been awaiting execution in our maximum-security penitentiary as his appeals languish in the courts. Two days ago, I was informed of his suicide. He circumvented the prison's guardrails designed to prevent just what occurred. I'm told he found, probably during the hour of exercise allowed him each day, a metal top cut from a can of soup or hash. At lights out, he used the serrated edge to cut both wrists, then lay covered on his bunk as guards checked on him from the small window they use to make sure death row inmates obey the rules. It was not a quick death. For some time, as life literally drained from his body, he resisted whatever urge would have been natural to save himself by calling for help. At some point, the loss of consciousness would have made whatever pain he suffered in the ordeal moot. But he wanted to die. I don't blame him. He had lost the one thing none of us can live without—hope. Do I mourn his death? No. Humanity paid a high price for his time on earth. But do I condemn the needless suffering he endured? I do, and so should you."

# CHAPTER 41

# A Personal Matter

The remainder of Dan's grilling tracked all such hearings. Pro forma questions regarding respect for legal precedent, separation of powers, and individual freedoms guaranteed by the Bill of Rights in the US Constitution. When asked if he owned a gun, Judge Borders said that he did—a hunting rifle and a pistol. Was he a member of the NRA? "No."

His testimony complete and the hearing declared over, Dan spent a few moments mingling among senators, shaking hands, and accepting compliments. As he was about to leave the room, Brock Jamerson appeared at his elbow. He introduced himself and asked Dan if his time permitted an interview. Dan said it did. At Jamerson's suggestion, they entered a nearby coffee shop. When they were seated, Jamerson asked if he could take notes, to which Dan agreed.

"How do you feel it went in there today?" Jamerson asked.

Dan chuckled. The hearing was behind him, and so was the tension it produced. His mood turned light and almost carefree. "I should ask you that question," he said with a smile. "You must have sat through hundreds of these."

Jamerson nodded. "Dozens, anyway. You scooped the paper on Otis Hazzard's death. We were set to report that in the Sunday edition, and now I'll have to revise the story."

"Sorry for the extra work," Dan said. "It seemed to me it went well today. I hope I'm not being unduly optimistic."

"It went well," Jamerson confirmed. "One of the better performances I've seen, and I'm using the word 'performance' in its best sense."

"Thank you," Dan said.

"Since I'm a nosey reporter, I know your wife has MS. That's a tough one. How is she doing with it?"

Dan's first inclination was to deflect, groping for a polite way to say none of your business, but in fact it was Jamerson's business, or his paper's business. "She's coping well," he said. "Thank you for asking."

"Any chance her health could impact your service on the court?"

"That's a bit premature. I'm not on the court."

"You may be soon," Jamerson said with conviction. "I've learned to read that bunch pretty well. You impressed them. I'd be surprised if you aren't their choice."

"That's gratifying to hear. What about Sidney Callahan?"

"A very nice man and a pretty good lawyer."

"And his chances?"

Jamerson stared off, as if reading Callahan's odds on a far wall. "Pretty good may not cut it on this. Not for this court seat. I see him up here all the time, pressing the flesh and chatting up his old cronies. There was a time in this state when that might have been enough, but those times have changed." He jerked his thumb in the direction of the building they had just left. "Did they ask you anything in there that you didn't expect?"

"Not really. I knew the assisted suicide issue would come up.

One could argue that it really isn't relevant to an appellate position like the court, but I wasn't about to object."

"Smart," said Jamerson. "They don't like to be told that whatever they are interested in is beside the point."

For the next thirty minutes, Jamerson jotted notes from Dan's answers to questions ranging from his hobbies (fly-fishing, boating) to the Otis Hazzard case. Sensing they were finished, Dan got up to leave and shook Jamerson's hand.

"Where are you parked?" Jamerson asked casually.

"Over in the old Turner & Feinberg parking lot. I wanted to walk this morning."

"I'm headed that way. I'll walk with you."

By now, it was nearly noon. The perfect weather had turned raw, with dark clouds moving in from the west. "We better hustle," Dan said.

At the parking lot, Jamerson said, "By the way, do you have any objection to me interviewing Andrew Prescott? I hear he's a friend of yours."

"And a neighbor," Dan added. "Who told you about Andy?"

"One of your courthouse regulars."

"Ah," said Dan with a grin. "Protecting your source?"

"Something like that."

"If you decide to interview Andy, you'd be well-advised to brush up on your astronomy. That's his passion."

"Well, for a man who can't tell the Big Dipper from a solar eclipse, that's going to be a challenge." Then, after a pause signaling a change of subjects, he said, "You probably don't remember, but I was in your courtroom the day you ruled that the knife in the Hudgins case was inadmissible. That prosecutor was pretty steamed."

"Yes, she was," Dan agreed. "I knew I had seen you somewhere before."

Jamerson looked toward the menacing clouds. "Funny

coincidence that we're in the Turner & Feinberg parking lot. I'll bet you brought your children here every December to see the 'real' Santa."

"We never missed one for what must have been a decade. Even when the kids were past the Santa stage, they loved it. A sad day when this store went out of business."

"Yep. I thought about that on the day I spent in your court. There was a young woman there with a Turner & Feinberg shopping bag. I hadn't seen one of those in years. Say, you don't happen to know the woman I'm talking about, do you? Really good looking. A fox. I'm embarrassed to admit it, but I followed her to the clerk's office after the hearing in hopes of meeting her. She got away before I could score an introduction."

Dan paused, as if concentrating, before saying, "There were a lot of people in court that day. Can't help you on that one."

"I understand," Jamerson said, remembering Dan with the bag on his way to the parking lot. "I need to interview Prescott. I'd be looking for some human-interest stuff."

"If Andy agrees, I certainly have no objection."

As Jamerson watched Dan drive away, he couldn't shake the feeling that the judge knew more than he let on about the woman with the shopping bag. Dan remembered seeing him, a reporter, but not her? A woman that good looking and nicely shaped who asked the clerk to see Dan on a "personal matter"? And how did he end up with the same bag she brought to court and carried with her when the clerk led her toward his chambers? If she delivered that bag to him after court, there was no way the judge could have forgotten it. Or her. No way.

# CHAPTER 42

# Letting the Chips Fall

On the morning after their Tex-Mex dinner, Glen arrived early at Jillian's office. When he mentioned the difficulty of finding a place to park and the gaggle of nuns outside the courthouse, she explained that Beaufort was experiencing a steadily increasing number of tourists and protestors, most of whom feared that Judge Border's elevation to the supreme court would increase the prospects for his Jury of One concept. She said the staff in the clerk's office photographed the best protest signs and posted them on the bulletin board in the lounge.

Jillian closed her door and kissed him lightly on the mouth, telling him that his "I can wait" comment was about the sweetest thing she'd ever heard. As he booted up his laptop, she pushed her door open before taking a seat beside him.

"Show time," he said as he adjusted the screen. "What I'm about to show you comes from the case I was working on in Dallas. A repo man showed up at this guy's house to get his car. They argued. The homeowner told the repo man to get off his property and went back inside to get a rifle. When he opened his front door holding the weapon, the repo man plugged him with a Luger. He lived, but he's disabled now. For his damages suit, we prepared this simulation. Using laser mapping, we were able to recreate the house and driveway to exact scale, and the avatars for repo man and victim match their heights and weights. That red line is the bullet trajectory."

With his index finger, he traced the roof lines and sidewalk as a way of highlighting attention to detail, but her attention had shifted from the display to him. Gone were his cowboy threads, but the blue eyes were a constant.

Back in the moment, she studied the screen, sipping her coffee. "This is so much better than a verbal description. I assume someone was lying?"

"You bet. The repo man swore that the homeowner raised the rifle and was about to fire. The homeowner insisted the weapon stayed at his side and that when he saw the Luger, he was in the process of closing the front door."

"Then self-defense wouldn't save the repo man."

"Exactly. We were able to establish the red line by analyzing the wound path and computing the trajectory. It couldn't have happened the way repo man said it did. The jury awarded twelve million. Interviews with jurors after the verdict confirmed the power this presentation had. The homeowner's lawyer told us it made his case."

"So you can use it to make my case?"

"It all depends on the variables, and you've got a few. The one that I would worry about is the dead guy's intoxication. He could have been twisting and turning from booze in a way a sober man would not. It's the old story of computers—garbage in, garbage out."

Glen left to catch a noon flight out of Savannah. Back at home, she took the Morgan file out on her patio to assess where things stood. As she adjusted the chair cushion, she could feel Max Ritter's stealthy stare. Instinct prompted her to stick out her tongue, but she thought better of it. One day, she would send him an unmistakable message to mind his own business, if he had any, but today, her mind was in decision mode.

Up until now, she had remained ninety percent sure she would not indict Alana Morgan. Her budding romance with Glen flourished under that assumption. She thought of him as her unpaid consultant, and no rule she was aware of required her to forfeit a private life to do her job. So they went to dinner? So they kissed a few times? Who cared, with the possible exception of Max Ritter? As long as they weren't involved as prosecutor and expert witness, there was nothing wrong with being involved as whatever they had become.

What had they become? The clues added up to something special. His extra effort on the Morgan case said all she needed to hear about how much he wanted to help her. She knew she shouldn't constantly compare him to Connor Nalley, but she did it anyway. Connor would never have attached enough importance to her work to put himself out like Glen Coleman had. Whatever she could have done to make Connor happy and advance his career would have been met with an expectation for more. Connor was an owner, while Glen felt like a partner.

What she had seen that morning in her office, with Glen's computer simulation, made indicting Alana less remote. With a tool like that, she could persuade a lot of people of a lot of things. But at the moment, she wanted only to convince herself to close the Morgan file, sweeping the runway clean for a takeoff or landing with Glen, whichever it turned out to be.

Her problem was that the evidence of Alana's guilt leaned one way, while the realities of indicting her leaned another. The ghost of Hazel Hudgins still sat on her shoulder because Alana taught school, and by all reports from the administration, she excelled at it. A failed prosecution of a popular teacher, coming on the heels of the Hudgins debacle, could seal Jillian's fate at the polls.

Jillian wanted to believe Alana's account of what happened but found herself fixated on Alana's failure to tell Rutherford about Toby Morgan's warning shot over her head. *How could she forget that?* And why had Alana lied about receiving Holly's phone call at the Elkhart place? *Where was she?* Perhaps she was in the bed of some lover at another location, and so what if she was? Alana was single, and her desire to protect the identity of whomever she was sleeping with would be understandable.

And then there was the matter of insurance. By some friend-of-a-friend, "you didn't hear it from me" phone calls, Jillian learned that Toby's life insurance policy was still in effect at the time of his death, with Alana as beneficiary. *Did she know that when she killed him?* In the days following Jillian's interview with her, Alana had applied to the company for the $50,000 proceeds.

And what about the ballistics? It was all well and good for Glen to testify that he had never seen a body respond to a gunshot to the chest in a manner that would have resulted in Toby's shoulder wound, but did that mean it couldn't happen? A good defense lawyer would smell the weakness, and she had to anticipate a defense expert contradicting her star witness. Would her expert's testimony be enough to convince a jury of Alana's guilt? And did her eagerness to take her crush on Glen to the next level fatally compromise his ability to testify?

And just how much stock should she take, or would a jury take, in Alana's threat to kill Toby leveled in her divorce deposition? That had been many years earlier, and in the heat of a bitter divorce, people said lots of things they couldn't be held accountable for.

"Our job as prosecutors," Frank Walthall had told her early in her employment, "is to present the case, not decide the case. That's what they pay the judge for." By that principle, Jillian should seek an indictment and let the chips fall where chips fall. But here again, she came face-to-face with the ghost of Hazel Hudgins. She knew this election reality should not weigh in her decision, but it did. Better to hold off a final resolution until she heard back from Glen.

She stood up, frustrated by her inability to reach a decision. She walked back inside, but not before glancing at Max Ritter's window, where the blind was reliably parted. *When will he get a life?* she wondered.

⊙  ⊙  ⊙

The rest of Jillian's week saw the usual parade of DUIs, shopliftings, break-ins, and assaults. Because she appeared before Judge Borders on an almost daily basis, she was in a better position than most to note changes in his habits and demeanor. Maybe it was the pressure of the supreme court appointment, or perhaps he was having problems at home, but whatever the cause, he was less patient with attorneys, cutting them off in mid-sentence and scowling at the kinds of arguments to which he historically showed benign, if not smiling, indulgence. He grew abrupt with witnesses as well, urging them to get to the point and thereby injecting himself into the case of the lawyer questioning that witness. His recall of facts suffered from whatever was causing this malaise. She had never seen him grumpy, but now he frowned as if the weight of whatever explained this change exerted gravity on his facial features. *Maybe,* she thought, *his wife's health had deteriorated. Or his own.*

One incident in particular stood out. A lawyer defending a man charged with breaking and entering a local pawnshop called a witness who gave the defendant an alibi, insisting they were together on the night the break-in occurred. On cross-examination, Jillian asked the man how he could be certain of the date, as several weeks had passed. The witness testified he remembered "because it was the night that fellow was shot up in Seabrook, that Morgan guy." She glanced at the judge to gauge his reaction and for an instant thought she saw faint but discernable alarm in his face. Later, in a phone call from Glen, she tried to describe it but found no suitable words except to say her impression had been visceral. "Just a gut," she said. "He seemed upset." The trial continued, the defendant was acquitted, and she thought no more about it except as one more example of how a man whose presence had been reliably stable had become erratic.

# CHAPTER 43

# Andrew The Celestial

Two weeks after Dan's hearing before the Judiciary Committee, his photo appeared in *The State* with three others rumored to replace the retiring Oliver Cox. A photo of Sidney Callahan appeared also. With the selection rumors fresh in his mind, and after a particularly contentious day in court, Dan decided to take Andy up on his invitation to visit the observatory.

Devil-Fish Point sat just east of Beaufort on a spit of land jutting from St. Helena Island into the Sound. From it, an eagle circling at fifty feet on a clear day could see across the Sound to and beyond Edisto Island. Its name derived from William Elliot's 1859 book *Carolina Sports by Land and Water*, wherein Elliot described, "a monster measuring from sixteen to twenty feet across the back, full three feet in depth, having powerful yet flexible flaps or wings, with which he drives himself furiously through the water, or vaults high into air: his feelers (commonly called horns) projecting several feet beyond his mouth, and paddling all the small fry, that constitute his food, into that enormous receiver . . ." In antebellum days, it became sporting to harpoon these giant rays as a means of propelling a trailing boat faster than any tide or sail. While the fertile waters for devilfish lay between Bay Point and Hilton Head Island, one of those monsters beached itself on what then became known as Devil-Fish Point.

A few private docks protruded from a shoreline essentially unchanged from the era of Elliot's accounts. Houses on the Point dated from the early 1900s, eclectic in design and use. There were no subdivisions, only enclaves accessed by dirt roads that dead end at the water's edge. Year-round residents would watch over vacation homes out of habit and because there was little else to do in the winter. Pine trees predominated. After sunset, the Point turned spectacularly dark, without streetlights and with very few outdoor flood lights, a proven deterrent against crime were there many crimes to deter. On a moonless night, the stars above the Point competed only with each other for the eyes of earth, one outshining another in such profusion that they reorder a person's priorities, or so Andy Prescott told Dan when asked why he had spent almost $200,000 on his observatory there. He named the place Star-Splitter.

Dan turned down the lane and a buck, a doe, and a fawn stood in his path. Only the doe registered alarm, bolting into a thicket lining the lane. He waited for the others to clear. Ten yards farther, he encountered a sign nailed to a pine tree: *Quiet, please. Worship service in progress.* Andy's Buick confirmed his presence.

Dan slowed, damping the sound of his engine in obedience to the sign's command. The SUV rolled to a stop beside the Buick. As he walked down the flagstone path leading to the back door, he gazed up, focusing on the Big Dipper as a constellation he recognized among thousands he did not. Andy was the only one he knew who could stand at the back fence and take you on a tour of the heavens with the ease of a man counting change from his pocket. He heard a piano, a vibrant series of staccato runs, as he reached for the knocker. After a minute with no sound but the piano, he opened the door and entered the main room, lit dimly by two table lamps at opposite ends of an ancient leather couch. The aroma of cedar bid him welcome just before Andy called from above.

"Fix a drink. I'll be down in a moment."

"Take your time," Dan said, walking toward the small kitchenette he knew to be just off the main room. He groped for the light switch, mixed a bourbon and water, turned off the light, and returned to the couch, sinking down into what felt like a cloud.

The dominant feature of the room was a turret in its center. It housed circular steps leading to the telescope and sealed off all light from below. The couch warmed his trunk and thighs as the drink warmed him inwardly. He kicked off his loafers, breathed deeply of cedar and bourbon, and began to look about the room.

On the far wall, between floor-to-ceiling bookcases, he saw the framed poem to which Star-Splitter owed its name. Wanda had had it specially printed in a fine font on parchment when the observatory was christened. Written by Robert Frost, the poem tells the story of a man so desperate to own a telescope that he burned down his house to collect the fire insurance, with which he purchased one. Andy knew it by rote.

The door to the turret opened and Andy's head appeared from behind it. "You've got to come see this," he said, beckoning with his finger.

Dan entered the turret and began to climb. Its steps were illuminated by fractional lights built into the step above. Andy, reaching the top, held open the upper door, against which Dan could see him silhouetted.

"Step into the cathedral," Andy instructed. "You've picked a glorious night."

Dan arrived at the top, paused to get his wind, and sipped his drink before looking up.

"Welcome to heaven," Andy said, still in shadow. "This is as close as I'll ever get, but you may get lucky." He chuckled faintly.

"Beautiful," whispered Dan, seemingly unprepared for the radiance of the canopy above him.

Andy tugged at his elbow. "Come look through the scope," he said, but Dan stood still.

"In a minute," he mumbled.

"I understand," said Andy, turning. He walked a few steps to his telescope, leaning into the viewfinder mounted on the side of the barrel.

They now stood twenty feet above the ground, at eye level with a stand of pines in the distance. In the stillness, only the piano music stirred, piped from below into three small speakers mounted behind them. Somewhere from within, Dan sensed an ache.

"I know what you're thinking," Andy said softly. "You're acknowledging God, the supreme being who constructed this loveliness. You're telling yourself that a night like this is proof positive of an all-powerful Him."

"It pains me to admit it, but you're right. Am I that predictable?"

"No, you're that human. It's a feeling that caused me to pay more for this property than any sane man would have done and spend more on a telescope than I spent on all the cars I ever bought combined. It's why I'm here tonight."

"But you're an atheist."

"Yes," Andy murmured, "but you don't have to be one. Exalt in it, in Him. It won't bother me."

Dan lowered his gaze to the horizon as an automated, economical lighthouse winked against the darkness. He vibrated his glass. The watery clink of ice cubes had something in common with the stars, or perhaps the piano. He looked up again. "It is inspirational," he said, but his voice portended more sadness than awe.

Andy spoke, very near him. Dan hadn't heard him approach. "I want to show you my slice of the sky, but you can't see it without the scope." He extended his arm southward, to a spot not far from the horizon. "That's the constellation Hercules. If you look closely, you can just see what looks like a star, but it's actually a cluster of them. We call them globular clusters. That's M13 in sky-speak."

"But that's not your slice."

"Mine is a little northeast of that, near a galaxy called MGC 6207. As I say, it's in deep sky, invisible without the scope."

"How far away?"

"About thirty thousand light years," Andy said. "Not far at all."

"Sounds far."

"Does it? The next Hubble telescope expects to capture light from the origin of the universe, billions of light years away, if you can imagine."

"I really can't."

"And we prefer marble for headstones because it is thought to be durable, lasting a few centuries at best. Time is the ultimate force in the universe. What we call God is only time, nothing more and nothing less. Once I figured that out, I finally began formulating some answers I can live with. I worked it out right here at this telescope. I'd had this feeling for years that the solution had something to do with a telescope. Strange, eh?"

"God is only time?" Dan repeated.

"Well, what would you call a force that can change a newborn infant into a wrinkled old man? That can combine universal dust to form planets? That creates a mighty river from a millennial drip of water, eases the bitterest loss, and turns grass into milk? Why, anything that powerful would be said to be omnipotent, magical, supernatural. God."

Dan shook his head. "I'll need to think about that one. There's a flaw in your logic, but at this moment, it isn't coming to me."

Andy clapped a fraternal hand to Dan's shoulder. "Don't examine my theories too closely. You'll take all the fun out of my philosophies."

"Do you ever worry that your views could have . . . consequences?"

Andy scoffed with a slight hissing sound. "You mean the afterlife nonsense? Take a look around, Daniel the Just. This is it, my friend. This is all there is, and isn't it enough? Of that I am sure, and as much as I may speak lightly of other matters, myself included, of course, I'm quite serious about that one."

"Why so?"

"Because if we all lived on that assumption, that we get one chance to do the right thing and no chance to be redeemed by some last-minute dispensation, I think we would try harder here on earth."

"Humanism to the rescue."

"And isn't it about time? Look at the Middle East nightmare. Muslims blowing themselves up to go see Allah and a bevy of celestial virgins. Mother Goose is stark realism by comparison. I tire of seeing ignorant people manipulated by such misguided claptrap. And frankly, Christianity isn't much better. People need to spend less time eating pie in the sky and more time cleaning up our planet."

Dan emitted a low whistle. "What's gotten into you tonight?"

"Can you honestly say you believe in heaven? Or hell?"

Dan's grin dissolved into a pensive stare, out toward the Point. "I'd like to believe I'll see Paul again, but I can't say that in my heart of hearts I think it will happen." Paul was Dan's older brother who died of a rare blood cancer when Dan was in college.

"Isn't that the desire that keeps the whole myth alive?"

"Maybe so, but let's change the subject."

"Okay, I'll stop. Enough is enough. I'm just glad you came. As much as I love the solitude here, it's nice to have someone to bounce things off of." Andy beckoned him toward the telescope. Standing next to the viewfinder, Andy made some adjustments.

"You'd think you could aim it at what you want to see more closely, but it doesn't work that way. Finding a specific star is tough, even when you star-hop from ones you know well."

"Why is that?"

"For one thing, they move across the sky, so you have to track them, a bit like shooting skeet. There, I've got it now. The area you see in the eyepiece is my slice of the sky. I could study it every night for the rest of my life and never run out of objects to focus on. I might be seeing a distant earth without knowing it. There could be fifty earths within this circumference. Or five thousand."

Dan leaned down, placing his eye at the viewfinder. "How big a slice is this?"

"Hard to estimate, but I'd guess at least three hundred light years from one side to the other. Imagine the distances involved when crossing the space encompassed in a fifteen-centimeter lens requires that much time."

"Impressive," Dan acknowledged.

"I'll say. You're seeing something you've never seen before."

Dan looked up at him and winked. "I do that every day, don't I?"

Andy replied, "I suppose you do."

Dan straightened. "A few months ago, I met a young woman who was having car trouble, and it turns out I entered her divorce decree a few years back. She came by my office to return the jumper cables I loaned her. We talked for a while. She's a single mother raising a kid, no money, and I ask myself if a person like her needs God or a god to function—"

Andy interrupted. "Back to a subject you were anxious to leave?"

"And I conclude they don't. She can work hard, get an advanced degree if she wants, move to California if she tires of Beaufort County, remarry, or do any number of things. For her, your humanism makes sense. Then I think about poor Hazel Hudgins, utterly defenseless, stabbed to death like some rabid dog, and I wonder where the justice is if divine justice doesn't exist."

"Wasn't that awful? I don't remember a more brutal crime since I've been here, and of all the people to be a victim of it, Hazel deserved it least."

"Agreed," said Dan.

"But why does Hazel need justice?" asked Andy. "It sounds cold to say, but she no longer needs anything. Justice is for those of us left behind, isn't it? I think Claire is in many ways a tougher case than Hazel, who led a full life and was nearing the end of it regardless. Claire, on the other hand, can't do much to change her situation, unlike the young woman you mentioned. Claire is stuck. I have such empathy for her. I've been careful to keep my heathen views to myself around her lately."

"That's thoughtful of you, but is that out of consideration for her or the weakness of your theory where her condition is concerned?"

"Ouch. That was a sharp one."

Dan smiled. "You'll get me back. It's simple justice."

"Damn right I will. By the way, is she pretty?"

"Who?"

"The woman who borrowed your jumpers."

Dan paused. "Very pretty, with character to match if I've read her right." He sipped the last of his drink, a knot in his stomach as Alana's image passed before him. "I'd better be going. Claire will think you've talked me into a trip to Tibet or something."

"No chance. I'm not a mystic, merely an honest, good-hearted sinner who tries to do a little good in the world."

Dan laughed. "If bullshit is a sin, you better pray there is no God."

"By the way," Andy said. "There is something I've been meaning to ask you about your Jury of One idea. It's a touch personal, so feel free to tell me to go to hell, to that hell I just denied exists. If you were that man you sentenced . . . what was his name?"

"Hazzard. Otis Hazzard. I guess you know he died by suicide."

"I read that. Did it surprise you?"

"Not really. A tragic life and a tragic death."

"If you had been in Hazzard's place, would you have done it?"

"You mean would I kill myself?"

"Yes."

Dan rubbed his chin before replying. "I don't know, and isn't that the point? I can try to put myself in Hazzard's shoes, but in the end, it's not possible. The decision is so personal. But I believe in his right to choose it, or mine, for that matter."

They descended the circular stairs. As Andy walked him to the door, Dan paused at the poem hanging on the wall.

"Here are the key lines," Andy said, pointing to a stanza near the end.

*Bradford and I had out the telescope.*
*We spread our two legs as it spread its three,*
*Pointed our thoughts the way we pointed it,*
*And standing at our leisure till the day broke,*
*Said some of the best things we ever said.*

Dan read them, then glanced back at the turret. "I'm not sure these were some of the best things we ever said, but I enjoyed it. Thanks, Andrew the Celestial."

"Any time, Daniel the Just."

# CHAPTER 44

# Blame Game

Jillian had just showered when the call from Glen Coleman arrived.

"What are you doing?" he asked in a chirpy voice. "Missing me, I hope."

"Drying off after a long shower. Can I call you back?"

"Absolutely not. I want to picture you just the way you are."

"You're sick."

"Lovesick, maybe."

"Aww, that's so sweet. Where are you?"

"Boston. I'll be here a while."

"Well, at the risk of puncturing your fantasy balloon, I really do need to get dressed and call you back."

"Yes, do that. I have some thoughts on the Morgan case."

As anxious as she was to hear his thoughts, it was late afternoon, after a full day in court, before she had a chance to return the call. Back at home, she poured herself a glass of chardonnay and walked out to the patio. When the blinds parted in Max Ritter's unit, she took a chair with her back to him.

"So, where are we?" she asked when Glen answered.

"I'm here and you're there, which sucks," he said.

She laughed. "You know what I mean. Where are we with the Morgan case?"

"It's a tough one, babe."

She couldn't remember him calling her babe, and to her mild surprise, she liked it. "Are you in a bar? I hear bar noise in the background."

"Of course. It's after five, isn't it?"

"Morgan?"

"I talked to some of the others who do this work. I told you I'd never seen a case with both front and back entry wounds, but I found a guy that had a similar situation. He did a reconstruction using a dummy with the same height and weight as the victim. In his case, the shot to the chest wasn't enough force to turn him."

She sipped her wine. "Which supports your theory that Toby Morgan was shot in the back first."

"It does and it doesn't. He used a different, less potent caliber bullet and assumed the victim was facing the shooter, whereas Toby was drunk and lurching, so he could have had what amounted to a head start in turning his back to her."

"Or he could have just as easily been lurching the other way."

"True. We'll never know. As a prosecutor, do you have to prove how it happened, or only that it couldn't have happened the way she says it did?"

"I'll need to do some research on that. My gut is that it is a bit like motive. In a murder case, you don't have to prove motive, but juries like to know why something happened, so it always helps. Here, we're going to have to make a strong case for that shot in the back because otherwise it looks like self-defense."

"Sounds like you're closer to a decision to charge her."

"I'm still . . . conflicted. I can't make the case without your testimony, so I'll be relying on your judgment as to whether it's winnable."

"I haven't given up. I'm a pro, remember?"

"When will I see you?" she asked.

"Best guess is a couple of weeks. I miss you."

"Miss you, too."

⊙  ⊙  ⊙

The following evening, Harper Kline introduced Jillian at the local Rotary club. Harper in front of a microphone wasn't risk free. "Listen up, fools," she began. "Tonight, we have an important speaker, so I want all you rednecks, come-heres, Christmas-and-Easter Christians to pay attention." Laughter rippled across the room. "My dear friend and our esteemed solicitor Jillian Pillai is running for a full term to replace Frank Walthall, who you all knew because he was a longtime member of this club. Jillian is smart, she's honest, and she loves her job. After she speaks, each of you is going to contribute to her campaign for two reasons. First, because she's going to impress you as a dedicated public servant who is best qualified for the position. And second, because I'll be standing at the door with my hand out when you leave. Don't even think about telling me you didn't bring your wallet, or you'll mail a check, or you already gave, or any other crazy-ass excuse you can come up with. I know, I know, Rotary is nonpolitical, so if it makes you feel better, you can write SPCA on the memo line, but make the check payable to the Pillai Campaign Fund. All you cheapskates out there better pony up, because I know where you live and I'm coming for more if you try to weasel out of your fair share. Now here's Jillian." The crowd loved it.

Jillian spoke about themes she knew would resonate with the local businessmen, businesswomen, and retirees who comprised the membership. She highlighted a crime rate that made Beaufort one of the safer counties in the state to live and to raise a family.

She praised local law enforcement and the courts, assuring her listeners that when it came to prosecuting criminals, she couldn't ask for more cooperative partners. She talked about how much satisfaction she got from the work she did and closed with a plea for their support.

"Frank Walthall was such an institution in this town. He was not only my boss and my mentor, but he became a friend as well. How do you replace decades of dedicated service like his? How do you compensate for the loss of the experience and judgment he possessed? The answer is you don't. No one can replace Frank Walthall, and that includes my opponent in this race. Frank told me on more than one occasion that when he left office, he hoped I would succeed him. He couldn't have predicted he would leave us so soon, but the confidence he expressed in me inspires me to be the kind of professional prosecutor he was, and I hope you'll give me the opportunity to prove him right by electing me solicitor for a full term." After a round of polite applause, she offered to take questions.

Dot Francis, who owned the flower shop, wanted to know if Jillian saw evidence of gangs in the county. Jillian did not.

Bert Bateman, a pharmacist, asked about drugs. "Marijuana, some cocaine, and more and more oxycontin," she replied.

She fielded the remaining questions with ease until Art Usher, who Jillian knew to be a lieutenant in Jerry Higginson's campaign, stood to ask why she tolerated the presence of illegal aliens like Rodrigo Lopez, who they all knew murdered poor Hazel Hudgins.

She chose her words carefully. "I did not know Hazel as well as most of you, but I feel very personally her loss to this community. By all accounts, she was a wonderful lady. I regret that Mr. Lopez was not convicted. My office and I did the best we could with the evidence available to us. We do not enforce the immigration laws. That is a federal responsibility. It is my understanding—"

Usher, a small, goatish man with a jaw that jutted from his

bony face, cut her off. "We've got that open border down in Texas that lets these people in to kill nice people like Hazel, and no one wants to take responsibility."

"As I said, the federal—"

Usher interrupted again. "Typical politician. Why don't you send the sheriff down there to the migrant trailers to check their papers? Because you don't want to know, that's why. If you did, you'd find out half of them are illegal. Maybe all of them."

Jillian was about to reply when Penny Frost, a part owner of All Green, where Lopez worked, stood. "Just a moment," she said. "I'm as sick about Hazel as the rest of you, and the possibility that one of our employees committed that horrible crime has put me on some medication I never thought I'd have to take, but we do our best to screen out illegals, and we report them to ICE whenever we find one. Lopez had forged papers, and they were damn good forgeries. And you may not want to admit it, but without the Mexicans and Guatemalans, everyone in this room would be doing their own yard maintenance, and that includes you, Art Usher." A smattering of applause erupted as she resumed her seat.

Usher appeared determined to have the last word. "All I'm saying is that we need these illegals prosecuted, and we need someone as solicitor who takes the problem as seriously as I do." And Usher wasn't finished. "Another thing," he said. "You dropped the charges against Lopez, and I know for a fact that someone saw him come out of The Happy Clam that night with blood on his shirt."

"I really can't comment on what any potential witness did or didn't see."

"Yeah? Well, I can. There's a Mexican named Fernandez that has told half the town he saw Lopez that night, that his shirt was bloody, that he had a knife, that he was running like a bat out of hell. And you didn't even make Lopez stand trial. I know Jerry Higginson, and you can be sure he would have made Lopez face a jury."

In her response, Jillian strove for a tone of patient understanding, but her frustration produced something closer to a parent soothing a rowdy toddler. "The decision to prosecute," she explained as Usher turned his back on her to leave the meeting, "is a complex one, taking into account many factors, some of which are judgment calls. We must evaluate available resources, likelihood of a successful outcome, credibility of potential witnesses, and admissibility of evidence, all balanced against the public's right to bring criminals to justice. At times, and the Lopez case was one, those are difficult decisions." She paused, fighting back the urge to lash out and blame Judge Borders. "These are very difficult, complex decisions."

As Jillian received her complementary coffee cup emblazoned with the club logo, she reflected on what had just happened. These good folks were angry and scared and needed someone to hold accountable, and it would be she, not Judge Borders, on the ballot.

Maybe the nolle pross of Lopez had been a mistake. A trial, despite being doomed from the outset, would have sent the message that she would go down fighting. Usher, Higginson, and their crowd could have slammed her for losing, but not for lack of effort.

No, she concluded, a nolle pross made sense. Loss at trial would mean that Lopez could not be tried again should stronger evidence of his guilt surface. The late witness or jailhouse confidant she still harbored hopes of identifying would be as useless as a chandelier on a camping trip.

At the door, Art Usher walked past Harper Kline with a contemptuous sneer, but from the others leaving the meeting, she raised $1,141.

# CHAPTER 45

# The Beer Test

Brock Jamerson placed a call to Andy Prescott. With the possibility of the Borders selection increasing by the day, the paper needed some human-interest background on the maybe chief-justice-to-be. Because Dan had alerted Andy to expect a call, he did, and agreed to be interviewed at his home. Wanda Prescott was away on the morning Jamerson arrived.

After offering coffee, Andy reminded Brock that he was hardly an objective interviewee. "Dan's one of my oldest and dearest friends," he said.

Jamerson responded with a knowing chuckle. "I didn't figure the judge would send me to talk to one of his enemies."

"I don't think he has any," Andy said.

"Come on," Jamerson pleaded with exasperation. "You can't be on the bench that long without making some. Every case has a loser, and surely some of those aren't fans of His Honor."

They sat in the Prescott den. Andy arose to adjust a blind to block the sun in Jamerson's eyes. "There, that's better," he said. Returning to his chair, he said he assumed Jamerson meant the kind of enemy that stalked you or threatened your family. "If you mean disappointed litigants, then, of course, there are those."

"What's he like on a personal basis? Does he pass the beer test?"

"I'm sorry, I don't—"

"Is he the kind of guy you'd enjoy having a beer with?"

"Oh, I see. Most definitely." Andy stood. "I'll pace a bit if it's okay with you. My circulation isn't what it used to be."

Jamerson laughed. "Yeah, mine's not either, and I'm half your age. So what's he like when he's not in court? You must see him often."

"They live just across the way, he and Claire." Andy motioned with his head in the direction of the Borders home. "If I had to describe him, I'd say he was friendly, sincere, dependable, with a good sense of humor. You couldn't ask for a better neighbor or friend."

Jamerson nodded, making notes. "Does he drink?"

"An occasional beer, a cocktail, a glass of wine. I've never seen him drunk, if that's where you're headed."

"And his wife? I've been told she has some health issues."

"Yes, MS. It's no secret. But she is coping well with it and so is he." He glanced toward the house as he paced.

"What does he do for fun?"

"Fly-fish, though not as much as he once did. He was a duck hunter when his son was still at home, but he doesn't do much of that these days. And he loves his boat."

"Tell me about the boat."

Andy paused. "Nice boat. My wife Wanda and I have been on it many times. Sailboat that sleeps four comfortably." Andy grinned, as if in recollection. "He bought it after he won a big case years ago. Named it *Car Pay Diem* after the accident that supplied the money. Clever name, don't you think?"

"So he keeps it here?"

"At a dock not too far. He doesn't go out on it as much because

Claire has trouble getting on and off with her . . . condition."

Jamerson stood. "Thanks for the coffee. Before I go, what do you think of his Jury of One idea? I assume he's discussed it with you?"

Andy ceased pacing. "I'd rather not go into anything we've talked about, but I think it's a splendid concept. In fact, if you've got another minute, I'll show you my clipping file. You'd think I was some kind of groupie, keeping this stuff, but I can't help it. Dan's as close as I'll come to a star." He walked to a mahogany bookcase and from a drawer beneath the lowest shelf took a bulging folder. "Look at this. *New York Times*. And this essay from *The Atlantic* on rethinking end-of-life options. Here's a feature story from San Francisco. My neighbor has begun a national conversation."

"On a very controversial subject," Jamerson added. "By the way, where's that dock you mentioned? I got a couple of photos of his courthouse, and the paper asked me to get some fodder for the files. Figured a shot or two of the boat would check that box."

Andy gave directions to Timber Gate Lane. "The house isn't easy to find because it's set back from the road with lots of privacy vegetation. I can't recall the exact address. Just ask someone for the Gilroy house."

# CHAPTER 46

# No One's Business

On Timber Gate Lane, Jamerson suffered the same indecision that confounded Alana on the night of the shooting. He saw no markings that distinguished one address from another. Rather than wander randomly through yards, he looked for a sign of life. After driving up and down the lane, he caught a glimpse of a woman through the foliage. He parked on the shoulder as the woman, her back to him, opened the trunk of a car.

"Excuse me," Jamerson yelled.

The woman, small and frail, stood on spindle-like legs that might collapse. She turned and took a moment to locate him. "Come closer," she urged, waving him forward.

As he approached, he saw bags of mulch in the trunk. "If you're unloading those, I can help," he offered, thinking some muscle for some information would be a fair trade.

"Praise the Laaawd," she said with an accent Jamerson would have expected to find farther south. "That man at the store put them in, but I had no idea how I'd get them out. No idea what-so-eva. Each one weighs about what I do." Her gray hair scattered in the breeze. From her neck hung glasses from an elastic strap. Fumbling momentarily, she put them on. "There. That's better. I can see you clearly now." She appraised him with eyes that had once been blue but which the rheum of age had watered down, their pupils retaining only a tinge of color.

He picked up a fifty-pound bag. Lifting it to his shoulder, he asked, "Where to?"

She led him to a bed of newly planted hydrangeas. By the fourth trip, he was sweating. "I'm Brock Jamerson," he said, catching his breath. "I report for a Columbia newspaper. Doing a story on Judge Borders. Some personal stuff to fill out his public profile for our readers. I understand he keeps his boat somewhere around here. The Gilroy place?"

"I'm Edna Poindexter." She turned to point a boney finger at the house next door. "The Gilroys live there, though they don't spend much time in South Carolina. I'll bet you didn't know you'd be doing manual labor for an old lady but I sure appreciate your help. Those hydrangeas thank you, too."

"Happy I could help. Do you know the judge?"

"Oh, quite well. I've known him and Claire for years. Their children, too. Ever since he bought that boat, they've been coming here, in the summers mostly. They're lovely folks. After my husband died, they made it a point to invite me to go out with them. We had some wonderful cruises. One weekend, they invited me to go for a sail, but I wasn't home, so I missed it. I hated not being with them because now that the kids are grown and Claire is ill, they don't use the boat much. It wouldn't surprise me if he sold it."

Jamerson raised his eyes above hers to look in the direction she had pointed. "From what I've learned about him, he's not the partying type, so I'm guessing noise from the boat hasn't been a problem over the years." He couldn't think of a more subtle way to inquire about any raucous tendencies, any splatter of mud on the family portrait.

"Oh, good heavens, no. When they were teenagers, the kids would play a radio on deck, but that was pretty much the extent of it. I can still picture them sunning themselves and diving off the stern. Such a happy family. And now it appears he might be our next supreme court chief justice, which makes me happier than I can tell you."

He asked if she thought Dan would make a good justice. "Absolutely," she said. "My late husband always said you could tell a person's character by the way they cared for their boat. Dan is meticulous in that way. In fact, the last time I saw him, after that birthday sail, he came in the late afternoon, just to make sure everything was shipshape, I imagine."

Jamerson took a visual survey of the area surrounding them. Neatly trimmed bushes in well laid out beds complemented a tree he guessed to be fig. "You keep all this up by yourself?"

"Laaawd, no. I use All Green for maintenance, or I used to before Hazel Hudgins was killed. I guess you heard about that?"

He nodded, the sweat on his face now cooling from a breeze. "I happened to be in court the day they tried to link that guy Lopez to the knife."

"Hazel was my dear friend, and when I think of what that Lopez did to her—well, I weep every time I think about it. And it wouldn't surprise me if Lopez had come here to tend my plants. You know he worked for All Green. Me living here alone, it could have been me he stabbed in my own yard!"

"What did you think when he got off?"

"I won't lie . . . it upset me. The law is the law, and I guess Dan had his reasons for doing what he did, but I wish he hadn't."

Jamerson left to take a few photos of *Car Pay Diem*, while Edna went inside to the window in the library on the second floor where she kept an eye on things. She saw Jamerson walk to the end of the dock, step aboard, bend down while shielding his eyes to peer inside the cabin, then retreat back to take his photos at a wider angle. She thought back to the evening she watched Dan carry a bag onto the boat not long before sunset. *He's here to do some maintenance,* she had assumed.

She had gone back to reading until she heard another car pull in. Back at the window, she saw a woman emerge, slam the door, and walk-run rapidly around the house and onto the dock. Edna turned out the library lights for a better view. Dan greeted the new arrival in what appeared from that distance as an embrace. *Is that his daughter, Christina?* No, this woman was older. Edna's curiosity now fully aroused, she lingered at the window. Minutes passed. By the light of the gas grill on the stern, she could make out Dan and the woman raising glasses in a toasting gesture. She picked up the binoculars she kept in the windowsill. *That is definitely not Christina.* When it was dark, they disappeared into the cabin. *None of my business,* Edna thought, as she lit her reading lamp and returned to her book.

She had begun to doze when the slam of a car door jolted her awake. Back to the window, and in enough time to see the car the woman had arrived in throw gravel in its haste to leave. *Maybe an argument,* she had guessed. The woman sped away, and seconds later, Dan followed in his SUV. *How strange,* Edna had thought. The kind of thing she would long remember, but not the kind of thing she would mention to a reporter doing a story on dear Dan Borders. *None of my business, and none of his either.*

☉ ☉ ☉

Jamerson's second stop that day was Jillian Pillai's office. He left his card and asked her secretary to have her call to schedule an interview. "You might mention I was in court for the Lopez hearing."

The secretary lowered her voice. "If I were you, I don't think I'd bring up Lopez."

# CHAPTER 47

# Lost Credibility

Glen arrived early at the San Diego airport for his connecting flight to Charleston. Seated in the boarding area, he played again the voicemail from Samantha. Jillian had asked over Tex-Mex whether he had any college girlfriends she should be jealous of, and he answered honestly that most were married with children. Most, but not all, and Samantha fell into the "but not all" category. She had married one of his fraternity brothers shortly after graduation, then showed up at the five-year reunion single again. Houston, where she lived, became a frequent stop on Glen's travels. Samantha combined smart, sexy, and the best money to be found in Texas, a trust fund lubricated by oil. She could thank her maternal grandfather for that. On a site visit to land he was assured got two drops of rain in a good year and held beneath it "just about that much oil," if any, the old man bought it anyway. Geology surveys showed it likely to play out sometime in the twenty-second century.

Glen could list several reasons why Samantha made sense, reminding himself of those reasons every time he touched down at George Bush Intercontinental. Just when the smoldering commitment embers were about to burst into flame, she uttered a single monosyllabic word that hit like a big bucket of water. "Nope," she said when he raised the question of children. "Not doing that. Already had my tubes tied, and nobody's going to untie them now or ever. I'll be all you can handle and all you'll need. We can get a dog if you're lonesome."

Glen liked dogs but loved children and couldn't envision life without them when the time came. Excuses to stop in Houston turned into excuses to avoid it. Samantha moved on, or he thought she had until she tracked him down in San Diego, where he was lecturing to a group of FBI recruits. They spent a long weekend in an airport hotel sharing some tears, sex, and bad meals. Glen brushed the dust from that list of reasons why she made sense, but the giant "nope" on the other side of the ledger carried more weight. Besides, he had met a woman named Jillian in South Carolina.

He landed on schedule at Charleston International. In a rental car, he headed to Beaufort, his mood along the way buoyed by the pines and oaks San Diego lacked. By deleting Samantha's voicemail, he put her in his rearview mirror, figuratively and literally. Jillian was waiting, and he couldn't get to Beaufort fast enough. Her email earlier in the week promised home-cooked Indian food. While in California, he had worked on the Morgan case because he knew how much was riding on it for her. Pleasing her had unexpectedly become a priority. An extended call to the medical examiner and some supplemental materials fit nicely into an opinion he knew she'd like. He stopped to buy wine and flowers on the way.

She met him at the door with a kiss and a drink. He handed her the bottle and bouquet. "A man bearing gifts," she purred. "What could be better?"

"How about some good news on the Morgan case followed

by that aromatic dinner you promised which, by the way, I could smell from the parking lot."

Jillian adopted her best Southern belle imitation. "Why, Mr. Coleman, you're giving me the vapors."

When he retreated to her bedroom to change into jeans and a pullover, she called from the kitchen to remind him to leave his dirty laundry on the floor and she'd take care of it. As he did so, she stuck her head in the door long enough to ask for his preferred spice level. On a scale of one to ten, with one being wimp and ten being what she called "resurrection hot," he chose eight. *My kind of man*, she thought, though she had thought that often since his last visit.

In the kitchen, she cut the stems and arranged the flowers while he opened a bottle of wine she pointed to. "We'll save yours for dinner," she said. Over a candle-lit table, she offered a toast to his safe return. "Now, what about Morgan? Can't wait to hear it."

Glen leaned back, adopting a philosophical look but with a hint of the cat that swallowed the canary. "Remember that colleague I told you about that had a similar situation, the one who reconstructed a shooting with a dummy he made?"

"Very well."

"I borrowed the basic idea but adapted it to Toby Morgan. It was easy enough for our people to create the dummy from the autopsy and crime scene photos of the body. They even dressed him like Toby. The folks in our lab went all out."

"Because you told them to?" she asked, sipping her wine.

"Because I told them a special lady needed their help."

Jillian laughed. "Okay, cut the crap."

"I brought some images you need to see." He left her long enough to retrieve his laptop from the bedroom. As it booted up, he named the medical examiner as the source of what he was about to show her. "Here are CT scans from the autopsy. This first one is the fatal shot. The wound path runs front to back in more or less a straight line, with entry just above the nipple at the fourth rib. You can see the bullet back there at T4." Glen moved his cursor to the impacted vertebra. "It severed his spinal cord, so even if he had survived, he'd be a mess."

"Wouldn't a bullet go through the dummy?"

"Good question, and that's where it gets a bit trickier. We needed a tissue simulant and used different blocks of ballistic gelatin. Over that, we put three millimeters of neoprene, which is a skin simulant. Using the same .38 ammo your girl used, fired from fifteen feet, which she says was the distance between them, we adjusted the blocks of gelatin until we were able to reproduce the fatal shot. I just don't see a way that shot could turn a one-hundred-eighty-pound man around."

"So, if he came at her straight on, like she said, he most likely fell backwards, faceup, yes?"

"That's how I see it. Then we have this other CT scan of the second bullet. The wound path here isn't straight because it hit bone. The bullet hit him in the back just below the right shoulder, glanced off the top of the scapula. We weren't able to reconstruct the second shot—too many variables."

Jillian studied the scans. "If I'm hearing you right, you can't give me an opinion that the shot in the back came first, as he was walking away, but you can say to a near certainty that her explanation doesn't hold water because the shot to the chest would have put him down."

"There's something else. Remember I asked about the parking lot being paved? I grilled the medical examiner about any dirt or debris in the chest wound. Her report didn't mention any, but I wanted to nail it down. She confirms the absence of anything the average driveway would be made of. Even if it is paved, it's likely to have some loose material on it. And as she said, blood sticks to everything."

Jillian's face registered excitement. "That might tie into something else I've been thinking about. Do we have to prove what happened, or is it enough to show it couldn't have happened as she said it did? You asked me that very question."

"I remember."

"Suppose, just hypothetically, we can show through your shot reconstruction that it couldn't have happened as she said it did. And suppose further that this clean chest wound proves that her account of turning him over couldn't have happened, either. When you combine those two lies with the one about where she was when her daughter's call came in, who would believe her self-defense statement to the investigator or, if she took the stand at trial, her testimony?"

"Her credibility gets lower by the minute."

"Glen, let me ask you this. You've seen a lot of these. What do you think happened? I'm not asking what we can prove happened, but what's your best sense of what went on here?"

"I like the question because it's the right one to be asking. I think she shot him as he walked away."

"I think so, too. Okay, enough shoptalk. You must be getting hungry."

# CHAPTER 48

# Can't Wait

At the table, with Glen's flowers set between them, he looked up long enough to tell her that whatever it was he was eating was "past delicious."

"We call it kadhi pakora. Dumplings in a yogurt sauce. Glad you like it. Cooking is one way my family has stayed connected to our roots. If you think this is good, you should try my mother's salli boti. Curried lamb. I've tried to make it, but I can't duplicate hers. She swears she gave me the whole recipe, but I think there is a spice or two she's holding back."

"I'd love to meet her," he said.

She refilled his wine glass as she stood. "Now for the main course. It's called vindaloo, curried pork. That's what you've been smelling." She returned from the kitchen with a steaming bowl of darkly pungent meat in one hand and a smaller bowl of rice in the other.

With his knife poised over the vindaloo as if he was about to go spearfishing, circling for the perfect victim, he asked if she had reached a decision on prosecuting Alana Morgan.

"Not a final one. I want to close the file."

His face registered surprise. "Oh? I assumed what I put together made the case against her stronger."

"It does. I still want to close this file."

"Why?"

"For two reasons a professional prosecutor shouldn't consider. First, I like her, and I think she did us all a favor, regardless how it happened."

"And second?"

"Remember when you told me you could wait?"

"Sure."

"I'm not certain I can. It will be weeks, maybe months before Alana Morgan can be tried. That's a lot of waiting for both of us, whereas I can close the file now. Tonight. My mother always advised me to play hard to get, so she wouldn't approve of me admitting that."

"You're a professional," he said. "You'll do what's right."

"I'll tell my mother you said that." Reaching for his hand, she said, "I can say this only to you. I desperately want to keep my job, and to do that, I have to find a way to win the election. Without patting myself too much on the back, I would have won handily had it not been for Hazel Hudgins. The Lopez snafu handed an election gift to Jerry Higginson, who is a moron. I need a win, and not just any win, but one that gets me in the papers and on the internet. Like my two reasons for wanting to close the file, charging Alana for political advantage is also bogus."

"I understand your dilemma," he said. "But didn't we agree before we sat down that we think she shot him in the back?"

"We did indeed," she said with a fret.

"Those crime scene photos I mentioned could have been clearer on where she was when she fired the shots. Any chance we could pin that down?"

"I could ask the deputy on the scene if he can be more specific. Or I could ask her. So far, she has cooperated."

Jillian looked up, running splayed fingers through her long black hair. "With your opinion, which is huge, and the life insurance she stood to get, and her big fib about where she was when the call from her daughter came in, I could get her indicted in ten minutes. But would a jury convict her?"

"And if you lose? Not saying you will, but . . ."

"If I lost the Morgan case, I'd be in worse shape. She's a popular teacher. Indicting her would be what the football people call a Hail Mary. I would have to win it. So," she said, inhaling deeply, "in answer to your question, I haven't decided."

# CHAPTER 49

# Playing Defense

I n her office, and not due in court for another hour, Jillian sipped coffee over the morning newspaper, which was getting thinner with less content by the week, or so it seemed.

The lead headline this morning announced the support of state Senator Bradford Bridges for Dan Borders as the next supreme court chief justice. Bridges sprinkled his endorsement with words like "seasoned" and "mature," assuring his constituents of Dan's commitment to "the South Carolina tradition." Of Dan's Jury of One idea, Bridges said little, conceding it was "novel" but insisting "other strengths" had persuaded Bridges to back the judge from Beaufort County.

Jillian pondered the local implications. Her judge appeared headed for appointment. That would mean an upcoming vacancy on the circuit court bench, and she spent a minute running through her mental file of local attorneys who might be in line. Given her near-daily presence in that court, no one had a keener interest in who filled the position. She could list two or three who would be a pleasure to try cases before, and an equal number who could be relied upon to make life difficult for her or, God forbid, for Jerry Higginson.

Thinking back to her most recent discussion of the Morgan matter with Glen, she called the only number she had for Alana Morgan. The call went to voicemail. "Good morning, Ms. Morgan, this is Jillian Pillai with the solicitor's office. Before we close the file on your ex-husband's death, one of our investigators would like to meet with you at your former home in Seabrook to go over a few things. I appreciate the help you've given us in sorting out the facts, and hope you'll agree to this request. It shouldn't take much time, and we can schedule it at your convenience. Please call me at the number on the card I gave you when you came to my office. Thank you."

Two days passed before Jillian received a reply, which also came by voicemail. "Hello, Ms. Pillai. This is Alana Morgan. Please direct all further communication on Toby's death to my attorney, Joe Roan. I'm sure you know how to reach him. Thank you."

*Well*, thought Jillian, *that is an interesting turn of events. Perhaps Alana anticipates being indicted, and perhaps she was right.* The grand jury met the following week, giving Jillian just enough time to draw up a bill of indictment. Glen's availability to appear before a grand jury would assure the result Jillian expected. All that remained was for her to pull the metaphorical trigger.

Still, she wavered. Roan was an experienced defense attorney who could be relied upon to call an expert of his own, and that expert could be relied upon to dispute Glen's testimony. Roan would demand a jury, which was his right. Defense lawyers with guilty clients wanted a jury, confident they could convince at least one juror to find reasonable doubt. And that was all it took.

And then there was the matter of celibacy with Glen, at least until the trial was over. He would now be her expert witness, and she had to keep their relationship on a professional footing. Her instincts told her this might be the real thing. Her mood brightened when she saw him, and when he left, she felt a momentary panic she would never see him again. No man had ever come close to affecting her that way, and if that wasn't love, she didn't know what to call it.

But in addition to Glen's charms, she knew him to be an excellent witness. He could sell snow to the Eskimos, as the expression went. With him as her star witness, she liked her chances in front of a jury. And she repeated to herself again and again during the weekend of her decision that she needed a win.

Over Indian food on Sunday evening, she told him she had reached the decision to indict Alana Morgan. "And," she added, "at the risk of complicating things, I'm getting awfully attached to you."

He held her stare as if she had offered him a gift. When he left after a dessert of kheer, a sumptuous rice pudding, she called her mother.

"Mom, I think I may have met *the* one."

"Well," said her mother in a tone that left Jillian momentarily wondering if it was "*Well, it's about time*," or "*Well, your father and I have been afraid of this*."

"Well," her mother continued, "this is a first. Tell me about him."

A week later, the newspaper headline and story, "Local Teacher Indicted for Murder," became the only topic of conversation in the county. It featured a faculty photo of Alana taken from the high school yearbook along with a grainy black and white of the driveway of her Seabrook home.

In the Borders home, Claire saw the story first. "Dan," she called out, "they've indicted that Morgan woman. The teacher. Isn't she the one you've been working with on the monument controversy?"

From an adjoining room, Dan found his voice in time to say, "Yes, the same. I'm sorry to hear that. She's had a tough time, and she seems like a nice person."

CHAPTER 50

# The Final Straw

$A$sked for comment on the indictment, Joe Roan was quoted as calling it, "a sad case of prosecutorial abuse," and that his client was guilty of nothing more than protecting herself and her young daughter from an abusive, drunken brute.

Dan read the paper's account of Alana's indictment like a man listening to his doctor explaining biopsy results and discussing treatment options. The only good outcome of this nightmare—a decision not to charge Alana—had been eliminated. Now he and she faced two possibilities, each spelling disaster. The first was that her case would be assigned to the other circuit judge. In assuring her that he would try her case should she be charged, Dan had promised more than he could deliver with full confidence because of the way cases were assigned to judges. To spread the workload evenly among the circuit court judges, clerks assigned new cases to the next judge in the rotation. At the beginning of a new court term, each judge was given a docket of the cases assigned to him or her. The chances were therefore one in two that Alana's case would be assigned to the other judge, a judicial lottery that Dan could not afford to lose but was powerless to affect.

But winning the judicial lottery meant he would have to sit in judgment of Alana, an outcome he had dreaded. By any standard of judicial ethics, he must recuse himself, thereby allowing his colleague to try the case. But to remove himself from the outcome violated the promise he had made to Alana that night. *Will she keep me out of it?*

Roan could be counted on to advise her early, probably in their first meeting, that to adequately defend her, she needed to tell him everything, and that whatever she told him was protected by the attorney-client relationship. Full disclosure by her was essential, he would stress, to avoid surprises sprung on him at trial. Dan Borders had given the same advice to defendants he represented before his elevation to the bench.

For two weeks, Dan sweated like that patient whose doctor kept postponing their appointment to discuss his biopsy results. Unable to eat, he lost weight, leading Claire to suggest that he needed medical attention and to observe, only half in jest and with some impatience, that "we can't both be invalids."

At the beginning of the third week, the docket for the new term showed Alana's case assigned to Judge Dana Highsmith. Dan felt both relief and dread. To lose control of this case was to lose whatever small control he had left of his life and his future. He picked up the docket sheet and walked to the clerk's office, where he asked Circuit Court Clerk Vivian Patterson if she could spare a few minutes.

Jillian saw the assignment of *State v. Morgan* to Judge Dana Highsmith as an answer to a small prayer. Highsmith, a petite woman in her early forties, had been on the bench only two years, having come from a practice focused on insurance defense. Despite limited exposure to criminal law and no trials as a defense attorney, she had shown herself to be a quick study once on the bench. Jillian's experience in front of her had been positive with rulings that some members of the local bar perceived as biased toward prosecutions. In Jillian's mind, chances for convicting Alana Morgan improved the moment she saw Judge Highsmith's name on the new docket sheet.

In the middle of Jillian's preparation for trial, she received a note from Vivian Patterson informing her that the Morgan case had been reassigned to Judge Borders. She promptly confronted Patterson, who instructed her in none-too-friendly terms to "take it up with the judge." After consulting Judge Highsmith, who denied any role in the change and indeed did not know of it until Jillian showed her Patterson's note, Jillian sought a meeting with Judge Borders "on a matter related to the Morgan case." He declined.

His refusal to meet supplied the veritable "last straw" for Jillian, who still seethed over the Lopez case, convinced Judge Borders got it wrong by his search and seizure ruling. An adverse ruling in the Morgan case, on the admission of her evidence and particularly rulings related to her expert, Glen Coleman, could cost her a conviction. And if Judge Borders refused to meet with her to explain the reassignment of the case from Judge Highsmith, he would have no choice but to give that explanation in response to a motion she planned to file.

From her bookshelf, heavy with musty old copies of the *South Carolina Reports*, she took a copy of the Rules of Civil and Criminal Procedure and turned to the rule governing judges.

Canon 3E(1): Disqualification. A judge shall disqualify himself or herself in a proceeding in which the judge's impartiality might reasonably be questioned, including but not limited to instances where (a) the judge has a personal bias or prejudice concerning a party or a party's lawyer, or personal knowledge of disputed evidentiary facts concerning the proceeding.

On what basis could she get Dan Borders disqualified? Her first inclination was to zero in on his relationship with Joe Roan. If she could establish a repeated acquittal of Roan's clients, it might show "personal bias or prejudice." She asked the clerk to bring her the file on every criminal case in which Roan had represented the defendant while Judge Borders presided. Over the course of several days, she examined all seventy-eight files. After setting aside those rare cases in which Roan pleaded his client guilty, she found sixty-one convictions to eleven acquittals. While Roan's success ratio might have been better than most of his competitors, it hardly established a pattern of sweetheart rulings in his favor. So much for that theory.

# CHAPTER 51

# Standard Procedure

The prospect of establishing a personal bias or prejudice in favor of Alana Morgan seemed at first to be remote at best. As far as Jillian was aware, the judge and the defendant didn't know each other and had never met. An internet search led her to a Facebook comment by Frances Mellencamp, a member of the Historical Society, which in turn led her to the Society's Facebook page. There she learned that Frances served on a subcommittee comprised of Alana Morgan, Judge Dan Borders, and a man named Randal Stephens. Jillian tracked down Stephens and spoke to him by phone.

"I don't like to throw dirt on nobody," Stephens said. "You know what I mean?"

She did.

"I mean, it's a free country, and everybody's got a right to their opinion."

"Go on," Jillian urged.

"Them two, the judge and the teacher, Miss Morgan, they got some radical ideas where our monument is concerned. She strikes me as one of them pointy-head liberals, and Lord only knows what she's teaching them kids."

"You meet with them?" Jillian asked.

"Sometimes. Sometimes I gotta work. You might want to call Darling Moore, our president. She's as upset about this monument business as the rest of us."

"Where do you meet?"

"Library."

The public library stood two blocks from the courthouse, so Jillian walked. There she confirmed that on various occasions Judge Borders and Alana Morgan met in the small conference room, with and without Randal Stephens. Then she called Darling Moore.

"Well," said Darling in breathless confidence, "I am the last person in this county to spread gossip, but I do believe our judge and this teacher are soulmates when it comes to that sacred monument. She joined our organization, and in the first meeting, the very first meeting, she spouts this hairbrained idea." But no, she had never seen the two together anywhere except the library, and no, she had no reason to think there was anything "going on" with them. "With Dan Borders? Don't be silly," she told Jillian.

When Jillian filed her motion to disqualify based on a personal bias by Judge Borders in favor of Alana Morgan, it cited, "personal friendship and mutual philosophical alignment of interests where matters related to the county's history were concerned, thereby creating an appearance of impropriety." Joe Roan promptly filed his objection. The hearing on Jillian's motion was set for three in the afternoon.

The courtroom was empty except for court personnel when Joe Roan and Alana entered, taking their seats at the defense table. Jillian stood stiffly at her table, as if anticipating a backlash from her motion. Moments later, Judge Borders took the bench. He avoided eye contact with Alana, though he could feel her eyes on him. He had not seen her in weeks, nor had they spoken.

"I must tell you, Ms. Pillai," said Judge Borders in a voice of reasoned tolerance, "that I was quite surprised to get this pleading."

She replied, "With all due respect, Your Honor, I was quite surprised to learn this case had been transferred from Judge Highsmith. I assure you it is nothing personal and that it was filed only after careful deliberation."

The judge nodded, then turned his head toward Joe Roan. "Mr. Roan, do you wish to be heard?" When Roan stood, the judge gazed at Alana, who sat with her hands folded in her lap and an expression of assured tranquility. Their eyes met for a millisecond, confirmation of the other's affection. *This would work out*, they seemed to say.

"I've noted my opposition, Your Honor," Joe Roan said. "I'll leave it at that and to the court's discretion."

Judge Borders nodded again. "Ms. Pillai, your duty is to represent the people of the state to the best of your ability and judgment, and I will extend to you the benefit of the doubt that these were your motivations. In a jurisdiction as small as this one, I am often called upon to judge people I know. At times it seems most of the litigants who come before me are known to me, often as friends. Between church affiliations, civic duties, and my lifelong presence in the county, I know just about everyone. If I disqualified myself on those occasions, I'd preside over very few cases. Several years ago, I tried a case brought by the fisheries and game folks that involved a man I'd fished with for twenty years. Two members of my wife's bridge club fell out over a contract, friends we'd known for years. The list goes on. The test is not whether I know one of the litigants but whether knowing them would prejudice me for or against them.

"As a practicing attorney, I was once sued by a client who wasn't happy with a result. There was no merit to his suit, and it was dismissed, but when my former client came before me in my capacity as a judge, I recused myself to avoid even the appearance of a prejudice against him. I honestly felt I could have tried the case without holding his suit against him, but in that instance, discretion dictated that I remove myself.

"I do know Ms. Morgan, as you suggest. We have worked together at the Historical Society on a matter of interest to the county. It goes without saying that this is volunteer, unpaid service. She invited me to speak to her class at Beaufort High. Outside of those two instances—work on behalf of the society and my Law Day lecture—I don't think I've had any personal contact with her."

Jillian shifted her gaze to the paper on her desk. Without looking up, she said, "My motion also references the change of judges. This case was initially assigned to Judge Highsmith. Why is it now in front of you?" She lifted her eyes to Dan's, as if to point two focused, accusatory beams of suspicion.

"I appreciate your confusion, Ms. Pillai. You are still relatively new to our procedures here, where there is a well-established pattern of judges retaining jurisdiction over cases involving litigants that have previously appeared before them. I use the term 'previously appeared' advisedly. Ms. Morgan was a litigant in a divorce I entered in 2002, and because it was done by deposition, we never met face-to-face. Nevertheless, I granted her a divorce and therefore concluded I should try the current case based on having previously decided a case in which she was a litigant."

Jillian nodded, conveying that she wasn't buying any of it. "That strikes the state as quite a reach, sir. A 2002 divorce?"

"Reach or not, I instructed Ms. Patterson to follow what I consider standard procedure here. Your motion is denied."

# CHAPTER 52

# A Knowing Stare

Longtime residents noticed the changes in their town in the weeks leading up to the Alana Morgan trial. Beaufort's dependable, pastoral pace had been replaced by something closer to the annual state fair without the livestock competitions. Sidewalks usually as abandoned as cemetery paths leading to seldom visited graves now pointed an increasing number of visitors toward the courthouse. The closer Judge Dan Borders's appointment to the supreme court came, the more opponents to his Jury of One concept arrived to register their displeasure.

Dan knew that on one level, the practical one, this made no sense. Should he be appointed, his power to bring about the death chamber he advocated would be zero. Such a radical change to the state's incarceration policy required major legislative action, highly unlikely in the immediate future. And if, against the odds, it passed, it was theoretically possible that the South Carolina Supreme Court on which he would sit would be called upon on some distant day to opine on various challenges to its constitutionality, as such challenges surely would be brought. But to rally opposition now in his small town seemed the equivalent of protesting a high school science class on the grounds that it could eventually lead a student to perfect cloning. Cause and effect were simply too remote.

He knew, however, that on another level, that of modern America, the controversy made sense. People felt powerless to stop changes all around them, changes that foretold a far different future, if not for themselves then for their grandchildren. This anger at their own impotence drove them to all manners of aberrant behavior, from storming school board meetings to online rants and manifestos. More people seemed to be asking, "Who do I see to stop this?" or "Where can I go to get my complaint heard?" He and his small hometown were neither the person nor the place for answers, but they were both as close as some could come, so come they did.

Death penalty supporters espoused the theory that society, and not the convicted life-without-parole Jury of One individual, had the right to say who lived and who died. To take that decision from juries, they argued, abrogated one of the most fundamental protections enjoyed by law-abiding citizens. A few death penalty opponents came, too. They argued in what they admitted to be counterintuitive logic that consigning the decision to die to inmates would lead to more deaths, not fewer. Nuns came all the way from a monastery in Travelers Rest, wearing their habits in lieu of signs protesting their opposition to suicide in any form and for any purpose. Paid employees of a national association of nursing homes came to protect the industry's bottom line, lest the Jury of One concept accelerate the right-to-die and assisted suicide trends gathering increased public acceptance. Cynics came to accuse those same nursing homes of warehousing people in a vegetative state to collect their rents.

Over a period of weeks, the presence of these folks, young and old, in shops and along the sidewalks, created a small storm in Beaufort. Through it all, Dan tried to stay invisible except in court and on the rare occasions when he walked to a local café for lunch.

During a court recess, he walked to the Seabiscuit for soup and salad. He passed a street preacher standing on a homemade box bellowing scripture. A block from the courthouse, an elderly nun passed. Her pious face flared in recognition. She grabbed the arm of the nun walking with her, and together they caught up with him at the curb.

"You're the judge," she said kindly. "Judge Borders. I've seen your picture in the paper."

"Hello, sisters. How are you?"

"Couldn't be better. It's the Lord's day, and we are glad in it. I just want you to know that I pray for you. Being a judge can't be easy. At the monastery, we make it a point not to judge, but you don't have a choice, do you?"

Touched by her empathy, Dan gave her a boyish grin. "As they say, it comes with the territory."

She placed an enfeebled hand on his forearm. "You're a busy man, and I won't hold you up. Just remember there is help for those hard decisions. He is only a prayer away. God bless you in your work."

"And you in yours, sister. And thank you for speaking with me."

It was nearly one-thirty, and the lunch crowd had largely dispersed. At his request, the hostess seated him in a booth at the back. Just as he finished ordering, he looked up to see Joe Roan and Alana enter. They took a table near the front, and when seated, he could see both clearly. Roan's office was a block from the restaurant, so it didn't strike Dan as remarkable that an attorney and his client would be having lunch nearby. What did stir him was the lighthearted banter they engaged in as they perused their menus, ordered their meals, and waited. Dan's view of her was in profile, and she was obviously unaware of his presence. Nothing in her demeanor suggested she would soon go on trial for murder. She chatted as she might have with a girlfriend, smiling often and gesturing with both hands in conversation he was not close enough to hear. Joe Roan, wearing no tie, appeared equally relaxed.

What did their cavalier attitudes portend? *Possibly,* Dan reasoned, *no, certainty of an acquittal.* Alana must have assured Roan she had no reason to worry, but how could she have explained such confidence? No jury had been selected, so there was zero possibility she knew someone on it that could be counted on, even if eleven others disagreed. Maybe Roan had found an expert witness with compelling testimony. Or perhaps they were relying on a legal or evidentiary flaw they had spotted in the prosecution's anticipated case. Or, God forbid, Alana had told Roan about Dan.

As his soup went from hot to cold, Dan stared at her. *She really is very pretty,* he thought, with looks enhanced by a charming, indefinable allure that had attracted him from their first discussions of a Confederate monument. And beyond that appeal, she seemed to "get him," understand emotions that he held close. At that moment, he envied Joe Roan, in full knowledge that the fateful, ill-advised night on the boat and the shooting that followed sealed him off from any possibility of a casual lunch with her, soon or ever. *I should hate her,* he told himself, *for all she could cost me.* Yet no sooner had the thought entered his head than it was replaced by the reality that the one he should hate was himself. Despite his assurance to her that "it would all work out," he doubted it would.

Roan pushed back from the table and left for the restroom. As Alana's gaze roamed the room, her eyes fell on Dan. She held his stare, a stare that might have come from across the room at a reunion of once-close classmates after a long separation, a flicker of recognition before some forgotten hurt resurfaced. It was a stare that said, "I know you, or I always thought I did." There was tension in it but also tenderness, with each sorting out what it meant through the prism of their shared experience. Without words, he tried to convey his profound regret that so much of what she had overcome, her bootstrapped efforts to raise herself up, now seemed in jeopardy. Toby, an anchor to all her ambitions in life, now threatened in death to pull her under. *You don't deserve this*, Dan thought.

*Nor do you*, Alana's gaze seemed to say. *To keep your promise to me, you'll have to betray all the values that define you. Every one of them.*

Roan's return broke the stare.

# CHAPTER 53

# Another Romance

Reporter Brock Jamerson called ahead to confirm his appointment with Jillian to avoid a fruitless return to Beaufort. She greeted him in her outer office when he arrived. This late in the afternoon, the courthouse was quiet, when closing doors echoed throughout the building. A new courthouse, under construction just down the street, gave the old one a feel of temporary space. Stacks of banker's boxes loaded with files attested to the move in the not-too-distant future.

"Welcome, Mr. Jamerson," Jillian said, shaking his hand. "It's not every day we get a visit from the Columbia press."

"Call me Brock."

"Then Brock, please step into my office." When he did, she left her door open, seating herself behind her desk. "So, you wish to talk about Judge Borders?"

"I do, but before we get into that, I'd like to talk about you. You're on the ballot in a few weeks. How's it looking?"

"I'm optimistic. It's stressful, I admit. I've never been through a campaign before except for Frank's, my predecessor's. I had just joined the office, and you could hardly call his a campaign because he had no opposition. Did you ever meet him?"

"Never had the pleasure. What's your opinion of your opponent, Jerry Higginson?"

"On or off the record?"

"First on. Something I can print."

"Okay, how's this? 'I welcome the competition. He's a nice person, but I believe I'd do a better job.'"

"And off the record?"

"He can't make a living in private practice and needs a steady paycheck."

Jamerson smiled. "There are a few of those in this state."

"But I am not one," Jillian said. "I happen to love prosecuting and have no interest in private practice."

Jamerson scribbled a note. "Any chance you might one day aim for higher office? Being so young, you've got a big head start."

Jillian laughed. "I'm young, true, but not so young that I would answer that one."

"I've seen you work. Are you aware of that?"

"No. When?"

"I came down for the Lopez hearing because our judge was news with his Jury of One idea, and he's still news, as you know."

Jillian took a deep breath and let the air out slowly. "Lopez. My Waterloo. Don't print that. It sounds too defeatist."

"Okay, I won't. It was a tough setback, and I've sat through a lot of them. For what it's worth, you did a good job."

"Thank you. I felt like I should have won."

"Borders's ruling on the knife was a killer, no pun intended. Any hard feelings about the judge?"

"At the time, yes. I've mellowed. I've also done some additional research. As much as I hate to admit it, he may have been right on the law."

He eyed her skeptically. "Oh? I read the motion you filed to disqualify him from the Morgan case. Some might see retaliation in that."

"I hope he doesn't see it that way. That was not my intent."

Jamerson shifted in his chair. "I couldn't make it for the hearing. Did he explain his decision not to recuse himself?"

"He tried. He entered her divorce a few years back and claimed that gave him the right to try this case. And he said he knew her from work on behalf of the Historical Society. That their only contacts had been at the library to discuss the possible removal of the Confederate monument from the courthouse grounds. Oh, and he spoke to her class at the high school. If he disqualified himself from every case in which he knew one party or the other, he'd never try a case. I suppose he has a point there. He knows pretty much everyone."

Jamerson's face registered doubt. "You're sure he said their only contact was at the library?"

"And the high school. He was adamant about that. Why?"

"When Alana Morgan was indicted, I saw her photo and knew I'd seen her somewhere before. It was here, in court, for the Lopez hearing. She was sitting near me. She's the kind of woman you don't forget."

"Well, if she was there, I've forgotten her, but I had a few things on my mind that day. Maybe the judge didn't notice her either. The courtroom was packed."

Jamerson nodded. "You're probably too young to remember Turner & Feinberg, the department store. They went out of business years ago, so I was surprised to see the Morgan woman with one of their shopping bags that day. I followed her to the clerk's office and was standing behind her when she asked to see the judge on what she called a personal matter."

"Oh? Are you telling me she met with Judge Borders?"

"I didn't see her enter his chambers or see them meet. But

later, as I was about to leave, I saw the judge carrying the same bag to his car. Wonder what was in it?"

Jillian's eyes narrowed. She drummed her fingers on her desk as she thought through it. "I guess it's possible she gave it to someone to deliver to the judge. Still, it's curious. Maybe she met with him and he forgot."

Jamerson scoffed audibly. "I wouldn't have forgotten . . . I can swear to that. Anyway, I know you're preparing for the Morgan trial, so I'll get out of your hair. I'll be there, incidentally."

"You're coming down from Columbia?"

"Like I said, the judge is news. His chances for the big court seem to be improving. I'll see you there. How do you like your chances of a conviction?"

She smiled. "I wouldn't have indicted her if I didn't think I could win. Still, you never know what a jury will do."

Jamerson stood to leave. Halfway to the door, he turned back. "By the way, and this question is off that record we talked about. I interviewed Joe Roan about the judge months ago, and now I see he's representing Alana Morgan. I've done some nosing around. Have you heard anything about them being an item?"

Jillian's mouth parted faintly in surprise. "Roan and Alana Morgan? As in, romance?"

"Yeah. That's the rumor. You didn't hear it from me."

# CHAPTER 54

# Wasp Attack

On the morning the Morgan trial was scheduled to begin, Claire Borders fixed a big breakfast in anticipation of Dan's long day ahead, but he had no appetite, moving scrambled eggs with his fork after a couple of bites. With ample time to read and watch television, she had homed in on *"Local teacher charged with murder"* as she might have followed a soap opera, prodding Dan to share any gossip from the courthouse.

"I really can't talk about it, Claire."

"Well, I understand you can't talk about the case, but can you at least talk about her? All you've said is that she showed some courage in proposing that the monument be moved. What's she like? Is she the kind of person who could kill her ex?"

When he didn't answer, she continued. "I have to think that insurance policy has something to do with it. Teachers make so little money." News of the insurance policy had hit on the day scheduled for Claire's bridge club, where speculations and predictions on Alana's fate fit nicely between no-trump bidding, crabmeat canapes with trimmed crust, and sherry.

Dan discarded his napkin onto the table and stood. "I need to go."

"I thought I might drop in on some of the trial. Would that bother you?"

"It's been a long time since you came to watch me work. Why today?"

"Because I'm so curious to see what she looks like in person, how she acts. I hear she's very pretty, which you wouldn't know from that picture in the paper."

"Suit yourself. If you come, I'll see you there. If not, I'll see you tonight."

The marsh around Distant Island had begun its annual pilgrimage into winter. On stalks of spartina grass, a rising tide of brown inched toward the green of summer like doom replacing hope, or so it appeared to Dan through his gloom and pessimism about today's trial.

From his first day as a judge, Dan had donned his black robe with a priestly reverence for the responsibility it invested. As a boy, like most boys, he passed through a stage of superhero absorption. Muscled men with capes brought justice to capeless masses too weak or too frightened to defeat evil, in the same way a judicial robe cloaked him with powers not to be entrusted to ordinary citizens. With that power came responsibility, the weightiest of which was to decide. Sitting at his desk in a shirt and tie, he possessed the same power, but putting on the robe authenticated it to those who would appear before him that day, and to himself.

That morning in his chambers, with the Morgan trial set to begin, the robe that had always been a source of extra strength hid weakness. It covered up his dinner on the boat and all that came after. As he put it on, it weighed him down, as if the cotton had absorbed within its folds Toby's death and all the lies that were demanded to keep Dan's role in it secret.

After buttoning his robe, Dan turned to the window behind his desk. Trees visible from it furnished a living calendar of sorts, fall foliage being his favorite. Today, storm clouds on the eastern horizon promised autumnal winds that would sweep yellow and gold leaves from their branches. He had stood here many times before, taking a quick inventory of the cases on his docket but also reflecting, however briefly, on the need to be attentive and impartial. He stared at the trees in the distance. Some of them had been saplings when he first entered this office. He liked to think that he, like them, had grown in the interval, but this morning, he faced the reality.

As he stared, a wasp hovered in his line of sight. After a minute, it landed on the muntin, peering inside. It slowly made its way from one side of the pane to the other, as if seeking a point of entry. Dan couldn't remember seeing a wasp behave like that. After returning to its landing spot, it lifted off but resumed its hover. Now it began attacking the glass, flying with increasing force against it. It was as if it had decided that the only access to Dan's office, and to Dan, would be through the glass. Each assault brought a fresh impact, a more determined dive or thrust. *Why is it doing this?* Dan wondered. *What is driving this futile insistence?*

He came back to the decision that haunted his waking hours and refused to let him sleep. A prescribed sleeping pill left him too groggy to function. The flask he kept in his nightstand helped him fall asleep but not stay there. His clerk had commented on his weight loss. Some extra gray in his brush caused him to wonder if his hair was thinning due to stress. How many times had he walked the floor at night dreaming up creative ways to contact Alana without being seen or leaving a trace? He could ask her, "Are we still good?" and she would know what he meant. If she said yes, maybe he could sleep. He felt fatally trapped.

He had two options—either recuse himself or try the case. The right choice was obvious; the difficulty came in making it. He knew with indwelling certainty he should take the bench to announce that he could not try Alana Morgan and that, for unspoken reasons and after "due consideration," he was reversing his prior decision and recusing himself. It would all be over in a minute.

But it wouldn't be over. In a minute or perhaps a lifetime. He had promised her, and himself, that if she stayed silent on the events of that night, it would all work out. He owed her that.

*But come on,* he thought. *Who was he protecting?* Recusing himself blew them both up. Had their dinner on the boat become public, he could rightly have been accused of a flagrant indiscretion, but no more. Claire would have been shocked, so managing things at home would have been a challenge. Publicity would have been negative but survivable. Fatal to his supreme court chances? Maybe. What was the old joke about Murphy's Law? What could go wrong that night did go wrong—hardly a joke. *"Trouble comes from the direction you least expect it."* He could hear his mother saying that. And what, he wondered for the thousandth time, had Alana Morgan told Joe Roan? Roan could be sitting in court this very minute in full knowledge of everything that happened.

Roan would know Judge Borders's indisputable obligation to recuse, his violation of every judicial ethic by trying this case.

Dan thought about one of his favorite films, *A Man for All Seasons,* in which Sir Thomas More refused to give oath acknowledging Henry VIII as the supreme head of the church, knowing such refusal meant death for treason. What was the harm, More's family and friends asked? Oaths are just words, nothing more. They can be disavowed inwardly as they are spoken outwardly. Save yourself, Thomas! Take the oath, they had urged. At his beheading, More ascribed to God's will his reason for eschewing the oath, but Dan felt the oath went beyond God, that More came to a deeper secular reckoning between the man More considered himself to be and the man others would have him be. It wasn't God's will, but More's, who found itself unable to cast aside the essence of personal integrity, even upon pain of seeing life ended.

It pained Dan that he could not find More's courage within himself. He roused from his reverie beside the window in time to see the wasp take another furious run at the windowpane. Glass protected him, and it was time for him to protect Alana, as he had promised. And protect himself. He headed to the door leading to his courtroom.

# CHAPTER 55

# A Surprise

From his chair behind the bench, Judge Borders looked out at a courtroom lacking a single vacant seat, the crowd swelled by the number of prospective jurors. At the defense table, Joe Roan and Alana Morgan sat patiently. Roan made notes on a legal pad, occasionally glancing behind him as if seeking someone in the audience. A witness, perhaps? A handkerchief, vibrant red, sprouted from his charcoal-gray breast pocket and matched his tie. Alana, her hands folded in her lap, wore a simple navy dress, as appropriate for church as for court. A small gold cross hung from a necklace. She stared at Dan with a look that conveyed neither confidence nor concern, as bloodlessly dispassionate as a mannequin. At the prosecution's table, Jillian Pillai's steely gaze suggested a take-no-prisoners mood.

As soon as the clerk called the case, the state against Morgan, Joe Roan stood. "Your Honor, I must begin this morning with an apology to the court and to the prosecution for what I realize will be an inconvenience. Some recent developments have caused my client and me to revisit the matter of a trial by jury. I'm aware we demanded one initially and that prospective jurors have been summoned today because of that demand, but the change was unavoidable. My client desires to waive a jury and have the matter tried by the court. To the extent the state has been inconvenienced and that needless expense has been incurred because of this last-minute decision, we are indeed sorry." As Roan resumed his seat, Alana continued to stare straight ahead.

Judge Borders kept his eyes focused on Roan. "As counsel is well aware, court approval of the proposed change requires acquiescence by the prosecution." Then, shifting his gaze to Jillian, he asked, "Ms. Pillai, what is the state's position?"

Jillian stood, hesitating, as if prisoners might have to be taken after all. "I request a recess to consider our response, Your Honor."

"Request granted. Will fifteen minutes be enough?"

Jillian returned to her office to consider her options, the most obvious of which was to withhold her consent. But why would Roan waive a jury in a case like this? With no witnesses to the alleged crime, it would likely be decided by expert testimony and the credibility of the defendant should she choose to testify. Roan was cocky enough to believe he could convince at least one juror of damn near anything, and one was all he needed. It made no sense, at least to Jillian.

And because it made no sense, she naturally assumed she was missing something. Roan enjoyed a reputation as a crafty, skilled lawyer, while Jillian was still learning the ropes. Was this some kind of trap? Some checkmate tactic that Jillian in her naivete and inexperience had never heard of? She had tried only a few cases in front of a jury, while Roan had litigated dozens. Would Frank Walthall have scoffed at Roan's waiver, a scoff that would have said, in essence, "Oh, that old ploy. I see what you're doing, and I'm not falling for it." For reasons Jillian couldn't discern or guess, waiving a jury was in Roan's client's best interest. Maybe that alone was reason enough to withhold her consent.

Like Roan, she had a right to demand a jury, but such demands by the prosecution were rare. Jillian and those in her position usually reserved that option for drug cases, as leverage against defense counsel in negotiations over a plea deal. Too many jurors in Beaufort County and elsewhere coped with the damage to their friends and families caused by drugs. Guilty users and pushers went out of their way to avoid the wrath of such jurors, who were inclined to put their heads on spikes as a warning to others. Far better to plead guilty for a short stay in the local slammer than to play the penitentiary lottery with a jury.

Consenting to Roan's request would leave guilt or acquittal solely in the hands of Judge Borders. Did she want that? Yes, she'd been severely disappointed by his evidentiary ruling in Lopez, and as much as it pained her to admit it, she had come to believe he might have been right on the law. Based on his comments to her after that case, he may well have convicted Lopez had the knife been admissible into evidence and had the decision been up to him instead of a jury. Should she try to persuade a dozen jurors of Alana's guilt, or take her chances with a single judge? How much confidence could she have in Judge Borders? It came down to that. Something Frank Walthall said more than once came to mind. *"If there's anything Judge Borders can't stand, it's a liar. When defendants lie to him, they dig their graves deeper."* Jillian was confident in her ability to satisfy the judge that Alana was a liar. She could hear the ghost of Frank Walthall telling her to trust him.

Jillian's other option was to renew her motion to have the judge disqualified from the case. He had explicitly represented in the hearing that his contact with Alana had been limited to library sessions discussing the monument and his Law Day talk. According to Brock Jamerson, who was sitting in the front row today and therefore available as a witness, Alana had delivered a shopping bag personally at this very courthouse, a bag he was seen carrying a short time later. But what proof did she have that they met on that occasion? Jamerson didn't see them exchange the bag.

He acknowledged the possibility that she delivered it to a clerk or secretary, who in turn delivered it to Borders. Maybe they met in a hallway, briefly exchanged greetings and the bag, and he simply forgot? To challenge him a second time, and on such flimsy proof, risked offending the judge about to preside over a trial she needed to win.

While Jillian pondered, Judge Borders returned to his chambers. The wasp, he noticed, was gone. As soon as he was seated, a clerk asked if he had time to take a call from Kennedy Mosby. "I'll make time," he said.

◉ ◉ ◉

Mosby greeted him in something of a conspiratorial whisper. "Good morning, Judge. Picked up some chatter in the capitol today that I thought I'd pass along. Tom Wentworth stopped me in the hallway to tell me he's decided to support you for the court, but he doesn't want that word out. He's got a revolt on his committee from some old timers who feel loyal to Sidney Callahan. If the vote were held today, Tom tells me Callahan would be the pick. He's postponing that vote so he can meet individually with several he thinks he has a chance of bringing around."

"I see," said Dan. "Anything I can do?"

"Stay positive and hope for the best. I didn't want you to be blindsided in the event this hits the press."

"I appreciate that, Kennedy."

Dan swiveled in his chair, thinking this news was just what he needed this morning. So what if the committee now favored Callahan? Depending on what happened in his courtroom today, it might not matter anyway. At the moment, Dan was more concerned about which decision Jillian was reaching down the hall.

Dan knew that Roan's waiver meant one of two things. As

the client with the last say in such decisions, Alana demanded it without telling Roan why and against Roan's advice, which Dan hoped was the case. Lawyers had a way of guiding clients to decisions, always couched in "their best interest." The challenge for the client was to figure out who "their" referred to, the client's or the lawyer's. And, like an inquisitor in a dungeon charged with extracting a confession from a hapless captive, there were tools of the trade, each more persuasive than the last. It often began with a version of "This is my profession, trust me," escalating to "You're paying for my advice, so take it," to "I may have to sever our attorney-client relationship unless you cooperate," and finally, the legal equivalent of the inquisitor ratcheting his pain index on the rack to ten, "I didn't want it to come to this, but I may have to sue you for violation of our retainer agreement in that you failed to . . . [fill in the blank]." It took a tough client to resist such pressure from her lawyer. Was Alana tough enough to insist Roan waive a jury?

In the dreaded alternative, Alana had told Roan the whole story in violation of her pledge. "I can't help you unless you confide in me," Roan would have said. "We can't afford to be blindsided at trial, and the only way to avoid that risk is to tell me everything." If she had told all, and Roan was sitting beside her in court pretending not to know it, his law license would be toast along with Judge Borders's when and if the case blew up.

Back in court, Jillian motioned to Joe Roan for a sidebar beyond the hearing of his client or the judge. In a whisper, she said, "You're sure you want to do this?"

Roan ventured a quick glance back at the defense table, where Alana sat staring straight ahead. "Between you and me, not my choice, but yeah, I'm sure."

Roan returned to his chair. Judge Borders studied him, reading his body language. He looked for any trace of friction between lawyer and client, any sliver of disunity that might signal his preference for a jury had been overridden by a determined defendant. He saw none.

In a tone of finality, Jillian stood and announced, "Your Honor, I join Mr. Roan in expressing my apologies to potential jurors for this inconvenience, and the state is ready to proceed."

# CHAPTER 56

# Tick . . . Tick . . . Tick

"Your Honor," Jillian said as she began her opening statement, "this is an unusual case because the deceased is unusual, having gunshot wounds both front and back. The state contends that the defendant, Ms. Morgan, shot her ex-husband, Toby Morgan, in the back before firing a second shot that killed him. Before she was indicted, she gave statements to the crime scene investigator and to me about the events of that night, but as you will hear from an expert, this shooting could not have happened as she says it did. Since there is no dispute that she killed him, the only question is whether it was done in self-defense, in which case you should acquit her, or done to rid herself of a man who admittedly tormented her and made life difficult for her and her daughter, in which case we ask that you find her guilty of murder or at the very least manslaughter."

"Thank you, Ms. Pillai. Mr. Roan?"

Roan stood as Alana kept her gaze focused on him. With no jury to impress, his demeanor was closer to a docent in a museum than to a flamboyant trial lawyer. He kept his hands cupped at his sides, speaking without notes. "Judge, as much as it hurts me to agree with a prosecutor, I must confess that Ms. Pillai states the issue quite well. But any expert who comes before this court takes an oath to tell the truth. Anyone who claims this can't be self-defense doesn't know what he or she is talking about. We are confident that when all is said and done, the court will see the state's case for what it is—a misguided, ill-conceived, and frankly cruel effort to inflict additional hardship on a woman who has already experienced enough of it."

"Thank you, Mr. Roan. Ms. Pillai, call your first witness."

Jillian called SLED agent Ben Rutherford, who nodded toward Judge Borders as he approached the clerk to be sworn in. He had appeared in this court, and before this judge, many times.

"State your occupation for the record," Jillian instructed.

"I'm employed by the State Law Enforcement Division as a crime scene investigator."

"And how long have you been so employed?"

"Fourteen years."

She led him through a description of the 911 dispatch that night and the scene at Alana's house upon his arrival.

"May I look at my notes?"

For guidance, Jillian looked to the judge, who in turn looked at Roan. "No objection," Roan said.

With one hand, Rutherford extracted glasses from the breast pocket of his SLED shirt and, with the other, placed a file on the top rail of the witness box. "I arrived on the scene at 9:50 p.m. A white male later identified as Toby Morgan, age thirty-two, lay dead in the driveway. He had been shot once in the chest and once in the back near the right shoulder."

"And was this woman present when you arrived?" Jillian asked, pointing at Alana.

"She met me in the driveway."

"Please tell the court what else you found."

"Deputies from the county arrived before I did, so crime

scene tape had already been put in place. In the house, I met a very frightened young girl, age eleven, who gave her name as Holly Morgan. On instructions from her mother, the defendant, she remained locked in a bathroom during the entire ordeal and claimed not to have heard or witnessed anything that went on outside between her parents. I then advised the defendant, Ms. Morgan, of her rights and took a statement."

As Rutherford recited Alana's account of Holly's frantic call, Toby's intoxication, getting him to hand her the gun by promising they would talk about their future, his walking away only to turn, scream, and put her in fear for her life, and her two panicked shots, Judge Borders saw himself defusing a bomb. *Tick . . . tick . . . tick . . .* he could hear the timer, see the wires leading to his destruction. All it would take was a single stumble, an inconsistency obvious to everyone, to trigger an explosion heard around the state. What would he do when it came? He didn't know. *Tick . . . tick . . . tick . . .*

From a banker's box in front of her, Jillian lifted a plastic bag and from it extracted a pistol. "Agent Rutherford, I show you now a weapon that I will ask be marked as state's exhibit number one. Do you recognize it?"

"Those are my initials on the tag. It's the gun the defendant turned over that night."

"And did you find spent shell casings?"

"Yes, ma'am. Three empty shell casings in the weapon."

"Three? But I thought your testimony was that the defendant fired two shots."

*Tick . . . tick . . . tick.*

"Yes, ma'am. Examination of the weapon took place back at the lab, where it was inventoried and dusted for prints. I wasn't aware of the three spent casings until then, so I couldn't ask her about the third shot."

"Did there come a time when you learned of her explanation of a third shot?"

"I was present in your office when you interviewed her. She said the deceased fired a shot over her head when she first arrived on the scene."

"And she mentioned no such shot when you interviewed her on the night of the shooting?"

"She did not."

"I see," said Jillian, glancing at Dan. "What did your examination for prints reveal?"

"It appeared an effort had been made to wipe the grip and trigger clean. On the barrel, we did find prints."

"And were you able to match those?"

*Tick . . . tick . . . tick.*

"One set belonged to the deceased, the other to the defendant."

Jillian approached the witness stand holding a sheet of paper. "I show you now what I will ask be marked as state's exhibit number two. Can you identify it?"

"That's a plat of her property."

"And did she show you where she was standing when the deceased gave her the weapon?"

"Right here in the driveway," he said, pointing.

Handing him a pen, she asked him to mark the spot. "Label it *A*. Was the defendant certain about where she stood?"

"She didn't say exactly where she was standing. She said she dropped the gun after she shot, and that's where we found it."

"How would you describe that area?"

"It's a driveway of sorts. A mixture of dirt and sand."

"And would you also mark the spot where the deceased was found. Label that *B*. And did you measure the distance between *A* and *B*?"

"Fifteen feet more or less."

"So, five yards. Turning your attention back to your interview at the scene, did the defendant tell you where she was when she learned there was a problem at home?"

"She said she was walking the old Elkhart place, thinking of buying it."

"Thank you, Agent Rutherford. Answer any questions Mr. Roan may have."

Roan stood. "Was Ms. Morgan upset when you arrived on the scene?"

"Shaking badly. I'd say she was in shock."

"You testified she claimed to have been at what is known in the county as the Elkhart farm when she received the call from her daughter. Do you know if she subsequently purchased that property?"

"It is my understanding that she did."

"And as part of your investigation, did you check 911 records?"

"Ms. Morgan, the defendant, had made numerous complaints."

"The nature of which were . . .?"

"Fear of her ex-husband. Trespass on her property when he was drunk. Brandishing a firearm. Threats to burn down the house. That kind of thing."

"Did you find any record of him calling 911 in fear of her?"

Rutherford appeared to struggle to suppress a wry grin. "No, nothing like that."

"And was she cooperative with you at all times?"

"Yes, sir."

"No more questions. Thank you, Agent Rutherford."

# CHAPTER 57

# Blood and Dirt

Medical examiner Rhonda Todd was sworn in as the prosecution's next witness. She was gaunt, with sharp, angular features, vacant eyes, a sallow complexion, and hair pulled back in Dust Bowl severity, as if the corpses she spent so much time dissecting dictated her diet and makeup. Jillian solicited the findings of the autopsy.

"On examination," Todd said in a flat, matter-of-fact voice, "I found a large tear in the posterior wall of the aorta approximately twelve millimeters distal to the insertion of ligamentum arteriosum. Sub adventitial hemorrhage was prominent in the descending thoracic aorta. The left pleural space contained large quantities of blood. Entry wound was found in left medial chest wall, T3 dermatome, entering superior to the fourth rib. I found no exit wound. The bullet lodged in the T4 vertebrae, shattering the vertebral body and pedicle and lodging in the vertebral foramen, severing the spinal cord."

"And you recovered the bullet?"

"I did. A .38 caliber slug."

"And," Jillian followed, "based on those findings, were you able to determine a cause of death?"

"Exsanguination. He bled to death from an aorta ruptured by the bullet."

"Ms. Todd, it has been established the deceased was struck by two bullets. Can you describe the second?"

"That bullet entered from behind at the right shoulder region approximately five inches from the centerline of the spine. It flattened on impact inside of the flat bone of the right scapula. The scapula displayed a highly comminuted fracture with radiating fractures traversing toward the axillary border. The axillary artery and axillary vein were both severed. The bullet shattered the glenoid fossa and head of the humerus and was found lodged in the superior aspect of the humerus."

Jillian asked if there was any chance of that wound being fatal.

"Not unless he received no medical attention for several hours and bled to death. He had a high probability of surviving this wound."

"Are you able to opine on which shot came first?"

Todd shook her head faintly before saying, "I am not. I can say the fatal shot came from the front and the shoulder shot entered at an angle from the rear, but your ballistics expert will need to address the shot sequence."

Roan's cross-examination focused on the sequence of the shots. "So," he said, "as I understand your testimony, if I told you or the evidence showed that the first bullet entered the chest and the second the upper right shoulder, you found nothing that could refute that, is that correct?"

"As I said, we were unable to establish the sequence of the shots. A ballistics expert might, but not us."

Her reference to a ballistics expert was a perfect segue into

Jillian's next witness, former FBI agent Glen Coleman. After he was sworn in by the clerk, Joe Roan stood.

"I move this witness be excluded from testifying, Your Honor. We have it on good authority that the relationship between the prosecution and this witness is not entirely arm's length, so to speak, and therefore biased in favor of the state."

Jillian blushed a shade of crimson, on her feet and about to speak when Judge Borders held up his hand, palm out, commanding silence. Turning to Roan, he said, "I will permit the standard questions about compensation for Mr. Coleman's testimony, but nothing beyond that. We are not here to explore Ms. Pillai's private life, or yours either, for that matter. Your motion is denied."

Jillian sat down in a daze of sorts, torn between wondering which of her neighbors had spied on her *(sure it was Max Ritter)* and running up to the bench to embrace the judge. "Thank you God and Dan Borders," she whispered under her breath. For a moment, her doubts about leaving Alana Morgan's fate in his hands evaporated.

Glen recited education, experience, and a wealth of testimony in cases that would have qualified him as an expert in any court in the land. Roan's feeble challenge came to nothing, and he was careful to avoid any personal questions on compensation. Glen confirmed he was being paid at his standard rates, an agreement he had reached with Jillian just before the start of the trial.

Jillian, again composed, asked him for his bottom-line. "It is my opinion to a reasonable certainty that the deceased, Mr. Morgan, was shot first from behind, and that the force of that bullet turned him toward the defendant, who then fired the fatal shot to his chest."

Dan's mind traveled back to that night. He saw Toby lurching toward his truck, saw Alana raise the gun and shoot, watched Toby's shoulder jerk forward and turn toward her as he fell. Saw

Alana fire again. *Damn*, thought Dan, *this Coleman knows his stuff. He described it as if he were there.*

When asked for the basis for his opinion, Glen described a series of ballistic experiments using a dummy of Toby's height, weight, and build. Critical to his analysis was the bullet's path as testified to by the medical examiner. A particular challenge, he said, was establishing the proper amount of resistance to turn the dummy, so he used a range from little to great, and in ten out of ten tries, the dummy turned back in the direction of the shot, thereby exposing the chest to the second shot. Conversely, shots to the chest failed to turn the dummy so as to expose the shoulder. He confirmed the results with a sophisticated computer simulation which he showed to the court on a projection. Glen's testimony and the computer simulation took up most of the afternoon.

Jillian asked a final question before relinquishing him to cross-examination. Pointing to Alana, she said, "In other words and in laymen's terms, Mr. Coleman, the defendant could not have been defending herself from an out-of-control drunk but rather decided to shoot an unarmed, retreating man in the back."

Roan jumped to his feet. "Objection, Your Honor," but Judge Borders waved him off as he had done with Jillian earlier. "There is no jury here to impress, Mr. Roan. The court understands the question and the answer, and I can put both in perspective."

When his turn came, Roan hammered Glen. "Are you saying it is impossible for the shot to have come from the front, and equally impossible that the force of the fatal shot turned him to expose the right shoulder?"

Glen paused before answering, lifting his gaze as if preparing a response more philosophical than practical. "Impossible is a strong word. As they say, anything's possible. I'm dealing with forensic and ballistic evidence, and based on that evidence, the first shot came from behind."

"This dummy you used in your testing, the one on which you base your opinion, that dummy wasn't drunk like Toby Morgan, was it?"

Jillian jumped up. "Your Honor—"

"Mr. Roan, you're out of order with that question."

Roan shot back. "Your Honor, the question is admittedly frivolous, but the point is not." Roan again addressed Glen. "Can you say, based on your knowledge of ballistics and to a reasonable degree of certainty, that it would not be possible for a drunk man shot in the chest to stumble or lurch in such a way as to expose his shoulder seconds later?"

"Highly unlikely, but impossible? No, I can't say that."

"And you admit, do you not, that the deceased's drunkenness would be a factor impossible for a computer model to account for?"

"I concede that his drunkenness introduces an element I did not and could not measure. That said, I stand by my opinion."

Roan turned his gaze from Glen to Jillian. "No further questions."

"It's getting late, Ms. Pillai," the judge said. "How much more time will the state need?"

"We have two more witnesses, Your Honor, both of whom promise to be brief. In light of Mr. Coleman's testimony on the shot sequence, I'd like to recall the medical examiner."

Rhonda Todd returned to the witness stand.

"You are still under oath," Judge Borders cautioned.

"Ms. Todd, my question is a simple one. In your examination of Toby Morgan's body, did you find evidence of dirt or sand on his face or chest? You may consult your notes if you can't recall."

Rhonda Todd's head underwent a faint backward tic, as if she had discovered a fly in her soup. "I recall very well," she said. "There was no trace of dirt or sand, either face or chest."

"Did that surprise you?"

"According to Agent Rutherford's report, the deceased was

facedown on the driveway when the defendant turned him over with her foot. I would have expected some contamination from the driveway."

"Thank you. Please answer any questions Mr. Roan or the court may have."

Roan stood. "Ms. Todd, you have no way of knowing whether sand or dirt may have been wiped from the deceased's front at the scene, do you?"

"No, I don't. But I can say that a bloody wound coming into contact with dirt or sand would almost certainly retain some trace of it, no matter how great the effort to clean it up. I found none."

As Rhonda Todd returned to her seat in the courtroom, Judge Borders noted a sharp exchange of eye contact between Roan and Alana. For the first time since the trial began, he saw fear place a cold hand on her shoulder.

Jillian said, "For my last witness, I call Deputy Victor Blasingame."

Blasingame's testimony regarding his effort to reach Jillian by cell phone and the unavailability of cell service at the old Elkhart property caused the judge a stab of high anxiety. Here was a detail that would have been easy to overlook in Alana's hurried, fabricated explanation of her whereabouts when Holly's call came in. There is always some flaw in a lie. He'd seen it in countless cases. Now he saw it in his own.

"Court stands adjourned until ten tomorrow," he announced.

# CHAPTER 58

# Motion for Acquittal

Promptly at ten on the following morning, Jillian stood to address the court. "Having secured after court yesterday Mr. Roan's stipulation that a life insurance policy insuring Mr. Morgan in the face amount of fifty-thousand-dollars was in force at the time of his death, and that proceeds of that policy were payable to the defendant, the state rests."

"The prosecution rests," Judge Borders said. "Mr. Roan?"

"Your Honor, the defense moves for acquittal. The evidence is insufficient as a matter of law to support a conviction."

"Ms. Pillai? Your response."

Jillian left her table to take a position closer to the witness stand. She insisted that, based on the evidence, the court had ample evidence on which to base a conviction. "Unrebutted expert testimony is a powerful thing, Your Honor," she told the court. "Mr. Coleman's opinion that the first shot hit the deceased in the back has been contradicted only by the defendant's self-serving denial. Of course, she claimed self-defense. Who wouldn't after you'd killed your ex-husband to get him out of your life and collect his life insurance?

"Equally telling, Your Honor, is Medical Examiner Todd's confirmation of the lack of dirt or sand in Toby Morgan's chest wound. Recall that the defendant said he landed facedown in the driveway as a result of what she says was the second shot to the shoulder and what Mr. Coleman insists was the first shot. She says she turned him over with her foot to explain the fact that he was found faceup at the scene. But it couldn't have happened as she said because some residue of the driveway would have been present in the fatal wound. She shot him in the back, and when he turned, she hit him in the chest. That is hardly self-defense. As to turning him over, she lied, just as she lied about her whereabouts when the call from her daughter came in. We ask that you convict her as charged."

Joe Roan countered. "Why engage an expert to rebut testimony that on its face is insufficient to establish guilt beyond a reasonable doubt? I will admit," he continued, "that Mr. Coleman's opinion raises suspicions about what happened that night. He's an impressive witness, and his reconstruction evidence might, in another context on different facts, be persuasive. But the prosecution's burden, as this court well knows, goes beyond raising suspicions. On this evidence, the court must acquit Ms. Morgan."

At the moment Judge Borders turned his gaze and said, "Ms. Pillai," Jillian experienced Lopez déjà vu. As he had done then, he complimented her on her presentation, echoed Roan's praise for Glen Coleman's expertise, and admitted that the prosecution had raised "grave concerns" about the defendant's actions. "But beyond a reasonable doubt is an extremely high bar to get over, and I will share with you what troubles me most about this case. Mr. Coleman's opinion might be entirely accurate for a sober individual, but the movements of a man in Toby Morgan's advanced state of intoxication are unpredictable. Mr. Coleman, to his credit, admitted as much. For that reason, I'm holding that the state has failed to meet its burden of proof and that the defendant is hereby acquitted." He stared directly at Alana before saying, "Ms. Morgan, you are free to go."

Jillian collected her files as deflation crept into her body and spirit like a living thing. She hadn't bothered to note an appeal, certain it would be futile. She stopped at the witness room to see Glen, who waited there in the event he was needed for rebuttal testimony. There would be no rebuttal. Judge Borders had pegged his verdict on the weakness Glen had identified at the outset, Toby's erratic drunkenness. "It's over," she told him. "Verdict for the defense. Let's go to my place." On the way, she began the process of cheering herself up. "You were great," she told Glen. "Frank's advice was to always present the best case I could, and I did. The judge gets paid to decide."

They parked in front of her townhouse. Getting out of the car, she spotted Max Ritter's blind undergo its usual peep. Once inside, she changed into a sweatsuit, telling Glen she needed a run to unwind from the trial. In the community gym, she punished herself on the treadmill for thirty minutes of hard-earned, self-inflicted pain. As she toweled off and returned to her unit, she passed guest parking and made a U-turn back to the management office.

"Stephanie, I just saw Max Ritter's car in a guest parking slot. That's his maroon Fiat, is it not?"

She brought up the image on the security camera that surveilled the lot. "Yep, that's his. Weird that he would park there."

"Weird, but against the rules, right?"

"Of course. We usually let it slide when there are other spaces available."

"But you aren't required to let it slide, am I right again?"

Stephanie stared a moment, uncertain, then popped a bubble before saying, "This should be fun."

Jillian returned to her bedroom and raised her blinds to full extension. When she saw a tow truck drive in the entrance and position itself behind the Fiat, she waited for Max Ritter's blind to part before waving her arms in full view of anyone who cared to look her way. She needed a victory today, and this was a small one over an even smaller man, but it pleased her. She could count on Stephanie to let everyone in the complex know who had given the prying pest his due.

After the verdict, Judge Borders did not remain on the bench long enough to see Alana embrace Joe Roan in gratitude, or to see Jillian collect her papers and, with head bowed, exit the room. He returned to his chambers, took off his robe, and sat at his desk staring out the window. After a time, an imperceptible nod signaled a minor decision. He walked to his parked SUV and retrieved the Turner & Feinberg bag from the rear. Back in his office, he stuffed his judicial robe in the bag and made his way back to the car. That night, after Claire went to bed, he got very drunk, drunker than he had ever been. Just before passing out on the sofa in the den, he removed his robe from the bag and put it in the wood stove; by morning, it had turned to a fine ash.

The days that followed were the darkest in Dan's life. His sense of place in the universe had been dislodged, like a planet suddenly spinning out of orbit. What was it he had told Andy months before, when this whole nightmare began? Something about having a PhD in depression? Now he felt the full brunt of what he had insisted he was a stranger to. Such hubris. The weight of his descent bore down on him, leaving him flattened and unable to breathe. He measured the nearness of his despair by his distance from a handgun he kept in the bottom drawer of his desk at home. He opened the drawer, stared at the pistol, closed the drawer. *No,* he told himself. *Not that. Not a coward's way out. Not the route taken by Otis Hazzard. Not that.* Yet days later, after no sleep and little food, he opened the drawer again, moving the pistol up to a middle drawer. *If it gets to the top one,* he acknowledged, *I'm in real trouble.*

# CHAPTER 59

# Alana

Alana returned to her teaching duties with what seemed like the weight of the world lifted from her shoulders. With the trial behind her, she could begin to enjoy the Elkhart property she looked forward to fixing up. Equally enjoyable was the $50,000 from Toby's life insurance to supplement her savings. Holly participated fully in school activities now that her commute from school was a mere ten minutes instead of the previous forty. She would be driving one day, giving her mother yet more time for herself.

Students greeted Alana with a mix of welcome and, at first, wariness. She was, after all, the woman who shot her ex-husband, which, if nothing else, served notice on the students that she was not to be trifled with. Jokes behind her back drew surreptitious laughter, but those eventually faded along with the wariness. Not since her pre-Toby high school days could she recall being happier at Beaufort High.

She thought often of Dan Borders. Their fates would be forever linked by the devil's bargain they made and kept. When she reflected back on the risks he took to follow her that night and the exposure to ruin he faced by remaining the judge of her case, her admiration for him exceeded what had already been high on the night of their aborted dinner. She had never met anyone like him and knew she never would again. The Dan Borders of the world came along once in a lifetime, if at all, and she had been both the object of his attention and, she hoped, his affection. She wanted only the best for him, including a seat on the supreme court.

When she tired of grading papers, she thought about what might have been had Holly's phone call come later or not at all. As she drove toward the dock that evening, she had willed herself into the platonic mindset that had served her well in her monument conferences with Dan, but her body was set on other things and sending her messages that were anything but platonic. She had not experienced sex in years. The touch of his hand, a look containing a hint of hunger, a casual overture with a double meaning—any of these would have been enough to turn her into a lioness on the prowl. She would have devoured him, as she had done in her daydreams many times. Only the phone call prevented what might have been.

Would Dan have resisted? Would he have played the gazelle to her stalking lioness, or would he have given himself over to the inevitability of where their relationship had been headed all along? He was so decent, so thoroughly decent, that she doubted she could have seduced him, at least on that occasion. She knew him well enough to appreciate his sense of loyalty to his wife and his wedding vows. During one of those monument talks that strayed from the professional into the personal, he had confided his monogamy in marriage. She admired that even as she pictured them running roughshod over it on their way to the bedroom. And then what? Secret afternoons of stolen bliss? He wouldn't be a party to that. Would rumors have reached his wife? The internet? Holly's call had thrown the switch on two trains headed for a collision, but not the kind of collision she fantasized about on her way to *Car Pay Diem*. For a time, it appeared that the collision avoided would be infinitely worse than their human, naked impact, but thanks to Dan, that had worked out as he pledged it would.

⊙  ⊙  ⊙

Her first impression of Joe Roan had come when she sat in on the Lopez hearing. She took little notice of him, her focus centered on the judge, but as the hearing wore on, Roan demanded more of her attention by the same means he used to demand a jury's attention. Physically imposing for a man five feet, ten inches tall, his snug suits and weight-lifter physique radiated power. She didn't care for his voice, a bit nasally, or his haircut, but she couldn't ignore his ability to hold the crowd's attention, including hers. When Roan won his motion, Alana resolved to call him if she ever needed a lawyer.

That need came sooner than she imagined. It had been the interview in Jillian Pillai's office that convinced her the Morgan file on Jillian's desk wasn't going to be closed without a fight. In battle, she needed a burly, muscled lawyer. His secretary "squeezed her in" on the afternoon after her call.

Roan's office reflected its occupant, compact with touches that evoked power. On the top floor of the only high-rise in the county, which is to say the fourth floor, a highly polished brass plate graced a deeply grained walnut door. Inside, a rich Oriental rug contrasted nicely with hardwood floors. Winged leather chairs offered comfort to those in extreme discomfort. Coffee offered by his secretary came in china cup and saucer. She had taken only a few sips when Roan emerged from his corner office to greet her. Behind his ample desk hung a photo of a college-age Roan with George H. W. Bush.

She repeated her account of the shooting as she had imparted it to the prosecutor. He listened, his fingers steepled in thoughtful attention, nodded in appropriate spots, and took some notes. When she finished, he used an expression he was fond of. "Hate to tell you, hon, but your tit's in a wringer. Mark my words. Jillie's going to indict you. Come back and see me when she does. We'll work something out."

So Alana returned. When he quoted his retainer, she got up to leave. "Sit down," he ordered. "I said we'd work something out. I don't need it all up front. You're getting his insurance money, right?"

"Hopefully someday."

"So, pay me a thousand now, and we'll talk about the rest later."

"Am I going to prison?"

"Not if you follow my advice."

Weeks before trial, at the end of a discussion about testimony he anticipated from Glen Coleman, she told him she didn't want a jury. He looked at her with not-quite-patient indulgence. "Hey, hon, remember what I said about following my advice? You want a jury on this case. There ain't twelve folks in Beaufort who will convict a schoolteacher defending herself from a thug of an ex-husband. They should give you a medal for shooting the bastard. You're taking a jury."

"No, I'm not," she said just as firmly.

"Oh, so now you're the lawyer? May I ask why not?"

"Call it instinct. I watched Judge Borders in the Lopez hearing. I've heard good things about him. I believe he would be fair, so I'd like him to try my case."

"Hon, fair sailed with Columbus back to Spain. Fair has nothing to do with criminal trials. I don't want fair. I want not guilty."

She remained composed. "I'll take full responsibility for the outcome if I'm wrong."

"Damn right you will. Listen, hon, your trial is around the

corner. I've already demanded a jury on your behalf, and we're in the process of vetting potential jurors now. Why would you waive a jury? It's a nutso idea."

"Maybe so, but I'm the client and that's my decision."

Seeing her resolve, Roan switched tactics. "Tell you what, hon. The judge is going to be steamed when we show up on the day of trial and waive a jury. They hate it when lawyers do it, and I haven't pulled that trick since I got my license. But just for you, I'm not going to waive a jury until the morning of trial because I'm betting that between now and then, you're going come to your senses and follow my advice."

But a week before trial, their relationship seemed headed toward something beyond attorney-client, as the rumor mill had noted. His casual "hon" had become a term of endearment. After a late afternoon office conference, they had gone to dinner followed by drinks at his impressive house, which gave her a chance to take a fresh look at him, and at the deep-water dock extending from a lawn sloping to the river, and a power boat tethered to it.

On the night before trial, as he outlined what he and she could expect the following day, he made one more run at a jury. "Look, hon, you gotta trust me on this. You liked my house, right?"

"Love the house."

"Juries built it. This is what I do. And I care about what happens to you. Why are you being so stubborn?"

"I told you. I trust Judge Borders."

After the trial, she and Roan became lovers. She sensed Roan might be in deeper than she was. *He might even propose,* she thought. But he and Holly hadn't spent enough time together for her to assess him as a presence in her daughter's life, and after Toby, Alana was more protective of Holly than of herself. For now, an occasional sleepover at Joe's suited her fine.

Gradually, he and Holly developed the kind of relationship that reassured her mother. They even began a ritual of going to Hardees on Saturday mornings after Holly swore it was okay to revisit the place where she had come to realize the width of the unbridgeable gulf that separated her father and mother. They ordered breakfast biscuits, laughed, and speculated on how long it would take Alana to turn the Elkhart place into the home of her dreams. "I want to live at your place," Holly told him. "I think Mom's is haunted."

With Roan occupying more of her time and attention, Alana gradually consigned Dan to one of those memories she would always hold close.

As to guilt over killing Toby, she had little. At her trial, the word "malice" had been bandied about, and malice was indeed what she had felt that night, and in the years leading up to it. Now she could let it go. For all the bad breaks life had dealt her, she caught a good one. As she would believe for the rest of her life, she had gotten away with murder.

# CHAPTER 60

# Dan

A month after Alana Morgan's acquittal, the following article appeared in *The State* under Brock Jamerson's byline.

### BORDERS NAMED TO HIGH COURT

Beaufort County Circuit Court Judge Daniel Niles Borders was selected yesterday as Chief Justice of the South Carolina Supreme Court, filling the seat left vacant by the retirement of Chief Justice Oliver Bidwell Cox. In announcing the selection, Senate Judiciary Committee Chairman Thomas Wentworth called Borders the "ideal replacement, a man who will serve the state for a generation." Many attribute Borders's elevation to his Jury of One idea, first put forward in a law review article after a capital punishment case. The concept, which would place a death chamber in the state's maximum-security facility for use by those sentenced to life without hope of parole, has proved highly controversial.

Following a profile of Dan's career and biographical background
on his family, the article noted he was expected to be sworn in on
January 1.

In the weeks leading up to Christmas, well-wishers treated
Dan and Claire to a shower of congratulations and praise. A letter
from the retiring chief justice assured Dan of his new colleagues'
goodwill and high esteem. The governor wrote to say how much
he looked forward to Dan's contribution to the state. Both US
senators reminded him of an open door in DC should he ever
find himself in Washington. Old friends brought casseroles to the
house as they did when Claire's illness first became known. Brock
Jamerson scheduled an in-depth personal interview for the week
leading up to his investiture.

At Thanksgiving, both Christina and Ethan made it home to
add their homage and to savor Claire's sage stuffing that never
failed to evoke memories of their childhoods. They found their
father uncharacteristically moody, a brooding presence in the
place of what they had expected to be the mild euphoria he might
allow himself. Christina's concern was sufficient to ask her mother
what was wrong.

"He's just tired," Claire said. "Between his caseload at court
and the uncertainty of his selection, I think he's worn down. He'll
bounce back. The change will do wonders for him, and best of all,
we don't have to move."

After the kids left, promising to be present for his swearing
in, Dan took Banjo on a long walk. A wooded trail offered bare
trees and old leaves that crunched under his boots. The starkness
surrounding him fit his mood. In the side pocket of his hunting
jacket, he could feel the weight of the pistol he had taken from the
top drawer of his desk.

He thought about Alana and wondered if she was wrestling,
as he was, with the night of Toby's death. He wanted her to find

happiness, with Joe Roan or another, and to move beyond whatever misgivings she felt over the shooting. Yet he wanted her to feel that remorse because, without it, he had misjudged her, and if he couldn't be part of her life in the future, he needed to know that within her dwelled the empathy and compassion he felt certain he had seen. If she possessed those virtues, as he was sure she did, she would carry for the rest of her life the burden of having murdered Toby. Which brought him to the purpose of this walk. He needed to decide what *his* burden would be. What price should he pay for violation of his oath to be impartial, for failing to uphold the standards to which he had aspired and, except for one night, upheld? And, though he banished it from his conscious thought whenever it surfaced to haunt him, he had a price to pay for the night Toby died, a price beyond oaths and standards.

As Banjo sprinted after a squirrel, Dan put aside the denials that had allowed him to survive and function since that night in Seabrook. He had deferred this "come to Jesus" moment. Now it had arrived, a self-imposed demand that he confess—but not to Jesus—to himself. To get back to the man he had always thought himself to be. What was that indelibly memorable line he had read one summer in some John le Carré's spy novel? To "kill and not be killed is an illusion," or words to that effect. He had buried his illusion under a mountain of serious work, political intrigue, and soul-numbing worry that Alana would not keep her promise. Now, the inevitable call to account.

It began by acknowledging his motive in asking Alana to dinner on the boat. That one night. He relived it over and over, and he did so again on this walk in the woods. He pictured Toby handing her the gun, butt-end first. He saw her finger wrap around the trigger as Toby retreated toward his truck, saying he needed more whiskey if they were going to talk. In that instant, Dan knew she would shoot him. He could sense it coming, and he made no move to stop her. When Toby fell, Dan felt only relief that the one witness to his part in the nightmare was dead.

But after Alana ran into the house, Dan heard Toby moan. As he approached, Toby lifted his head. "Help me, Judge," he had mumbled as his eyes closed, wincing in pain. With the gun Alana had passed to him, Dan stood over Toby and fired a single shot into his chest. In the fleeting instant he took to comprehend what he had done, he could only think of the day he had carried Banjo's sire, riddled with cancer, behind the shed to end its misery. He returned to his car to wipe his prints off the gun, which was where Alana found him when the sound of the shot brought her back from the house.

What price should Dan pay for his crime? Was it enough to silently shoulder the guilt for the rest of his life, or did he owe it to Alana, to Toby, to the world at large to do penance? And if so, what form should penance take? He thought about confessing to Alana, to free her from whatever guilt she carried from the mistaken belief she was a murderer. But with no statute of limitations on murder, Dan could still be charged. Toby Morgan's ghost would taunt him always, but risk of a criminal charge in Dan's fifties and beyond was too high a price to pay. Maybe the answer wasn't penance. Maybe it was redemption.

Was redemption possible? Was it real? His high school English teacher had required the class to write a book report on Joseph Conrad's *Lord Jim*. On a training ship for duty in the merchant marines, an adolescent Jim had lost his nerve and with it the chance to join with other boys to save two seamen about to drown in a boating accident. Fear froze Jim into a spectator. Though his inaction on that occasion was cowardly, Jim saw himself as having heroic qualities, needing only another chance to prove them. He was looking for redemption. His chance came when, now seventeen, he signed on as first mate of a rusting hull named the *Patina*, carrying over 800 pilgrims to a hajj. One night, sailing in calm seas, the vessel struck something that sent through it a shudder, "hardly more than a vibration . . . and the ship quivered in response." Captain Gustav, believing the ship would sink quickly, lowered a lifeboat and exhorted Jim to save himself by jumping in. He jumped. The *Patina* eventually sailed safely into port, triggering a court martial of those who abandoned her. Jim, disgraced, again sought redemption, fleeing to other ports until he one day landed in a remote village. When the village chief's son, whose safety Jim had guaranteed, is killed, Jim offers his life in recompense, an offer the village chief accepts. Jim found his courage and, with it, redemption through his own death.

Dan patted his pocket where the pistol rested. *Was that the answer? Death, like Lord Jim's?* He looked down into an eddy of water pooling where the boundary of his property met Andy's. In the stillness of the afternoon, his reflection caught the light in a way that made for a faithful mirror. Each line and crease in his otherwise pleasant face attested to the prison he had built for himself. He managed a sardonic laugh before muttering, "Otis Hazzard and me. Cellmates." He reached into his pocket and withdrew the gun. Turning it over, one side then the other, he threw it into the water. He had decided to seek other redemption.

He looked over his shoulder at his home, where Claire waited in her chair. They had good years ahead and would enjoy them together. She could depend upon him to be there. Together, they would build a house at the lake that would rival Star-Splitter. How fortunate they would be to have homes in two such places. He would teach his grandchildren to sail in Beaufort, though he would sell *Car Pay Diem* and buy something smaller and less physically taxing, closer to the sunfish and skiffs he learned on. And to fly fish at the lake. A small boy or girl with a trout at the end of the line, shimmering in the early morning sun—that was something to look forward to.

☉  ☉  ☉

When Brock Jamerson came to Judge Borders's office for the scheduled pre-investiture interview, Dan announced he would decline the proffered supreme court seat. Claire's health demanded he stay close to home, and she needed him. Just that morning, he had mailed a notice of his retirement from the bench. He and Claire would be building a home on property they owned by a lake, and he looked forward to devoting all his energy to his wife and their future. A new organization, My Life, My Choice, had formed to push for the reforms needed to implement his Jury of One idea. He planned to write, lecture, and raise funds to make it a potent force for change. "The burden of deciding your own fate is a heavy one," he acknowledged to a stunned Jamerson, "but only by individual choice can we find some rough justice in this world and be at peace with the consequences."

When Jamerson asked if he could quote him, Dan smiled wistfully and said, "You may."

# CHAPTER 61

# Jillian

Jillian spent the weeks after Alana's acquittal in a campaigning fury. She left her office after lunch and went door-to-door in every precinct in the county, usually with Harper Kline at her side. After the first couple of neighborhoods, they fell into a pattern. Harper pounded on the door with enough force to wake anyone in the house or next door. When it was answered, Jillian stepped forward, introduced herself, and gave her elevator speech asking for a vote. She left a handout. When enough people asked who she was running against, it became obvious that Jerry Higginson had a name recognition problem. If the person answering the door was old or handicapped, Harper offered to give them a ride to the polls when the time came. Jillian's confidence surged whenever a potential voter knew her name. Evidently, she concluded, publicity surrounding the Lopez and Morgan trials had done what publicity, good or bad, does.

By election day, Jillian had difficulty keeping food down, a combination of nerves and excitement. She voted early, then made her way to every precinct to shake a few more hands. Harper had predicted the night before that she would win, but she refused to believe it. Fear of losing a close race kept her motivated to campaign until the polls closed. Exhausted but confident she had done all she could, she headed for the party Harper had organized. When early returns showed her with a commanding lead, a celebration erupted. Having her parents there added to the festive chatter that grew louder by the minute. The absence of Glen Coleman might have spoiled for her the perfection of the evening, but he arrived just in time to hear her take Jerry Higginson's concession call.

"I told Glen to get his ass here," Harper said, grinning, then gave a shrill whistle for quiet so Jillian could thank her supporters. As she took the microphone, someone in the back yelled, "Jillian for governor" to raucous applause.

Had Jillian been less distracted by the cheers of the crowd, handshakes by the dozen, and six people talking at once about some incident at a polling place, she might have paid more attention to Harper and Glen huddled in a corner. She learned later that he was confiding in her that he brought with him a marquis diamond ring.

When he asked her to dinner at Saltus, she guessed his purpose. In the confusion of the victory party, she had missed his confab with Harper, but not his whispered asides to her parents or her mother's barely concealed excitement. The handshake with her father had seemed something more significant than a hello or farewell. When he ordered champagne, she asked casually, "Special occasion?"

"Of course. Your election win."

"We already did that. Something else?"

"You know, don't you? You always know. Did Harper tell you?"

Grinning, she shook her head.

"Your mom?"

"No one told me. A girl can have a hunch, can't she?"

"If you say yes, I'm on notice not to try to keep secrets from you. Is it yes?"

She raised her hands, palms up, in innocent perplexity. "So, what's the question?"

"You're loving this, aren't you?"

"I intend to get engaged only once in my life. And I want to enjoy every second of it."

After bringing their glasses together in a toast, he produced the ring, slipping it on her finger. Sparks from the ring's facets matched those in her eyes as she gleefully admired it.

Several days later, he suggested they talk about children. "We've never discussed them," he observed.

She reacted with surprise. "I told you I love kids."

"Loving them isn't the same as wanting to birth and raise them."

"I want to do both. I hope you do."

He told her about Samantha and how her refusal to consider being a mother had driven him away. "I wanted you to know that because I love you too much to let you go, even if your attitude about kids matched hers. Can't tell you how thrilled I am about us being parents."

◉ ◉ ◉

After their wedding and a honeymoon in Mexico, Glen told her he wanted to learn to sail and that living so close to the ocean presented the perfect opportunity. They took lessons together and, with their newly developed sea legs, bought a twenty-one-foot skiff, docking it at the local marina. When their twins grew old enough to swim, their best days were spent exploring Beaufort's creeks and rivers on *Guilty Pleasure*, which Jillian named in tribute to her prosecutorial success and the delight she took in seeing the bad guys get their due.

About the time the girls entered first grade, the family

succumbed to the boatowners' compulsion to buy something larger, something that slept four. Jillian scoured the local marinas and the internet for deals. She had just finished a sentencing hearing for a drug dealer when a clerk mentioned Judge Borders and the rumor that his boat was for sale. Jillian reached him at his lake house. Yes, he said, it was good to hear from her too, and he named a price for *Car Pay Diem*. She and Glen were encouraged to inspect it, even take it out, and the key was available from Edna Poindexter, who lived next door and kept an eye on things.

On a bright day in early summer, when the breeze off the Sound called to every boater within its reach, Jillian, Glen, and the girls pulled into Edna's driveway. The hydrangeas she had planted on the day Brock Jamerson helped her place the mulch were now full grown. The twins, beyond excited and impatient to get aboard, hung on Glen's arms as Jillian rang the doorbell. Edna greeted them and insisted they come in for lemonade.

"I'm honored to have our solicitor visit me," Edna said. "I voted for you, incidentally."

"Then I'm the one who is honored," Jillian said.

"I knew this day would come," Edna said as she led them onto a deck overlooking the river. Seagulls dipped and rose near the shoreline, some taking up sentry posts on the dock's pilings as a few continued their effortless glides. "Dan and Claire so rarely use it now. And, should you decide to buy, I feel sure Chet Gilroy would let you keep it there. What darling girls."

"Thank you," Jillian said, eyeing her daughters as they sipped lemonade, oblivious to the compliment. "They are so excited, I'm afraid they'll jump overboard."

"Well," said Edna, "if they have any thoughts of doing that, best do it before the jellyfish arrive."

Glen said they knew the jellyfish well from their experience on the skiff. "Just a reminder that even the best things in life have their irritations," he said philosophically.

"And I assume you will sell that boat?"

Jillian laughed. "We certainly can't afford two."

"Should you decide to buy the Borders's boat and keep it here, I'll get the pleasure of watching your children grow up just I did with Christina and Ethan. If yours are as well-behaved as those two, as I feel sure they will be, life here will remain as peaceful as it has always been. In all the years that boat has been docked at Gilroy's, I can't think of a single crisis or drama. Pretty remarkable, really."

"Then the pressure will be on us to keep that streak alive," Jillian said.

Edna cocked her head reflectively. "I take that back. There was one incident, years ago."

"Oh?" Jillian said, more from politeness than curiosity. Like Glen and the girls, her mind was on the inspection and cruise they had come for.

"The strangest thing happened. Dan arrived in late afternoon. I spoke with him about seeing the family when they took a cruise the weekend before. He was by himself. He said he had come to do some maintenance or cleaning. Just about sunset, I heard another car. A woman in a hurry went around the house and onto the dock. Sometime later, maybe an hour after dark, I heard a car door slam. I got back to the window in time to see the car driven by the woman take off like a bat out of you know where, driving like there was no tomorrow. Dan's car followed. That was so unlike him, to leave in such a hurry. Maybe they had an argument? I never knew because it wasn't any of my business."

Jillian turned to Glen. "Why don't you take the girls over to the boat and I'll join you shortly?"

"The key is hanging on that nail by the steps," Edna said as they were leaving.

Jillian watched them before turning her attention back to Edna. "What you just said reminded me of an old case. What did the woman look like?"

"I couldn't say, dear. She was too far away."

"Was she a young woman?"

"Well, judging by the way she practically ran from her car to the dock, she couldn't have been too old. And women reach an age pretty early when they don't wear a bare midriff, which is the way this person was dressed."

Jillian tried to recall what Alana wore on the night of the shooting, but too much time had passed. "Could it have been his daughter?"

"No, I would have recognized Christina."

"Does the name Alana Morgan mean anything to you?"

Edna gazed across the river, narrowing her eyes for better recall. "Alana Morgan. No, should it?"

"Years ago, she was charged with killing her ex-husband up in Seabrook. I thought you might remember because the trial was in the news for several days."

"To be honest, I don't pay much attention to that sort of thing. The only trial I remember is when Hazel Hudgins was killed. Hazel was my friend, and I miss her to this day. They never found her killer."

Jillian felt the pang that the mention of Hazel Hudgins, even years later, always triggered. "We knew who did it. We just couldn't prove it."

"Who was it?"

"Lopez was his name."

"Oh, yes, I remember now. Lopez. That must have been just before Frank Walthall died."

"Actually, it was shortly after. I handled the case, and I'm still upset that we couldn't hold him accountable. Lopez was eventually deported, but that is small comfort for the memory of Hazel Hudgins. I also tried Alana Morgan, which is why I asked about her."

"I wish I could help. My memory isn't what it once was. I only remember the night I told you about because it was so unlike any other, and so unlike Dan to leave in such a hurry. I thought of asking him about it, but like I said, it was none of my business."

"Were you surprised when he declined the supreme court appointment?"

"Totally bowled over. I'll never understand it. I suppose he had his reasons."

On her walk from Edna's to Gilroy's dock, Jillian wondered again about what had puzzled her for years; where was Alana Morgan on the night she got the call from her daughter, and why did she lie about it? Could she have been the woman Edna saw? If Dan Borders followed her from the boat, could he have followed her all the way to Seabrook? Was it possible he witnessed Toby's shooting?

She looked up in time to see Glen and the girls on deck of the soon-to-be-renamed *Car Pay Diem*. They waved for her to hurry. Once on board, the girls gave her a tour of the boat they already considered theirs. As Glen started the engine and familiarized himself with dials and gauges, Jillian and the girls studied a navigation chart at the same table where Alana had reached across to cover Dan's hand on the night of the shooting. "All-hands-on-deck," Glen called. Topside again, Jillian and the girls stationed themselves at the deck cleats, preparing to cast off. The sun was approaching noon, Jillian was happy, and she dismissed any further speculation about Alana Morgan and Dan Borders. It had ceased to be any of her business.

High in an oak tree behind Alana's old house in Seabrook, the bullet she was certain killed Toby is still lodged, and at the old courthouse, the Confederate monument still stands.

## ACKNOWLEDGMENTS

I began this book years ago while living in Virginia. Confinement dictated by COVID brought me back to it in South Carolina. Encouragement and helpful suggestions came from Marilyn, my love and my partner. My doctor, Clark Trask, MD, helped me understand the path a bullet might take through a male victim. My gratitude to the talented folks at Koehler Books. To generous readers Walter "Cotton" Kurtz, Bill Ritchie, Carolyn Mason, Brian Robinson, Roxanne Cheney, Barbara Planchon, Wyatt Durrette, Cassandra King, Brenda Gael Beasley-Forrest, Donna Altman, Patricia Denkler, Katherine Lang, and Ted Hogshire, I can only offer humble thanks and a pledge that the next round is on me.

CPSIA information can be obtained
at www.ICGtesting.com
Printed in the USA
LVHW030454120423
744130LV00001B/46